**JAMES VELLA-BARDON** is the author of five books,
including *The Cream of Chivalry, Mad King Robin,
Hero Of Rosclogher* and *A Rebel North*.
His debut, *The Sheriff's Catch*, was the winner
in the 'best novel' and 'best historical fiction' categories
at the International Royal Dragonfly Book Awards 2019.

"The new king of historical fiction"
– *The Scotsman*

"Remember the name of rising author James Vella-Bardon"
– *Reader's Digest*

"Reminds me of works by today's masters such as
Bernard Cornwell, Conn Iggulden and Wilbur Smith"
– *Yorkshire Evening Post*

"Has what it takes to become a literary giant"
– *The Star*

"Sheer quality, historical integrity and emotional resonance"
– *The London Economic*

"A master storyteller, moving Abel through
a land of wonder and danger"
– *The US Review Of Books*

# Ring
# of Ruse

PART FIVE

*of*

The Sassana Stone

*Pentalogy*

JAMES VELLA-BARDON

TEARAWAY PRESS

Copyright
Published by Tearaway Press 2024
PO Box 477, Belrose West, Sydney NSW 2085

Copyright © James Vella-Bardon 2023
James Vella-Bardon asserts the moral right to be identified as the author
of this work.

ISBN: 978-0-6451230-7-4

Cover design and typesetting by Rafael Andres
Editing by Hatch Editorial Service

*To Jorge Pérez y Asenjo, who shared the journey from day dot. Gracias hermano.*

# Cast of Characters

# The MacGlannagh Tribe

Tadhg *Óg* MacGlannagh, Gaelic chieftain of the Mac-Glannagh tribe.

Dervila Bourke, Anglo-Norman wife of Tadhg *Óg*.

Muireann Mac an Bhaird, widow of Tadhg *Óg's* late son Aengus *Cliste*.

Lochlain, only son of Aengus and Muireann.

Cathal *Dubh,* Tadhg *Óg's* marshal (cavalry commander) and nephew.

Donal *Garbh* MacCabe, Scottish constable of the tribe's gallowglass troop.

Redmond O'Ronayne, a Jesuit and a qualified physician.

Nial *dhá chlaíomh* Ne Dourough, a bondsman in the service of Tadhg *Óg*.

# Spaniards

Francisco de Cuéllar, a sea captain shipwrecked in Ireland.

Abelardo de Santiago, a widowed marksman shipwrecked in Ireland.

# Sassenachs

George Bingham, English sheriff of Sligo.

John Gilson, an Irish renegade lieutenant in the service of Bingham.

Treasach Burke, an Irish renegade sergeant in the service of Bingham.

# The dead

Aengus *Cliste*, only son of Tadhg *Óg* and Dervila, husband of Muireann, father of Lochlain.

Cathal *Óg*, previous chieftain of the MacGlannagh tribe and called *An Faolchù* (The Wolf). Also the elder brother of Tadhg *Óg* and the father of Cathal *Dubh*.

Elsien van der Molen, late wife of Abelardo de Santiago.

Maerten van der Molen, late brother of Elsien.

Reynier van der Molen, late father of Elsien, Maerten and Pieter.

# The story so far...

*In the year 1588, Abelardo 'Santi' de Santiago, a veteran of the Spanish Army of Flanders, finds himself a reluctant member of the Spanish Armada which sets sail for England. Following the Armada's defeat by the English fleet at the famous sea battle of Gravelines, Santi's ship is wrecked on the western coast of Ireland. Santi somehow reaches the shore and journeys inland, where he quickly discovers a country that is oppressed by heartless English troopers that the natives call Sassenachs, which to Santi's Spanish ear sounds like 'Sassanas.'*

*Santi is himself hunted by English troopers, who have orders from their queen's viceroy in Dublin to capture and kill all Spanish Armada castaways. He is eventually seized by the brutal English sheriff of Sligo Town, who imprisons Santi and has him tortured. But thanks to an unlikely twist of fate, Santi flees Sligo with an invaluable emerald ring. He also rescues a revered Irish bard named Muireann Mac an Bhaird. Muireann leads Santi deep to her tribe's rebel kingdom of Dartry, where Santi receives the protection of its rebel chieftain Tadhg Óg MacGlannagh (the MacGlannagh). The MacGlannagh soon learns of Santi's exceptional sharpshooting ability, so that Santi is ordered to train the chieftain and his bodyguards daily in marksmanship.*

*Santi proceeds to distinguish himself among the tribe by rescuing a Spanish sea captain and defending the MacGlannagh's* tower house of Rosclogher during a siege by the English viceroy's army. He also rescues the MacGlannagh's nephew, Cathal the Black, during a raid on the English garrison town of Boyle. This last act of bravery leads the MacGlannagh to proclaim Santi as a true hero of Rosclogher and his adopted son.

Following his adoption, Santi notes how the MacGlannagh's nephew Cathal, and the villainous, Scottish mercenary leader Donal MacCabe, are both determined to wed the widowed Muireann. Santi also learns that the only way to restrain the ruthless Donal's growing power among the tribe is for Cathal to marry Muireann. This is because the marriage will ensure that Cathal receives Muireann's inheritance, making him the wealthiest man in Dartry.

However, Santi and Muireann find themselves falling in love with each other, with the two engaging in a number of secret trysts. One of these trysts is discovered by Donal's spies, and Santi shoots one of them dead. Santi is accused of murder while Donal also accuses him of raping Muireann. In making this accusation, Donal hopes that either Santi or Muireann will confess to their affair, which will besmirch Muireann's honour and compromise her union with Cathal. Yet Santi surprises Donal by accepting the accusation of rape, in order to protect Muireann's honour and to rescue her impending union with Cathal.

Santi's admission of guilt means that he is punished with a huge fine. Yet since he does not have the means to pay it, Santi finds his recently elevated status among the tribe being reduced to that of a slave. Santi spends many backbreaking weeks serving a local herdsman, until his fine is paid by a neighbouring, rebel overlord of the MacGlannaghs: the O'Rourke. The O'Rourke overlord orders Santi to help train a modern troop of pike and *shot, made up of Spanish Armada castaways and Irish natives, to fight the English on equal terms.*

*Santi trains the local troop mercilessly for days on end, then leads them to Doagh Mountain where they ambush and over-power a Sassana baggage train. Afterwards Santi learns from a Sassana captive that an Irishwoman who can ruin the Irish rebels' English enemies is being held captive in the English garri-son of Sligo Town. Santi reluctantly decides to somehow free the Irishwoman from Sligo Town. After tricking the town's guards to allow him inside, Santi learns from a renegade sergeant that the emerald ring in Santi's possession is a gift by the Spanish king to the mother of his illegitimate son. The ring is therefore powerful proof of paternity which could decide any potential succession dispute relating to the Spanish Imperial throne. Santi also finds out that Queen Elizabeth I of England has learned of the ring's significance and wants it, so that her viceroy in Dublin will never stop searching for it.*

*After breaking the captive Irishwoman out of Sligo Town, Santi learns that the MacGlannagh's lands are being raided by allies of the Sassanas. Santi and his troop march to Dartry and repel the MacGlannagh's enemies. In doing so Santi redeems himself by rescuing the tower house of Rosclogher once more.*

'. . .If you had been so wise either in divinity or policy as you would be taken to be, you might easily have considered that such loose persons as they are that broke out in Connaught could and should in no better sort be repressed than by the sword, which was the course adopted by Sir Richard Bingham . . .'

*— Sir Francis Walsingham to the Bishop of Meath,*
*24 June 1589*

# XLVI

## Rosclogher, Dartry, County Leitrim

### *5 – 7 August 1589*

I sighed aloud as the Croat and I returned to our feet. As I turned towards the fleeing O'Reillys, I raised my musket to take aim at their skiff. Each of my five shots were true so that the little boat across the lake was soon sinking below the lake water. The O'Reillys pointed frantically in all directions as they shrieked at one another in fear, caught as they were between the crannog and the edge of Manglana's town. Many furious tribesmen could already be seen lined up along the water, nocking arrows to their bowstrings.

'Do you think they can swim?' asked Dario.

His question went unanswered as I trudged back towards the keep, feeling both weary and lightheaded from the events of the day, the smell of gun smoke still lingering in my nostrils.

'I need a drink,' I said.

Dario followed me to the door of the tower house, and the sound of our squelching boots alerted the keep's occupants to our presence.

'Unbolt the door!' cried Dervila. Both her lady-in-waiting Saorla and the chieftain's sister flew from her side to obey her command.

Our approach had also disturbed the wounded O'Reillys who lay at our feet, who had each received a ball in the fusillade. One of their number had crept halfway towards the water, but Dario drew his *skene* dagger and set off after him. Within instants the fleeing O'Reilly had his head hauled back by his hair. He cried once for mercy before the length of the Croat's dagger was drawn across his gullet, rendering him a hissing, throbbing mass.

Dario whistled casually to himself as he wiped his dagger upon the corpse, then walked back towards the keep to finish off the rest. The iron door swung open as he knelt towards yet another wriggling enemy who groaned in protest as he bled profusely from the stomach.

'What are you doing?' asked Saorla from the doorway, observing the Croat, who tightly clenched the hair of the shivering enemy around his massive fist.

'But a mere act of mercy,' grunted the Croat. He pulled back the head of the wounded tribesman and placed his knife beneath the trembling man's chin.

'Shouldn't we take them hostage?' I asked, feeling somewhat disturbed by the sight.

Dario stared back at me in puzzlement as he momentarily refrained from both his whistling and the drawing of blood. 'Should we?'

'Their tunics are saffron,' added Mangala's sister, who had also appeared in the door.

Dario's eyes met those of the man whose life he was about to snuff out; then he flung the O'Reilly's head forward. The Croat returned his dagger to its sheath, then rose off his knee with a shrug and followed me into the gloom of Rosclogher Castle. Upon entering the tower-house we made our way towards the ladder which the two maidens had lowered, then climbed up the inbuilt staircase in the direction of the roof.

'The Scots appeared two days ago,' said Saorla, 'and demanded that they be let inside the tower to take the payment which was due to them. They abandoned the town to the O'Reillys when my lady refused their request.'

I ignored her as I stepped through the entrance to the roof and made for the water cistern. Dario and I silently washed our hands and faces in it as Manglana's wife approached us.

'It pleases me to see that you are in good health, Spaniard,' she said.

'And I am relieved that you are safe, my lady,' I replied with a flourishing bow.

A sly grin spread across her lips at my words.

'Are you truly relieved, Spaniard? One would say I almost met with a deserved end after allying myself for so long to MacCabe.'

'No, my lady. You defended yourself well.'

'Hardly,' she replied, rolling her eyes. 'Those curs would have taken us before the guns were reloaded.'

The truth of her claim could not be denied, so I chose another topic of conversation after swallowing yet a few more mouthfuls of water.

'Your town still burns, my lady. Many are killed, with many more wounded. We also have great plunder which needs to be moved into the keep.'

Lady Bourke closed her eyes and drew a deep breath, steadying herself for a few moments, while one of her maidens tucked some of her dishevelled hair back underneath her linen headdress.

'Ferry me across the water,' said Dervila at last, as her verdant eyes opened, 'that we may restore order and succour the wounded.'

Dario and I instantly led her and the other maids down the steps, but when we reached the floor below us, Dartry's queen stopped dead before us and called out into the hall.

'Lochlain, my love. You may come out now.'

At first there was heard no reply to her bidding. For a moment I felt strangely disappointed to discover that Muireann's son was hidden away with his grandmother in the keep while his people endured an attack by the O'Reillys. Yet as Dervila called out once again, her voice rose in distress.

'Lochlain, my boy! Are you there?'

We waited a while longer to no avail, so Manglana's wife ran towards the northern window of the floor. Dario, the maidens and I ran after her, reaching a chamber which had a ruffled blanket and some chicken bones against a corner of the wall. Dartry's queen released a piercing shriek of distress when she found that the hall was empty, then cast her head out of the window and screamed again. As she fell to her knees and shook in anguish, Dario thrust his head out after her.

'What happened?' I asked as I stepped towards his shoulder.

'There is an arrow shaft tied to knotted bedsheets upon the grass.'

'So he climbed out?'

The Croat cast me a pained glance at my stating the obvious, then fell to one knee and helped the stricken queen back onto her feet.

'Do not yet abandon hope, my lady,' he whispered. She looked back at him in confusion as we led her towards the steps.

The chieftain's wife clutched the Croat's arm and whispered beneath her breath, 'I promised his mother, promised her . . .'

Her gibbering hadn't ceased when we reached the bottommost floor and emerged from the keep. It carried on all throughout our brief passage across the water, with Dario and I rowing as hard as we could. When we reached the jetty she flew out of the skiff and ran towards the town, shrieking her grandson's name, her saffron-gowned maidens gathered closely about her.

'Follow her!' said Dario as he jumped out of the boat and coiled a rope about a pier. 'She might do him an injury when she finally finds him!'

Despite my great weariness at the events of the day, I heeded the Croat's command. One of the maidens could be seen slipping behind a smouldering wreck of a cabin as I ran past *Doire Mel.* As I closed in on Dervila's party, the ladies could be seen falling to their knees to speak to wounded tribesmen or ruffling the besmirched hair of dead youths in the alleys to ensure that it was not red like the prince's.

Cries of dismay abounded as the dead bodies of tribesmen were discovered, accompanied by the sounds of collapsing huts. We searched for Lochlain all over the distraught town, in which many familiar faces were discovered amongst the deceased. We even found Gorman's son Brian slumped against a cabin with his head split open. My heart sank as his foolish face gaped back at me even in death, and I dreaded the moment his kin would discover the loss of a son who had cost them so much to raise.

Further along the edge of the settlement, the daughters of mad Orla could be seen wailing upon their knees, gathered about the corpse of their mother, who had also perished from a blow to the head. The dead harlot still bore the demented grin which had been so disturbing in life, her glazed expression fixed upon the clouds overhead. In their haste the O'Reillys had beheaded few of their victims, so hope remained that Lochlain might at least be discovered dead if not alive. After the greensward had been searched from end to end, I returned to the cabins along the water's edge, fearing the worst and wondering if the young prince would ever be found. A chain of men had formed between the water and the town, quickly passing wooden pails from hand to hand as water was drawn from the lake and hurled upon the remaining fires.

'Lochlain?' cried Dervila behind me as one of the water bearers turned his head towards her.

Lady Bourke had already gathered her tunic and scampered off towards him, her cries of outrage and relief alerting her ladies, who swiftly made after her. We pursued the women at a cautious distance. Their mistress' face turned a scarlet hue as her grandson looked at her askance. I recognised Nial standing alongside the youth. The bondsman had just passed a pail to the man beside him, and he stepped towards the queen with a ready smile.

'This man honours the memory of his father,' he declared, gesturing towards Lochlain. 'With only a sword he put his life in great danger, defending a woman and child from a pair of raiders.'

At Nial's words we realised that the blood spattered across the face of Muireann's son was not his own, yet this did little to calm the youth's grandmother, who seized him in a crushing embrace. She next pushed him away and slapped him across the face so hard that his head flew sideways.

'Never disobey me again!'

A trickle of blood appeared on the boy's chin. Dervila raised her hand to strike him again, but we all gasped in surprise as the boy snatched the queen's wrist to halt her movement.

'Treat me not as one of your maids,' he snarled with a dark grimace, which was rendered more unsightly by his bloodied mouth, 'for I am the son of Aengus Cliste, and I shall always honour the memory of my father. He would not have me hide behind stout walls while my people perish.'

For once Lady Bourke appeared lost for words at the sight of her pup's claws, and it was but a few instants before she regained her composure.

'Indeed you are,' she hissed back at him, jerking her hand free of his grip, 'the son of my Aengus, and your life shall not be risked for the life of a cowherd's daughter!'

With that she whirled about angrily and marched off with her ladies still following closely on her heels, her face like a thundercloud. After she was gone, we stood about in awkward silence, still too shaken to speak after having witnessed the ire of Dartry's queen. The uncomfortable lull was broken when Dario appeared again, clapping his hands at the sight of Lochlain. The youth still breathed heavily after his confrontation with his grandmother, and his blood-streaked countenance appeared both anguished and confused.

Lochlain's eyes glimmered with tearful indignation, his stare possessed of a righteousness that reminded me of his mother, the woman I loved. I felt sorry for the lad, so I stepped towards him and laid a hand upon his shoulder despite my better judgement. His stare was both earnest and sincere as he looked at me, and I found I could not hold it for long.

'What would you have done in my stead, Spaniard?' he asked.

A deep sigh left me as my hand fell back to my side, and in the prince's stead, I took the pail of water borne by the bondsman and passed it on down the line.

'Seek not guidance from me, lad, for I always clashed with my elders and betters.'

I turned away and walked off as swiftly as I could, hoping in vain to get out of earshot before he asked the inevitable question. Yet he asked it before I had reached the nearest cabin, in a voice loud enough to be heard from *Doire Mel.*

'And do you regret it?'

I released another sigh of distress as I stopped in my tracks and stared warily about me. I beheld the smouldering piles of wood and wattle, the scenes of death and destruction which had become all too familiar during the many years I spent serving as a starving soldier. I turned to face the boy and stared right into his ochre eyes, which reminded me so much of his mother.

'Yes.'

Thereafter I made straight for the greensward, with Dario swiftly running up behind me. Together we found Ramos deep in conversation with Geraldine, who held a bloodstained blade out before him.

'I tell you that this is Cathal's. One of Nial's bluejackets has already confirmed it.'

Ramos pursed his lips as he observed the weapon, then lifted his head towards us.

'So there you are! Where in God's name did you end up? With mad Orla and her daughters?'

The sergeant did not stir when I told him that the mad whore had been killed, and his stoic expression barely registered the slightest disquiet when Dario told him how we had pursued the two boatloads of raiders.

'Fools. Nearly got yourselves killed over a stupid keep.'

'I beg your pardon,' protested Old Tom, 'but do you not mistake valour for foolishness?' These men risked their lives to rescue the stronghold of our master's first lieutenant.'

'And that is the problem with you Irish,' sneered Ramos instantly, 'all desirous of acts of valour to fill the songs in yet another hall. Yet if you fail to understand that this is a war we are fighting, the last bard will soon swing from a tree. I need able men to beat our enemy, not acts of valour. And if you two fools ever engage in another valiant act without my express instruction again, it will be your *last* act.'

He next addressed the Anglo-Norman, who had listened to his retort with a pained expression. 'Was there any other sign of the tanist?'

'None yet,' replied Geraldine sadly. 'The highborn O'Rourkes are still searching the banks of the lake.'

'How did the O'Reillys get here before us?'

'They must have passed through Fermanagh.'

Ramos' eye widened slightly in alarm when he heard this. 'Has Maguire also turned?'

'No,' snorted Geraldine. 'They must have passed through his lands unnoticed.'

Ramos stroked his whiskers as he cast Old Tom a look of the greatest cynicism. 'We both know that that is impossible.'

'Are you accusing Maguire of treachery? He has not declared himself for either side.'

'All I am saying,' replied Ramos tersely, 'is that something strange is afoot, which smells all too much like good old treachery.'

Geraldine slowly nodded back at him before replying. 'That smell is as common as peat smoke in this land. Yet of whom do you suspect it?'

'Perhaps one of our hostages can help us find out.'

'Alas!' cried Geraldine. 'None of the enemy were taken alive. All fought to the death or got themselves beyond our grip.'

'Do not fret,' said Dario, 'for our foolish and futile act of valour at the stupid tower has secured us four O'Reilly prisoners.'

Ramos served the Croat with a hard stare as Geraldine burst out laughing and slapped both the Croat and me upon our backs.

'Some welcome tidings at last!' he chortled. 'The Lord knows this has been both a trying and thankless day.'

'Then let us gather our men from along the lake and relieve them of their bucket-bearing duties,' said Ramos. 'It is time to bear both plunder and hostages into the keep.'

The men were rounded up and led back to the edge of the bog, where the goods we had abandoned by the trees were recovered. After a pair of runners were despatched to Keelooges to fetch Riona and Gilson, we made our way with heavy packs on our backs towards the jetty. Dario and his O'Rourke riders appeared not long afterwards, their mounts bearing the remaining panniers from Gilson's train. As a pair of kerns punted a skiff towards us, we observed Dervila rallying the town's survivors and issuing commands even as the wounded still sobbed and groaned in the dirt.

'Poor bastards,' said Dario, observing the tribesmen's efforts to haul the injured back onto their feet and gather up the newly orphaned. 'Lady Bourke has much work on her hands.'

'It serves the bitch right,' snapped Ramos, 'for placing so much trust in the Scots. Donal MacCabe was ever a ruthless and lowborn ruffian, and it was only a matter of time until he attempted to supplant Manglana. It is the curse of these people that you never know who is with or against you.'

'As with all peoples,' I replied faintly, my eyes fixed on the ground.

He frowned at me for a moment, then nodded. 'That is true.'

We followed the sergeant into the approaching boat, leaving Old Tom behind as we returned to the crannog. When we reached the tower-house, two of the wounded O'Rourkes Dario had not despatched had all but perished from their wounds. Another lay dead along the water's edge.

'Let us hope that the Jesuit returns soon,' said Ramos as he nudged one of the stricken O'Reillys with his sword point, eliciting no reaction, 'for these men are at death's door.'

The goods were taken into the keep. Then we emerged from the tower-house.

'Are there no other boats?' asked Ramos as he looked about him in boredom.

'No,' replied Dario, 'for the other one was sunk by Abel here.'

The sergeant frowned at me in irritation.

'When the next boatload returns,' he said, 'you must get the men to build a raft. One of those makeshift ones we used to build back in Flanders. Otherwise we will be standing here until tomorrow.'

His command was followed to the letter, and I sent a handful of natives to obtain logs from the woods. After the timber was carried back to the green, we bound it tightly together with many lengths of cow gut. In this way our goods were swiftly borne across the water well before nightfall, whereupon Ramos ordered that the raft be kept upon the crannog. The remaining rowboat was used by Dario to return to the town, where he ordered Ramos' militia to set up camp on the greensward.

The only men that remained behind with us were ten of the Spaniards, including Dal Verme and the Canarians. Old Tom also remained with us upon the crannog, so we had an unlikely reunion of the true heroes of Rosclogher. We were up late into the night after our companions had passed into slumber, long after Dervila and her ladies had returned to the keep with a strong guard of bluejackets.

'How many days since the siege was broken?' asked Pedro, licking his fingers after his last bite of horseflesh.

'Eight months to the day this Sunday,' put in Old Tom matter-of-factly.

'That long since we last saw action?' gasped Franco at his brother's shoulder.

'Well, we have more than made up for it in the last two days,' I said.

'Yes,' Pedro agreed, 'and it was the Lord's hand which saved me today. That is the truth of it. One of those bastards hurled a spear behind me which just nicked the edge of my throat.'

The young Canarian grimaced as he gently rubbed a gash on the side of his neck.

'Have you cauterised it?' asked Old Tom. 'The wound could yet putrefy.'

"'Tis but a scratch.' The lad shrugged, as he dismissively patted it with grubby fingers.

Geraldine and I swiftly exchanged knowing glances, after which the Anglo-Norman rose to his feet and drew his pipe.

'I need a pipe light,' he said, then shuffled off to climb to the hearth in the chieftain's hall.

'And you, Luigi?' I asked the lanky figure of Dal Verme, who had until then sat with a raised knee against the wall, silently staring into space. 'What do you think of all this?'

A few minutes passed before the Milanese mercenary finally spoke in a voice which was still haughty and contemptuous despite the travails of the previous two days.

'Even the blind could tell that there is treachery afoot. My fear is that the same hand which betrayed us during the siege has been at work once more. How else would the O'Reillys have known of the small force guarding the keep?'

'Do you suspect the gallowglass?' I asked.

'Who can tell for sure?' he replied, never once stopping to return my stare. 'It could be anyone close to the chieftain who still stabs him in the back, except perhaps for the bard and the Jesuit. That said, stranger acts of treachery have happened.'

We mulled over his words in grim silence until Old Tom reappeared down the steps, bearing a smouldering brand which he had picked off the chieftain's hearth.

'What is that for?' asked Pedro nervously, then fell silent as I wrapped the palm of my hand around his mouth.

I held him down while Geraldine pressed the ember against the wound in the boy's neck, which hissed ever so slightly before the stick was pulled away again to loud protestations from the Canarian's twin brother. The twins yelled and cursed at us, yet were eventually placated since they knew that what we had done was for the best.

The following day we crossed the water with Ramos, then marched with him to the greensward, where inspection was held before drill. While we trained, a number of herdsmen appeared through the trees along the southern ring of bog and made their way down to what was left of the town. I looked away from Gorman when the herdsman appeared in the company of his own son Shane and a half-dozen family members. A cry of grief was heard not long afterwards when they discovered the body of the *druth* Brian in the blackened, tamped-down alleyways.

Ramos relieved us from training towards midafternoon with assurances that our share of the booty held at Rosclogher would be fairly shared after Manglana returned from his campaign. The pinch of the pistol stowed away in my belt left me doubtful of his assurances, for I already knew that every officer sought to pilfer any goods to which his inferiors were entitled. Yet I was also mindful of the emerald ring which was hidden away in my ampoule, so I thought it better to take Ramos at his word and not seek out trouble by questioning his promises.

My ears were still filled with the howl of keeners as I made my way from the town, intent on avoiding scenes of misery or any rebuilding works. The events of the previous two days had greatly worn me, so that my own company and time to strategise were my only desires. As I trudged along the eastern bank away from Saint Mel, I was suddenly met by the sight of Gorman and his relatives gathered about a cairn, which they had erected upon the corpse of the *druth*.

The old herdsman's hand trembled as he lay the last rock upon the mound of stones, and tears flowed freely among the gathering as they stared on wordlessly at the grave of Brian. Other herdsmen had also returned from the heights of Dartry to the town to discover the lot of their relatives. We could soon hear the start of a death feast, yet this was ignored by Gorman and his family, who stood crestfallen alongside the remains of their slain kinsman.

As I observed them from afar I could not help but think of the number of times they must have wished he had never been born due to the amount of strife he had caused them during his lifetime. Upon thinking this I instantly berated myself and whispered a prayer for the departed soul of the fool who had persecuted me for nearly two months.

After an hour, Gorman's kinsmen began to drift off towards the town. Soon, only the elderly herdsman and his wife remained alongside the cairn. I was moved by the sight of them, and I had not the heart to abandon them to their grief. As I walked over towards them with a cautious gait, Gorman turned and beheld me wordlessly, his arms hanging limply by his sides. His wizened features bore an expression which I had seen all too often, as he struggled to understand the meaning of his son's passing.

'I should have let him join the creaght,' he said, 'but I thought it was safer here . . .'

It was hard to meet his lost stare as his voice trailed off, and my voice shook as I managed a whisper.

'You could not have known.'

Manglana's party returned to the town two days later, still blood-spattered and battle-weary from their raiding. They rode through the green but an hour past dawn, just as we were lining up to endure another day of punishing training. Manglana's host approached the town at a canter, their sounds largely muffled by the blood that had caked upon horse and man alike, only the clink of steel and dull hoofbeats revealing their presence. At the sight of the despoiled settlement a look of bewilderment shadowed their faces, and for a moment they reminded me of a pack of wolves that had discovered their defiled lair.

These horsemen were an ominous sight as they emerged from the trees and crossed the green, the rotten heads of slain enemies bouncing off their mounts' flanks like the faces of ghosts shaking in the early morning mist. Dozens of kerns followed in close pursuit, leading scores of lowing cattle which had been stolen in the raids and bearing cages of fowl upon their shoulders. Yet no cheer of delight was heard at their approach, for the townsfolk had not yet stirred after their efforts spent rebuilding the village.

Ramos ordered us to form square, and our attentions were quickly diverted from the returning party as it made its way down towards the banks of the lake. The kerns busied themselves with erecting posts and confines for the many heads of cattle which they had rustled from the southern plains. After the chieftain and his closest kinsmen returned to the keep, we saw and heard nothing more of them until the end of the following day, after more hard training had concluded upon the greensward. At the end of it Ramos lined us up and declared that the next day would be one of rest.

The news was welcome due to our sore limbs and aching backs, for we had barely had a day to recover from our frays against Gilson and the O'Reillys. The men were so exhausted that none visited the whorehouse or played dice that evening. Instead the whole militia immediately retired to their tents. I fell asleep as soon as my head touched the ground, yet any hopes of a late morning rise were dashed just before dawn, when Dario shook me hard by the shoulder.

'What is it?' I blurted irritably as he scowled at me.

'You have been summoned to Manglana's hall. The chieftain has requested our presence.'

I was baffled by his words, and I slowly arose from the ground, cursing beneath my breath as I reached for my sword.

'Bring the rifle, too, and make haste,' snapped Dario. 'They say that the gallowglasses will be here within the hour.'

'Constable MacCabe?' I asked in surprise, but the Croat's hasty departure left me alone in the tent with my unanswered questions.

When I poked my head out, I could see a trio of men in the early dimness. Ramos huffed aloud at the sight of me.

'By the love of the Virgin, Abelito,' he muttered. 'Will you hurry up?'

As I scrambled out of the tent, I found that Ramos and Old Tom were already in the Croat's company, and together we walked down towards the water. Just then the distant whinny of a horse was heard at our backs, and I quickly turned my head back towards the greensward.

'They have arrived,' observed Dario.

'Curse them,' snarled Geraldine at my shoulder. 'If they do not meet with his justice today, then there will be open revolt.'

'It is not for us to dispense justice,' said Ramos, 'although I suspect that it shall be served out heartily today.'

I suppressed a shudder at the sight of a mailed gallowglass warrior on horseback, who reined in his mount and glared at the town. We hurried towards the lakeside cabins of the highborn and made our way towards the jetty, where we swiftly boarded the skiff to the Rosclogher tower-house. Ours was a silent party that crossed the dark water, reached the keep and made our way up to the hall. The bluejackets upon the steps were many in number and looked fiercer than ever, especially following the battering which their master's pride had taken at the hands of the O'Reilly raiders. Yet upon noticing us their spears were instantly lowered, and they swiftly stepped aside to let us into the MacGlannagh's hall.

'Why are there twice the usual number?' I asked, but Geraldine cast a long forefinger across his lips for me to keep silent as the four of us stood before the gathered elders of the tribe.

The rare sight of the chieftain sitting alongside his wife greeted us at the other end of the hall, and although there was no fire upon the hearth, I found myself warmed by the sight of Muireann standing alongside the Jesuit and bard. A large party of bluejackets were also standing around us, and Nial stepped forward to silently wave at us, urging our party to stand on the chieftain's left.

'Load your rifle,' he whispered to me, and as I slowly drew the gun off my shoulder, I realised that all eyes in the room were still fixed upon the door through which we had entered.

The Marquardt was long loaded and returned to my shoulder – I could have reloaded it another dozen times – before the usual creak of the doors was heard. There stepped before us the constable Donal MacCabe, bedecked in his full armour and accompanied by his giant son Brogan and another half-dozen Scots. Freemen hastily moved aside and a heavy clank of armour was heard as the seven gallowglasses entered the hall in their long mail dresses, their domed helmets held in the crooks of their arms. They were ashen-faced to a man, though their lips curled in contempt. The *ogham* symbols scrawled on their axes appeared more ominous than usual.

Donal MacCabe's weapon was a beauty to behold, a snaphaunce rifle with an axe head at the end of its bore, which allowed it to serve as two weapons. As always, the mercenaries did not bow to Manglana or offer any words of salute. They observed the Dartrymen gathered before them with a frosty stare as they leant forward on their huge axes. On their part

Manglana and his wife said nothing, casting dark stares at the gallowglasses until Donal haughtily stepped forward.

'You summoned me, Lord?'

Manglana placed his hands upon the armrests of his throne and pushed himself to his feet. It was a sight which filled me with trepidation, for I had never seen it happen in these halls and it led me to expect the unprecedented. Indeed the sight of the chieftain rising onto his feet was to herald the longest address I would ever hear him deliver.

'My most loyal retainers declare me sheriff-slayer of Dartry and champion of the law,' he boomed, as we braced ourselves for his dragon breath, 'while those who would supplant me secretly accuse me of fratricide and claim that my elder brother returns to plague my lands in the form of a black wolf. Yet above all else, I am lord of Dartry and first lieutenant to our overlord *na Múrtha*, Brian O'Rourke of neighbouring Breifne.'

The chieftain fell silent as he glared at MacCabe – for so long that a slight scrape was heard when the Scot shifted awkwardly from foot to foot.

'Why do you tell me this?' asked the gallowglass constable. 'For I already know it.'

Dervila stirred in her seat, but her husband whirled upon her with a raised hand, urging her to remain silent. He then leant forward and glared at MacCabe.

'And have you not forgotten it?' yelled the chieftain. 'Have you not ridden to Rosclogher with your own banners unfurled, all while loudly declaring yourself lord of my lands?'

MacCabe snorted aloud at Manglana's accusation. 'But lies, my lord, and the idle talk of lowly churls.'

'It is you that lies!' screeched Lady Bourke at Manglana's side, finding herself unable to contain her outrage any longer. She flew to her feet and pointed an accusatory finger at the Scot. 'Lies! Blemishes and boils shall burst from your face for the slander uttered in the presence of your lord!'

'My face is already marked,' growled the Scot, 'from years spent fighting in your defence on an empty belly. In any event, I did appear to defend the town, yet it was you that would not let me into the keep.'

'What is your game?' roared the chieftain suddenly, ignoring MacCabe's attempt at sympathy and reason. As I observed the Scot, who stood in outraged silence, I savoured the day of reckoning which had finally dawned.

MacCabe's face turned a crimson hue as he puffed his chest out and rested his fists upon his sides.

'You do me ill by asking that, Tadhg *Óg* MacGlannagh. I have spilled blood and lost kin defending your lands. Yet since you ask the question I would happily answer it, if only to remind all present of my standing and the outrage of my treatment. For I am Donal MacCabe, your brother by marriage, he who fought by your side when the last sheriff was slain. I have saved your men from the field times without count.'

'How hollow do the faithful words of a usurper sound,' said the chieftain drily, 'in the very hall which he sought to claim for his own.'

'It is the men that became unruly, my lord,' protested MacCabe, his voice suddenly low and feeble, 'for how long do you expect them to fight on empty stomachs?'

'My men have also gone hungry, Donal,' retorted Manglana, 'for our first heads always go to your men! Your womanly rant shall not find my sympathy, for my tanist is lost and my town destroyed despite your being bound to protect them both! The destruction inflicted by the O'Reillys more than shadows my debt to you, Scotsman. Begone from my lands and consider our ties absolved. Take your men with you if they shall follow, but whatever you do, get out of my sight.'

MacCabe visibly bristled at the chieftain's words, and all present in the hall looked at each other in amazement at the banishment which had just been pronounced.

'You shall regret this,' seethed the Scot, but the chieftain's voice rose above his once more.

'On your knees before you leave, and swear that you shall honour my last command and never set foot in Dartry again.'

The constable's face reddened when he heard this, and a growl left his lips as he advanced towards the chieftain and his wife, his men forming a menacing ring about him with their arms were raised. Yet they had hardly taken two steps when a body of spearmen, who had until then mingled unnoticed among the crowd, stepped forward and drove their weapons through the necks of the approaching Scots. MacCabe and Brogan alone were spared death. They were beaten with the ends of countless spear butts as their dying fellows kicked the air and hissed upon the ground. Tribesmen quickly withdrew amid gasps of horror at the sudden violence, though the odd laugh of scorn was also heard as this incredible treatment of the constable unfolded before our very eyes.

The Scots' was a resistance which ended the moment it started. Brogan barely stirred as a half-dozen spear ends stroked his throat, and MacCabe was beaten to his knees amid the cracking of spear shafts. Yet even in the arms of utter humiliation and defeat, the Scots' spirit remained undimmed.

'Is this the reward for my loyal service?' MacCabe protested, as he held a spear end away from his chin in a bloodied hand.

Manglana growled as his fists quivered in fury. Then he slowly returned to his seat.

'You come to me, Donal Garve, having barely wiped the fat of my land from your lips, while my town smoulders on your account? And you would make demands?'

'But what shall become of my people?'

'They can work the mines of Thomond for all I care! Whatever you do, it shall be leagues beyond count from here, for you will never set foot in these lands again!'

'And what of your sister, my lawful wedded wife?' protested MacCabe defiantly.

Manglana raised his hand towards Dervila's ladies-in-waiting, and his portly sister stepped forth.

'Donal MacCabe, I dismiss you!' she cried, thereby pronouncing her divorce and leaving us to wonder if any further dishonour could possibly be cast upon the beleaguered Scot.

Donal's breathing grew heavy and quick at his rupture from Manglana's house, and it was clear that he suddenly feared for his life.

'Let none say that I killed my former brother,' roared Manglana as soon as the marriage was broken, instantly dashing our hopes that he might call for Donal's execution. 'Consider yourself fortunate to still draw breath. Now begone and make haste if you value the life of your own son.'

The chieftain's anger was discomfiting to behold, for he rarely showed his teeth. They wiggled as he shouted, his face turning as red as dulse. MacCabe had barely returned to his feet when he noticed the bluejackets binding Brogan's arms with long lengths of cow gut before hauling him back onto his feet.

'If you touch a hair on my son's body,' hissed the constable, shoving the spears at his back aside and returning to the centre of the hall, 'I shall return to Dartry with a greater army at my back and raze the very mountains to the ground.'

'And if you so much as dare take another step forward,' yelled Manglana from his seat of power, 'this here Spaniard shall blow your lying jaws off your face. I need not remind you of how much pleasure that would give him.'

No sooner had he said this than MacCabe stopped dead in his tracks, eyeing me warily as my finger quivered on the serpentine. It was all I could do not to shoot the man who had cost me so much in the way of suffering and dishonour, so it was a relief when he finally whirled about with a low grunt and stormed through the door.

For a time thereafter none spoke. Then murmurings from the more elderly members of the tribe were heard, which grew into a heated debate while the chieftain sat in pensive silence. As I slung my rifle back on my shoulder, Geraldine muttered beneath his breath with a frown.

'It is dark days indeed when a lord must banish his gallowglass constable.'

I stared back at the Anglo-Norman just as Donal's son was roughly led out of the hall.

One of the elderly members of the assembly stepped forward.

'My lord,' he said, 'have we acted in haste by expelling the gallowglass? The fighting season is still with us.'

'There is no reason, friend Seamus,' replied Manglana, 'to retain the services of those who would do us harm in return for payment.'

'Indeed, Lord,' said another elder. 'Better to use what wealth we have left to seek to ransom our tanist.'

'That would be both unwise and unnecessary,' sneered Dervila from the chieftain's elbow, 'for he would also seek to usurp us at the first opportunity.'

The attack of Dartry's queen on its tanist left me feeling stunned and angry, although none dared to openly contradict her. I was relieved to hear the chieftain rebutting his wife's words.

'Cathal *Dubh* has always been a loyal servant to me, and I have never doubted his good faith. At dawn tomorrow I shall despatch an envoy to meet with the grey merchants, that we may discover his fate and if we are able to ransom him.'

'You would put lives at risk for such a worthless whelp?' asked Dervila, but her words went ignored by all present as Manglana beckoned to his steward.

'Summon the witness, Malachy.'

As soon as he made this request, the small door to the hall opened once more, and there appeared the figure of Riona O'Malley. The witness had been fetched from her refuge at Keelooges only two days previous. Some semblance of colour had returned to her face following her rescue from Sligo, although her movement was still cautious as her brown eyes shifted warily from left to right.

The gathered freemen stepped aside respectfully as she passed through them, the crisp saffron of their freshly dyed tunics contrasting with the white one which she had received at *Doire Mel*. At the sight of it I studied the frowning features of Redmond O'Ronayne, who stood among the chieftain's closest retainers. Ever since his return with the chieftain's party, the Jesuit had busied himself with funeral rites and caring for the newly orphaned, yet he had also seen to it that the O'Malley witness had received all the care and protection that she required.

'All hail a woman without fear,' declared the chieftain as she bowed deeply before him, 'whose witness in Dublin shall have those Bingham devils clapped into chains and led to the Tower of London.'

Riona turned to acknowledge the bowing of the assembly members, then addressed the chieftain in a voice which was both clear and unfaltering, and which I thought verged on anger.

'Greetings, most worthy MacGlannagh. I am Riona of the Síol Owen O'Malley, of the O'Malley clan in Mayo.'

The chieftain sat back on his throne with a fleeting grin. 'A kinswoman of the famous Grania.'

'Yes, my lord, a kinswoman of Grania, she whose kin have suffered much at the hands of the Bingham brothers throughout the troubles caused by the MacWilliamship. After the rebels killed the sheriff of Mayo in February, our lives were crushed by Governor Richard Bingham. Our villages were razed to the ground as his men slew all those who fell into his hands.'

'I have heard tell of these matters,' replied Manglana tersely, 'yet were the Binghams not reined in by the viceroy?'

'That they were, my lord,' replied Riona, 'yet his lieutenants' outrages persist even now. Few places are safe and spies abound everywhere. After my capture I was fortunate to be rescued by these daring men; otherwise my end would also have been grisly.'

Manglana acknowledged her praise with the slightest of nods, and to a man we stiffened as his eyes flickered over the four of us.

'We have received word,' he said to Riona at last, 'that the Blind Abbot has proclaimed himself the MacWilliam, which would make him your overlord. This act shall spur the Binghams on to greater barbarity if they do not meet with justice.'

'Of a certainty,' replied O'Malley, 'for they are a law unto themselves, ignoring all orders from the Crown.'

'And therein lies the root of our quarrel,' continued the chieftain, 'but fear not. You shall be safe from harm in Dartry. Yet are you still prepared to bear witness in Dublin? After all it is much to ask any woman, especially one with child.'

'Yes,' whispered the witness as her hand slowly caressed the swollen lump at her belly, 'for the past is strewn with blood and ashes, yet it is for tomorrow that I am resolved to do this.'

Manglana fell silent for a few moments as he beheld the witness in awe, then drew in a huge breath and addressed her again.

'What you commit to is the greatest sacrifice one could ask for. I shall provide an armed escort to guide you to the Maguire's seat in Fermanagh, where you will be smuggled across the Shannon to our allies in Dublin, who have the viceroy's ear. Until then you will be provided for by my steward, who will attend to your every request.'

Riona bowed deeply, then gestured towards Ramos and the rest of us. 'Once more I offer my humble thanks for the gallantry these men showed at Sligo.'

To a man we bowed deeply to her as the chieftain addressed the O'Malley woman a last time. 'Retire now to the abbey, fair maiden, and recover your strength, for you have a long journey ahead and the hope of the whole of Connacht rides with you.'

The bowing witness stepped towards Geraldine and served him with an impassioned kiss on his hand, then served the same on Dario's, Ramos', and my hands too. She made her way back towards the door, and we faced the chieftain, who spoke to each of us in turn.

'You men are magi. The O'Rourke shall be overwhelmed to hear of your exploits. The goods you took from the enemy train number over a hundred ducats in value, which is not to mention the even greater prize you took from Sligo Town.'

His voice fell to a whisper as he leant forward and addressed me. 'And you, Juan: your debt to the Scot is no more, ever since his banishment from my demesne. As for what you owe me, it is already forgiven.'

So stunned was I by this absolution that the Marquardt all but fell from my hands, even as the burden of my fine fell from my shoulders like an unhitched yoke. My realisation of what had just happened had hardly sunk in when a rattle of chains was heard behind us and we turned to find the prisoner John Gilson being led before us. His fortunes had hardly improved since we had last seen him. His gold locks were dishevelled, his face and hands grimy. The Irish did not use prisons or detention except in the most extreme of circumstances, which meant that the renegade lieutenant had found himself leashed like a dog to a corner of the bluejackets' ringfort at the edge of the town. Although his presence did not inspire as much fear as that of the Scots, the revulsion on the faces of the freemen was akin to the stares they had served on the fallen MacCabe.

'Your wickedness is ended, Gilson,' said Manglana.

As Gilson raised his head to reply, I was amazed by his expression of unmasked hatred.

'Perhaps,' snarled the captive, 'but that of my master has barely begun.'

The chieftain frowned at the barely veiled threat. 'You know you have but one chance of a swift death, for many are those in Dartry who would tear you apart like oaten bread.'

'Do your worst,' spat Gilson, 'for I shall not betray the Crown. To aid rebels is treachery.'

'We are not rebels, since our loyalty also lies with the Crown. Albeit the one in Madrid.'

A few snatches of laughter were heard, which were in turn eclipsed by a roar of outrage from Gilson, who surprised everyone by springing to his feet and pointing an accusing finger at the chieftain.

'Yet do you confuse your sworn duty, MacGlannagh! Your titles were surrendered to Dublin by your own hand! In the eyes of the law you have reneged on your promises!'

'I do not answer to a crown that lets rogues like you do as they please. Or one which cannot even guarantee my people's safety. How many orders from Dublin have you ignored? But I need not discuss my actions with you. If tried by our laws you shall meet with certain death, but if you share your knowledge willingly, you may yet find us merciful.'

'And what would you have me tell you?'

'Of the Binghams' intentions.'

Gilson's eyes gleamed with a devilish amusement, and he grinned wickedly. 'Very well then; that is no secret. The trial in Dublin is but a farce, solely meant to reduce the uprisings in Connacht. In London the treasury is to be used to fund the counter-armada against Spain, since the Crown cannot yet afford to also suppress the rebellion in the west of Ireland. The Binghams have many friends close to the English queen who know that they are the only men who can restore some semblance of order in Connacht. The viceroy is a spent old fool whose last post was minding the queen of Scots, a simple task for which he proved incapable. He shall be told to call off his stupid trial before the year is out, when the Binghams will return to lay Connacht to waste. Once this suppression is accomplished, they shall claim those taxes that are rightfully due by law to the Crown, and civilise this land.'

'Who are you to civilise these people?' asked Ramos suddenly.

The captive returned his stare with one of amusement. 'And who is Spain to civilise the Indies?'

The sergeant grunted in annoyance at the prisoner's arrogance, then addressed him again. 'And what of the quarrel between the viceroy in Dublin and the Binghams? What is at the root of it?'

Gilson leered at the sergeant before he finally spoke the words that chilled me to my core. 'They say that it is a precious trinket, a ring. Stolen by some Spaniard.'

He stared at me when he said this, so that I blurted a mocking and uneasy reply of sorts. 'Or robbed by the Binghams, you mean?'

Gilson grinned. 'Or was it you, lowly horse thief? Stowing it up your backside and hiding it from your Irish allies? Some friend you are to them.'

I was so stunned by his accusation that I fumbled for a reply, yet the assembly's attentions were taken by the approach of O'Ronayne, who walked towards the captive with a raised cross and Bible, having clearly mistaken Gilson's revelation as a sign that he might also recant his heresy. At the sight of the approaching priest the captured lieutenant strained against the chains which bound him, then spat at the Jesuit and hissed.

'Keep away from me, idolator, for I worship in the church of Ireland!'

A sharp intake of breath was heard across the hall as O'Ronayne stopped dead in his tracks. The Jesuit appeared so flustered that his head resembled a red-hot pot on the boil. A seething hiss left his lips as he proceeded to strike the captive across the face with his cross. Then he grabbed his holy book with both hands and brought it crashing down on Gilson's head.

'Enough!' roared the chieftain. 'The prisoner will be made to talk tomorrow if he will not say anymore today. He has until dawn to confess all that he knows.'

The captive raised his bound wrists at the chieftain as he was dragged away.

'All you do is give them false hope and prolong their doltish old customs!' cried Gilson. 'Until they surrender they shall never be free of their suffering!'

# XLVII

## Rosclogher, Dartry, County Leitrim

### *7 – 10 August 1589*

After another day of hard training, I slumped upon my rifle at the edge of the green, observing the tribesmen. Some of them busied themselves with thatching the newly built huts of sod and wattle while others toiled to herd sheep and cows into the byre. Their exertions were hardly enviable and reminded me of my hellish days spent in the creaght, and so I felt relieved to form part of O'Rourke's militia.

'The town is all but rebuilt,' said someone behind me. I turned to find Ramos advancing upon me with Dario at his shoulder.

'No mean feat,' observed the Croat, 'considering these evil Protestant winds that blow no one any good.'

He had hardly spoken when a merciless easterly rippled the grass about our feet. A rustle of leaves was heard from the trees as we pulled the *brat* mantles tightly about our shoulders.

A few of the soldiers across the training ground cursed aloud and hurried into their tents while Ramos scowled.

'Holy host of the Madonna,' he seethed. 'That was a right Flemish devil breathing icicles up us.'

Our hands were trussed beneath our armpits, and we stamped our feet hard upon the ground.

'The locals say –' I began, but stopped talking as Ramos gestured for us to quickly follow him.

'Who cares!' he exclaimed. 'Let us hasten away to one of the cabins along the water. I'll be damned if I'm to spend a miserable night in a billowing tent while my balls shrink from the chill.'

We soon found ourselves seated in the cabin of Cathal the Black, where we were warmly received and served with blankets by his surviving retainers. We were also provided with mazers of beef broth mixed with sorrel leaves.

'You were saying about the locals?' said Ramos at last, having seemingly thawed enough to be able to listen to me.

'They say this is not usual weather for August and that it will surely improve soon.'

Some of the tribesmen stared at us when I spoke in Spanish, which led me to revert to Gaelic. 'We marvel at the composition of your broth, most worthy hosts. It is most heavenly in both texture and flavour.'

'Have you any tidings for us?' asked a wizened crone after receiving my compliment with the deftest of nods.

'O'Rourke has withdrawn his troops from the south,' said Dario, addressing her in fluent Gaelic, 'while to the west the Blind Abbot has proclaimed himself MacWilliam.'

'How do you know this?' I asked, feeling somewhat annoyed and excluded from their conversation.

Both Ramos and the Croat ignored me as they nodded gratefully to an aged Dartryman who passed them each a serving of beef.

'Have the troubles broken out again?' he asked. 'That's all we need through the winter, more mouths to feed.'

'More refugees mean more troops,' said Ramos with an evil grin, 'although you need not fret. For after an initial attempt at suppressing the MacWilliam, the Binghams were summoned away from the west at the viceroy's orders. They were ordered to repel O'Rourke's raiders in the Roscommon instead.'

'That is unheard of,' mumbled the crone, from a corner of the hut where she had taken up working her flax.

'Yes,' agreed the old man, who returned to the fire alongside his younger relations. 'That is an unexpected change of events. The Sassanas do not usually refrain from bloodshed.'

'Must be tactical,' remarked Dario, 'to buy themselves time.'

'It is most certainly tactical,' said Ramos, his mouth still full, 'and we cannot get the witness to Dublin fast enough.'

'God bless that woman,' said the old man as he crossed himself, 'for she has the courage of a lion and the devotion of a saint.'

'Indeed she lacks not devotion,' noted the sergeant drily, as he swallowed his last mouthful, 'for she has hardly stepped past the door of the abbey's chapel for as long as she's been here.'

'It is the hand of providence that guides her,' gasped the elderly crone, crossing herself wildly, with all of Cathal's retainers following suit. Ramos glared at them in annoyance as they broke into exclamations of 'God bless her', which spread about the hut like a gust of wind through the doorway.

'When is she to depart?' I asked, realising that Riona had been in the town for well over a week.

'Two days hence,' replied Ramos absent-mindedly, as he accepted a cup of milk which was passed to him, 'which reminds me that you must advise her to prepare for the journey tomorrow morning.'

'Why me?' I balked.

'Because Manglana has requested that you form part of her bodyguard until Enniskillen.'

The chieftain's instruction left me feeling baffled, if not somewhat flattered.

'Are you certain that he wants this?'

'Yes,' replied Ramos with a frown, 'although I am loath to risk the life of my sniper. Yet he has concluded that if you were good enough to serve Alba as bodyguard in Flanders, then you should be good enough to defend Riona until Fermanagh.'

'I wonder which task is more perilous,' I mused, causing Ramos to laugh aloud.

He proceeded to slap me upon the back.

'It will be child's play,' he chuckled, 'when compared to what you have been through.' He wiped a tear from his eye as Dario observed us in solemn silence.

'And what news of our master?' asked our eldest host. A score of faces turned towards us to hear what we knew of the fate of Cathal the Black.

For a while both the sergeant and the Croat hesitated to speak. At long last Ramos cleared his throat.

'The chieftain returned yesterday from his meeting with the grey merchants, but they had nothing to share with him except offers of merchandise. No word has been received of Cathal for good or for ill; indeed it appears that he has vanished without a trace.'

His tidings were met without so much as a stir or an utterance. The retainers merely stared back at him in puzzlement. They seemed to be as still as statues until their heads turned towards one another and the eldest among them found his voice again.

'These are strange tidings indeed. For what harm could the O'Reillys have done to a prisoner for whom they could fetch such a handsome ransom?'

'Strange tidings indeed,' agreed Ramos, 'for some word of his fate must yet reach us.'

'He shall surface again,' cried one of the younger Manglanas from beside the fire, 'for our master is cunning and has survived worse!'

Great cheers and exclamations of approval echoed about the cabin, sounding as desperate as they were heartfelt. Men still chattered about the fire as we readied to sleep upon the ground, wrapped in our blankets in a corner of the tanist's lodging as the wind howled outside like a belted hound.

It was late after dawn that I stirred again. Instantly worried about the time of day, I had reached out for my weapons when I realised that I had been relieved from duty until the witness had been safely despatched with Maguire. The crumpled mantles about me and the faintest of cries revealed that my two comrades had long abandoned me for training on the greensward, so I took my time to rise to my feet, taking full advantage of the opportunity to rest after sunrise.

Cathal's retainers had also disappeared, having taken their chattel from the byre to graze near the banks of Lough Melvin, so I drew the emerald ring from my ampoule, sheltering myself from view by pulling my blanket over my head. The cover was gently raised to risk some daylight, just enough to be able to view the ring, which I held close to my face. The series of events which had led to our reunion passed through my mind, though I could not believe that it was back in my possession.

Long minutes passed in which I took in the verdant sheen and the possibilities refracted through the bauble's light. At the sound of a slight rustle, I quickly slid it back into the lowest ampoule on the bandolier, then picked up my rifle. I laid both the gun and the belt against the boards of the hut, then pulled on my jacket and boots.

I then walked over towards the nearby structure of the abbey, sticking my head through the doors of the chapel to catch a sight of the witness, yet only a long line of empty benches greeted me as I turned my head from left to right. I wondered whether Riona tarried within O'Ronayne's lodging, so I approached the abbey's door and knocked on it, until at last the Jesuit's maidservant opened it, receiving me with a look of deep suspicion.

'What do you want?' she hissed.

'I am here on the chieftain's business,' I snarled, 'and must speak with Riona O'Malley.'

'She still sleeps.'

'Then wake her.'

The nasty biddy frowned back at me in annoyance, seemingly striving for an excuse to further frustrate me, but then she held up a hand as a gesture for me to wait. She next ran back into the house to do my bidding. With a sigh I waited at the door, grateful that the cold had subsided, though I wondered why the annoying old hen had not let me in. Moments later I heard a loud scream inside the house, which prompted me to crash the door open with my shoulder and run in the direction of the sound.

I was flooded with terror when I saw the maidservant upon her knees at the witness' bedside, alternately holding her face in her hands and striking the white face of Riona across its cheeks. I already feared the worst as I threw myself at the witness's side, and my jaw dropped at her ice-cold touch. I shook her hard even though I already knew that it was useless to do so.

'Fetch your master!' I cried at the gibbering hen, who scampered off with a whimper as I got back to my feet and leant over the ivory features of Riona.

I gently patted her stone-hard features as tears formed in my eyes, and I howled like a madman in the resolute face of death itself.

'Arise, O'Malley! Arise! Connacht yet needs you! Arise!'

Amid my screaming I was all but bundled over by the Jesuit, who appeared with a florid face and heavy sighs of exertion.

'The devil!' he cursed, then attempted a few pats of his own whilst he bent his ear towards her nostrils and held up her wrist, which he pinched tightly between his fingers.

He made a heart-wrenching series of attempts to revive her, with sharp slaps across the face and a desperate shaking of her shoulders. At last, he fell to his knees and held his face in his hands, though his sobs were barely stifled.

I had hardly had the time to recover when an almighty crash was heard behind us. We turned to find a pair of bluejackets with faces almost as pallid as that of the deceased witness. Behind them the old biddy screamed in indignation at the manner of their entry and waved her finger at their backs, even seizing one by the shoulder only to find herself swiftly shaken away.

'Father! You have been summoned in all haste!' cried one of them, still so startled by whatever distressed him that he had not yet even noticed the object of our grief.

O'Ronayne's face was fearful to behold as he staggered back upon his feet and stared at the two visitors.

'What is it?' he barely managed.

'The son of MacCabe!' exclaimed the kern. 'He is dying! You must come with us now!'

'Christ's bones,' swore the priest, though he made after them when they hurried out the door.

I also ran out into the daylight and saw O'Ronayne and the two bluejackets boarding one of the skiffs along the rebuilt jetty. The boatman had barely punted them away before another kern was seen running towards the abbey through the huts of the town, shouting for the Jesuit at the top of his lungs.

'Father! Father!"

'What is astir?' I cried, running up to him and grabbing him firmly by the arms. 'Speak, lad!'

'The Jesuit? Where is he?' cried the young bluejacket as he attempted in vain to shove me aside.

'Travelling to the keep as we speak,' I said, pointing at the lake, 'but what is astir?'

'It is the prisoner, Gilson,' gasped the youth. His jaw dropped at the sight of the shrinking boat upon the water.

He wrenched himself free of my grasp and ran down towards the banks of the lake, howling O'Ronayne's name at the top of his lungs.

'It cannot be,' I muttered to myself, then hurried in the direction of the ringfort.

I already feared the worst as I ran around the huts upon the edge of the town, forgetting that I was in full view of the militia, who trained upon the greensward.

'Abel!' boomed the sergeant behind me, yet I ignored him as I closed in on the walled structure ahead of me.

I was greeted by looks of horror upon the faces of its defenders, which only served to confirm my worst fears. None barred my path as I tore through the entrance and turned towards the inner wall to which Gilson had been chained. The lieutenant was as pale as the dead witness, barely breathing as he lay with his head in the lap of a stricken bluejacket. Gilson's clothes were covered with white streaks of vomit, and his breeches were heavily soiled. When I seized him by the arms and raised him towards me, he felt as stiff as a wooden plank.

'What happened?' I roared, shaking him wildly as his evil, blue eyes fixed themselves upon me.

'You are all finished,' he rasped, then chuckled, coughed and spewed upon my chest.

He shook so violently that I released him from my grasp. He twisted and turned upon the ground, holding his belly, until he was finally motionless.

'What can we do?' asked a distraught officer alongside the dying renegade.

'It is no use,' I replied, 'for it is arsenic.'

'Let us hang him upside down,' cried a voice from the doorway, which revealed Ramos, with Dario at his back. 'It is said to be a certain cure for poisoning.'

'Yes,' I snorted, as I made to leave the ringfort, 'a certain death more likely.'

I stumbled outside. Ramos and Dario followed me out, with some of the bluejackets trailing them.

When I turned to face them they all appeared confused, and for a few moments the very earth seemed to rise up and swirl about me while my knees buckled.

'Abel,' said Dario in a firm voice, wrapping his large hands about my arms to help steady me.

I swallowed awkwardly and strove to collect myself, and the sergeant appeared at the Croat's shoulder with a glance which appeared almost compassionate.

'What happened, son? Tell us all.'

'The O'Malley witness is dead,' I finally managed. 'Poisoned. MacCabe's son too.'

Ramos tottered away from me and turned his back upon us, and Dario had the look of one just condemned to death. My gaze fell upon the earth and remained there until Ramos at last looked away from the mountains and spoke again.

'Then all has been undone, in one fell swoop. For both our witness and our intelligence have been destroyed, and our only defence against MacCabe is now gone.'

His words sank into us like cold steel through the gut, and an unbearable silence lingered among us until the Croat spoke.

'So what do we do?'

Ramos walked back to the greensward, where the militia still stood in square formation, waiting on his instructions.

'I shall return to my duties until otherwise instructed, and it would be best that you join me. Take my word for it: by the time all the dust from this mess settles, you will want plenty of witnesses to have observed your every last movement.'

At his words we hurried after him, back towards the training ground, from which we dared not stray until our training was over. Yet Rosclogher was already astir as the chieftain's most loyal bluejackets crossed the water and started to kick down doors and ask questions of people all over the town. Men were dragged from their blankets and ferried across the water, and what fate befell them was unknown to us.

We were ourselves not spared the questioning which ensued, after the three bodies had been inspected at length by the Jesuit in the infirmary. Only two days after the murders, O'Ronayne led Ramos and me beyond earshot of the militia, to question our whereabouts in the days after our return to the town.

'For the love of the Virgin,' scoffed the sergeant, 'surely you do not suspect us of being involved in this tragedy? I allowed my men to rescue her from Sligo Town at great risk to my own operation.'

The Jesuit did not appear appeased by the sergeant's rebuff, and his face was drawn and pale when he replied in a hard voice. 'We must understand where everyone was at all times. It is the chieftain's orders.'

After we had disclosed all our movements and provided the names of witnesses, O'Ronayne walked away from the green.

'Any idea yet who did this?' Ramos called after him.

The Jesuit shook his head in annoyance. 'Not yet, but someone will pay. He is livid.'

His obvious reference to Manglana left us feeling less reassured about what the future held, given the huge strain the chieftain was already under to defend and provide for his threatened kingdom in the face of another merciless winter. Eventually most of the men and women who were taken away to the keep were allowed to return to the town. Some of them wore the odd bruise to the face or a broken nose. The household guard had not been gentle in extracting information, having been given free rein by their master to use means fair or foul to pursue the truth.

'It is a witch hunt,' said Dario, as we spotted yet another bruised tribesman with a torn tunic returning to his home.

'Inevitable,' I sighed with a shrug.

Rumour soon reached us that O'Ronayne had concluded the death of the witness had been caused by the use of arsenic, a heavy sprinkling of which had been discovered upon her pillow. The same deadly poison had also caused the death of Gilson, although it was uncertain whether the lieutenant had helped himself to the deadly substance, since no trace of it could be seen on his clothes or blankets.

As for Donal's son, it was concluded that the last jug of water he had been served was also envenomed. This would have been the worst news of all for the chieftain, and a source of great embarrassment, since it meant that he could not even guarantee the safety of his hostages within the walls of his own keep. Over the next two days tribesmen spoke of how one of the tower's kitchen scullions had disappeared without a trace, together with one of the horseboys. The disappearance of these two striplings only worsened the overall mood in the town, since the townsfolk desired a convicted murderer on whom they could vent all their anger.

This in turn gave rise to an evil rumour which grew with each passing day, one about the provenance of the poison, which could only have been obtained from one place in the whole of Dartry. Gossip long abounded about a secret apothecary which was maintained by the lady Dervila. All memories of her revered late son, Aengus, were swiftly forgotten, as were her contributions to the building of the infirmary and the upkeep of the abbey. Instead, men growled over their fires about how an Anglo-Norman could not be trusted, and how she might have furnished the poison which had removed any advantage afforded to her husband and all the Gaels.

These words were of course idle gibberish, yet the people of Dartry had suffered much over the previous months. They were desperate for a scapegoat whom they could heap with blame, as if the death of the witness and the captives had accorded them full rights to compensate for all their sufferings. Even the furious protests of O'Ronayne at these vile mutterings could not appease his flock, and things came to a head after most of the tribe had travelled to one of the heights of Dartry to honour the dead witness and bury her in a cairn befitting the highborn. It was a cold evening when we stood about with heavy cloaks and heavier hearts to pay our last respects to the lionhearted woman whose life had been so tragically taken from us.

As I observed the pale, bloated face of Riona disappearing beneath the stones, tears gathered upon my eyelids at the thought of the child which had died with her. Both my thumb and forefinger were moist as I pinched my eyes, and I bent over to conceal my hapless weeping. When the ceremony was over and the last rock laid, Manglana and his closest circle made their way back towards the path down the mountainside. It was then that all hell broke loose.

'Witch!' cried a man from the back of the gathering. A handful of mud flew through the air, landing directly in Dervila's face.

Dartry's queen fell to her knees as she held her face in her hands, and her husband turned crimson as more handfuls of dirt were flung at her.

'Guards!' he roared. A host of bluejackets fell about his party with their spears held out before them, and Ramos and I tried to seek out who had caused the protest.

'Murderer!' screamed another woman from the crowd, which surged towards Manglana's party.

'Stand back, you ingrates!' roared the chieftain as Muireann and his sister helped Dervila back onto her feet.

Meanwhile, the bluejackets formed a tighter ring about the highborn party, and the Jesuit stared about him with a bloodless expression.

'Take that, bottle lady!' cried another tribesman, referring to a nickname which had often been used to refer to Manglana's wife in reference to her many potions. Yet another handful of mud flew at the crouching party of the chieftain.

Ramos swiftly grabbed me by the shoulder and growled in my ear. 'This is getting out of hand, Abelito. Load your rifle.'

His instruction proved timely, as the hafts of the bluejackets' spears were soon seized by the furious Dartrymen. A savage shoving match ensued, with the bluejackets hurled back by the onrushing tide of bodies. The chieftain and his fellows were in turn jostled ever more closely towards a sharp cliff edge. It was then that Ramos grabbed me by the shoulder and nodded, leaving me to aim the rifle at the air and fire a shot. The sound of the blast caused the hard press of bodies to withdraw swiftly.

Ramos drew his sword and roared at the tribesmen. 'Back, whoresons! Back! Let none step forth again if you value your lives.'

So saying, he gestured to me again, and I was watched by the stricken faces of men, women and children as I swiftly reloaded the Marquardt at his back.

'The next ball goes through your face,' I declared, as I withdrew the ramrod from the rifle and stood with my legs apart.

I was emboldened by the fear of the fast-dispersing crowd as I held the gun to my shoulder and aimed it in their direction. The tribesmen ran down the bridle path like rats fleeing a flooding sewer, and when the last of them had disappeared, we took a moment to draw our breath. The sergeant and I exchanged a look of disbelief as I slung the rifle back over my arm. We turned to find Dervila being helped back onto her feet by her handmaidens.

The chieftain still stood before her with a drawn blade, too furious to speak and still shaken by the seditious act which had almost claimed his life. He wordlessly returned his sword to its scabbard as he slowly walked off through the ring of bluejackets ahead of him. Dervila's face was flushed as she, her ladies, the bard and the Jesuit made off after him. I thought I saw Muireann casting a swift glance in my direction, as Ramos and I remained rooted to the spot, observing the household guards swiftly following the women. When they were all gone, the sergeant issued a low sigh. He put his blade away and turned his back upon the cairn of the deceased O'Malley.

'Whoever flung that shit will be fortunate to get away alive,' he said at last.

'They shall have already fled Dartry' – I shrugged – 'for everyone needs more conscripts.'

For two days thereafter no one left the tower-house at Rosclogher, save for the odd band of kerns who were sent round the village to ask questions about the dishonour cast upon Dervila at Riona's funeral. Their querying appeared mostly symbolic, since no violence was employed and few questions were asked of the usual unruly specimens who inhabited the town. As I had predicted, two men and a boy had since disappeared from the settlement. None knew whither they had ventured, save a bluejacket who said he had spotted them walking off through the trees while he was busy flinging Gilson's corpse into the bog shortly after the standoff on the mountaintop.

Events gathered pace again in the morning, when we were met by the sight of Old Tom bursting through the trees along the bog as he led his blown mount by the bridle. The grey bags beneath his eyes were larger than usual, and he barely saluted us as he skirted the side of the green and hurried towards the town.

'He appears distressed,' observed Ramos with a frown of concern, then ordered us to form a square again before we could even get our breath back.

Yet our exertions were not to last much longer. A page from the tower-house soon appeared to summon us to a meeting with Manglana. As the sergeant and I made our way to the keep's upper reaches and entered the hall, I could tell that a matter of the greatest importance was afoot, for the chieftain and his wife were only accompanied by their most loyal retainers.

'Her passing is indeed a great setback, my lord,' said Old Tom, 'for safe passage through Fermanagh was agreed with Maguire at great expense to our lord *na Múrtha*.'

Manglana glowered back at the Anglo-Norman, then took a deep breath before he replied in a tone bristling with great restraint.

'Too many heads have been turned by a taste for enemy silver. Our vigil against treachery appears never to suffice in these dark times, for every precaution was taken to protect our charges. To think of the vile acts which have taken place in my own domain! Yet there are those among our people who wish for an end to the rule of the chieftains, who think the enemy's yoke is preferable to the coshery and livery, which they must currently endure.'

'And what of your prisoner?' asked Geraldine. 'Is word of his passing also true?'

'Have the tidings already reached Breifne?' said Manglana with a start.

'No,' said Old Tom, 'the Jesuit told me upon my arrival.'

The chieftain cast a dark look at the wincing O'Ronayne, then spoke in as low a voice as he could manage.

'We chained his corpse to a boulder and cast him into the lake at night. God forbid that his father ever learns of his passing, for we can ill afford to defend ourselves from an enraged gallowglass troop at this time.'

Old Tom nodded his understanding. 'And who were the perpetrators? Have they been met with justice?'

'Doubtless they were the men who disappeared from the town yesterday,' replied the Jesuit at a nod from the chieftain, 'a churl charged with serving the ward's food, together with one of my serving boys who came and went as he pleased, who was last seen serving the prisoner in the ringfort after he had changed Riona's bedding at the abbey. Somehow they were committed to an enemy agent who must have provided them with the arsenic.'

'And we are certain that the poison came from the enemy?' asked Geraldine with a scowl. 'Our overlord shall require a full account of what occurred.'

An uncomfortable silence hung over the hall before Dervila let out a loud groan of impatience and spoke up unbidden.

'There were missing stocks in the apothecary,' she said, 'although how that came to pass is beyond my reckoning, for it is guarded both day and night.'

'The bluejackets have assumed guard of it since the Scots were banished,' added Manglana. 'The responsibility for the lapse lies with Nial Ne Dourough and the two bluejackets on guard duty, who shall all be tried by month's end.'

I traded a look of surprise with the sergeant at the chieftain's reference to the bondsman. Muireann also stared at me, aghast at the revelation.

'And have any of them confessed to partaking in the murders?' asked Old Tom.

'They have all claimed that they are beyond reproach,' replied the chieftain, 'but the arsenic in the apothecary was missing, and that is beyond doubt.'

'Then your circle of trust grows smaller,' said the Anglo-Norman with a grimace, 'for in less than a month you have lost constable, tanist and sword master.'

Manglana bared his teeth slightly at the remark, and he squirmed in his seat until he could find a reply.

'Ne Dourough's innocence might yet be proven, and the tanist recovered,' replied the chieftain. 'Have you received word of Cathal *Dubh's* whereabouts?'

'Yes,' said Old Tom as he reached for the leather pouch at his belt. He pulled out a lock of raven hair. 'This is the proof that he still lives. It was borne to Castlecar by an envoy of the O'Reillys.'

'The Lord be praised!' exclaimed O'Ronayne excitedly. 'Cathal yet lives!'

For a moment we were all elated by the tidings, save for Dervila, who sneered openly. Manglana sat up in his throne with an expression bordering on hope.

'And what is their price?' he asked. 'It is fair?'

'Hardly,' replied Geraldine with a deep frown. 'They want seven *cumhals*.'

The chieftain's wife snorted as the rest of us stood in silence, and Manglana appeared downcast at the high cost of the ransom.

'Have you no hostages of your own?' asked Geraldine.

'No,' said the chieftain, 'for the ones we took did not survive their battle wounds. But we will pay the ransom for him, although it will greatly reduce our spoils.'

'That is indeed a sore blow,' replied Geraldine, 'for the winter shall not pass peacefully now that the chance to rid ourselves of the Binghams has eluded us. The passing of the witness is indeed a great tragedy, for besides being a worthy woman, it took a great effort to bring the Maguire to agree to her safe passage through his territory. We also received a pledge bearing the royal seal by the viceroy, who guaranteed that full protection would be afforded to her from the Binghams' rogues.'

'Indeed,' said Manglana, 'it is a great shame that no one else can take her place.'

'Why not?' remarked his wife, taking us all by surprise.

She rose to her full height amid a swirl of vestments, then stared at her husband as she made the declaration that left our jaws hanging.

'I shall myself ride on to Dublin in Riona's stead. The Lord knows I have seen enough barbarity from the Binghams to fill two whole books of outrages!'

For a time no one spoke as Dartry's bold queen stared back at us in defiance. She was met with expressions of fear and disbelief.

'Have you lost your mind, woman?' asked Manglana. 'Your life will be put at great risk. And what am I meant to do without my wife at my side?'

'What you have always done,' she spat back at him. 'Continue with your warring and whoring, yet I'll not squander the one chance which might save us.'

Manglana scowled at her following her tirade while the Jesuit made an attempt at reason.

'This is no hunting party, my lady,' he said gently. 'You shall stray into alien lands, and the way shall be fraught with danger.'

O'Ronayne shied away in fear as Dartry's queen whirled upon him.

'If I am the only man or woman brave enough to bear witness to Dublin, then there is no choice! I will leave you to your abbey while I bear witness in Dublin about these Bingham animals who hack my kin in the west to pieces!'

'There is much you may yet do to help our cause,' protested Manglana at last, rising to his feet. 'Women nurse the sick, cook meals, wash and mend clothes! Why must it be you that risks your life so needlessly at a time when your people need you most!'

'My people?' scoffed the queen with her most mocking expression. 'You mean those who call me "bottle lady" behind my back? Or who claim that I cast a spell upon you before you claimed my hand? Those wretches out there who forget that I bore them the finest son who should have claimed this earth? A son whose own murderer slipped our justice because of their own doltish ways?'

Her riposte bristled with menace and outrage, and we all cringed at the sight of Manglana's bunched fists as his authority was so openly disputed by his wife. When he nodded at the door we all scurried towards it, the furious argument between king and queen raging on behind us, seemingly without end. Word later reached us of how their squabbling had persisted late into the night, with Dervila insisting on bearing witness at the trial in Dublin despite her husband's great objections. As we sat in our tent in the warmth of the evening, Ramos chuckled to himself as he recounted the rumours which had been passed on to him by Old Tom.

'It is said that she hurled every accusation imaginable at him, from his mistresses and children out of wedlock to his dragon's breath.'

I thought of the chieftain's foul breath and loose teeth, which were a symptom of the calomel administered to him by the Jesuit, which was intended to ease his sharp agony caused by the French pox.

'That was indeed below the belt,' I said.

'The woman has spirit,' conceded the sergeant, as he picked at his teeth with the point of his dagger.

'Yes, she has ever been a restless one,' said Geraldine, who was seated between us. 'She has long been bored of Dartry, for she is an educated humanist and abhors the barbaric ways of her husband. It is also said that the Spanish sea captain, de Cuéllar, gave her aspirations well and truly beyond her position. They say his disappearance forced her to question what the cultured daughter of an educated Anglo-Norman had achieved with her life.'

The following morning the tidings only became more concerning when Ramos approached me on the training ground and pulled me aside.

'What is astir?' I asked, seeing him staring at me in disbelief.

'The mad bitch wants you to join her party.'

'What? Why me?' I asked, having no desire to partake in so dangerous an exercise.

'She says she feels safer riding with you, for you once saved her life.'

I remembered the time when I had rescued her during the hunting party, having swiftly hauled her off her horse before her falcon had slashed my face.

'Can you not contest the order?'

'No, although the chieftain has insisted that you are to venture no further than Inis Ceithleann. The crazy woman wanted you to accompany her all the way to Dublin, but you should be back here before the week is out. Geraldine is to ride with you, as well as the O'Rourke riders.'

On the next day, Geraldine and the sergeant led me across the bog, where Dervila and the O'Rourke riders waited. The mire shimmered about us in the torrent of rain as Old Tom explained the venture which lay ahead.

'The Sassenachs will not send a force into Fermanagh without Maguire's permission, since they would not want to provoke him. Even now he is torn between joining the rebel cause and keeping out of the fray.'

As I approached the horses, Dervila's voice saluted me.

'Ah, one with whom I can converse. My mind shall not become a barren desert of boredom.'

'At least until Enniskillen, my lady,' growled a hooded figure from the shadows, and I realised that the chieftain had arisen with some of his retainers to bid his wife farewell.

When I mounted my horse, one of the O'Rourke riders kicked his horse forward. The chieftain handed Geraldine a bugle and grudgingly saluted us.

'Blow upon it if you meet with trouble, and my sentinels shall summon reinforcements. Godspeed, my friends. Ride like the wind.'

'Farewell, husband,' said Dervila. 'We should return before Samhain.'

'Enjoy the fair land of Fermanagh and the hospitality of Maguire, Abelito!' called Ramos as we made off. 'They say it is a fine land, as yet unravaged by war.'

His words were ignored as we galloped towards the foot of the mountains. Dervila's gaze was serene beneath the hood of her cloak as we commenced our ascent beneath the height of Arroo.

# XLVIII

## ROSCLOGHER TO FERMANAGH TO ROSCLOGHER

### *10 – 11 August 1589*

O ur party rode for close to an hour in a grim silence as the daylight grew about us. We kept among the cover of the woods which bordered the lake, clinging to our eastward path. I could tell that Geraldine led us in the general direction of Rossinver, as the peak of Doagh mountain grew in the distance. The trees grew sparser as the boggy earth turned into a more level grassland, which allowed us to travel faster towards our end.

'A sightly land in fair weather,' remarked the queen at my shoulder, 'and it already feels like we have reached Fermanagh.'

'This is not your first visit, my lady?'

'Oh no,' she said with a start, 'heavens no. In days of peace, I was often a visitor to Maguire's seat with both Aengus and Muireann. We were always as happy as larks whenever we arrived in Inis Ceithleann to attend the great bardic competitions hosted therein.'

Her hawkish features softened when she referred to these events, and her eyes glistened with contentment at the memory.

'Days of happiness, my lady,' I said, 'which are to be treasured.'

'Days of yore and days of learning,' she replied, as her face assumed a steely cast, 'far from the brutish ways of my husband and his cow-herding thieves.'

My stare fell to the mane of the horse beneath me. I said nothing as we rode on with only the clink of the armoured horsemen to be heard for miles around.

'Do you also think that I have abandoned my duty, Spaniard?' she said at last. 'That I should remain at Rosclogher to keep my place and do my husband's bidding?'

'What I think matters not,' I said tersely, 'for I am but a mere soldier in the employ of *na Múrtha*.'

'Do not take me for a fool,' she hissed, 'for we both know that you are among the most learned men for miles around. Give me the opinion I have sought, and do not test my patience.'

Finding myself both rebuked and coerced in this manner, I drew a deep breath and collected my thoughts as I sought to attempt as diplomatic a reply as could be managed.

'Indeed I am well read, yet you may not be aware that I am also a freethinker, my lady. Like the Gaels, I believe that women should be educated in the same manner as men, so as to be learned enough to choose their own path.'

My reply seemed to appease her for a while, and she mulled over it as the domed helmets of the O'Rourke riders quivered from left to right, while we thundered on towards the lands of the Maguire. Dartry's queen passed her eyes over the great plain, which stretched out towards the mountains to our right.

'The path I have chosen is doubtless the right one, Spaniard. This land is possessed of a spirit which cannot be killed and which ultimately charms all off their feet. It cannot be broken. The people defending it might be killed, but its aura cannot be subdued by an act of man alone.'

She took a deep breath and met my stare.

'It is what the invaders fail to understand. They might tramp the land's fields, rob its gifts and violate its people, even live to a ripe old age upon its ground. Yet ultimately that same ground shall claim the alien in ways they cannot understand, for the soul of the land of Erin cannot be claimed by any.'

'Inspired words, my lady,' I replied, trying to keep a straight face. 'They would not go amiss on the lips of your poet bard.'

Her eyes narrowed at my words, as though she sensed a hint of mockery in them.

'My forefathers arrived in this land with hostile intentions,' she said, 'for they intended to convert and subdue. Their intention was also to suppress the natives, yet this land seduced them before their mission was even a quarter completed, and we became nearly as Gaelic as the Gaels themselves. The new enemy does not yet understand this, for it still sends its worst people against us, tosspots and ruffians who can only conceive of a heartless society like the one they left. Yet in time they, too, will be seduced.'

The ends of Dervila's lips formed a mischievous grin.

'And much as you may deny it, Spaniard, I know that deep down you are already seduced by the ways of this land.'

I was left feeling bewildered by her prediction, although I agreed with what she had uttered. My thoughts returned to our errand, though, as low snickers and whinnies were heard from the horses ahead of us, and I drew rein at the sight of Geraldine's raised hand. He looked over his shoulder and hissed commands at the rest of us.

'Halt, halt.'

Old Tom removed his helmet and dismounted before he strode back to us, the ends of his sweat-streaked hair stuck to his neck. His eyes blazed with reverence as he bowed to Dartry's queen and raised a gauntleted hand to help her off her mare. The horse kicked the ground as its highborn mistress slid off its back.

'What is this place, Geraldine?' she asked as her feet reached the ground. She looked about her from left to right. 'And what are we doing here?'

'This is a lesser-known path that the grey merchants use, my lady,' replied the Anglo-Norman respectfully. 'We are roughly five miles east of Rossinver as the crow flies, just along the borders of Maguire. We await one of his envoys, who shall guide us to his lord's seat of power.'

'Very well then,' she said as she raised her arm to me. 'Let us stretch out on the grass and engage in further conversation. If the lackey is not tardy, we may well be banqueting in Maguire's hall tonight.'

I took the queen's arm and led her beneath an old oak, where we sat on a bed of green grass over which there were scattered golden-red autumn leaves. Geraldine soon followed our lead with the most senior of the O'Rourke horsemen, followed by the twin horseboys Pirib and Pilip. The twins bore us wine from a skin and a light lunch of oaten bread and bog cheese, while we discussed the works of the likes of Erasmus and Machiavelli.

'Erasmus can take his writings and burn them.' Old Tom snorted. 'Who cares for these pacifists spouting high ideals behind the walls of a university?'

Dervila glared at her fellow Anglo-Norman as she helped herself to yet another sip of the claret, which had left her cheeks rosy and her eyes wide.

'Our Spaniard here cares greatly for the pacifist,' she said.

'What?' exclaimed Geraldine, casting me a look of the deepest disdain. 'You are also one who would conciliate with the heretic? After all your years of service with Alba?'

I cleared my throat awkwardly before I gently rebutted his accusation. 'I would not say that Erasmus advocates conciliation with heretics. He has urged for persuasion through debate, without the need for violence.'

'Ah,' said Geraldine, 'another who would turn the other cheek, until not one believer is left alive. So, you would take Erasmus' lofty ideas on the high seas to face the cannon of the sea beggars? Or use them in the field against the Binghams?'

Dervila stared at me expectantly, apparently hoping for me to come up with a witty counterargument based on my many readings.

'Ours is indeed a different situation,' I replied, then helped myself to more of the food. After a time, I lay back on my elbows, stretching my legs out before me.

Manglana's wife cast me a look of disappointment. Then she raised her head towards the riders who sat about the horses.

'The men are stirring,' she said. 'It looks like someone approaches us.'

Old Tom got to his feet and loosened his sword in his scabbard, the horseboy twins and the captain of the O'Rourke riders following his lead.

'Wait here, persuader,' he scoffed at me, then walked off with the other men.

The leaves crunched beneath their feet as they made their way towards the other horsemen, who had gathered with raised spears about the approaching rider. Lady Bourke and I watched Geraldine exchange a few words with the stranger. Then he turned about and called out to us to return to the horses.

'This is our man. Make haste and do not tarry.'

As we approached our mounts I cast a look at the envoy, finding myself bewildered by his sallow looks. He did not look that different from a highborn Dartryman at all, with his *brat* mantle wrapped tightly about his light mail shirt and his eyes peering at us keenly from beneath his long, brown fringe.

'My lady,' he whispered with a flourishing bow, 'my lord Maguire keenly awaits your arrival at his hall.'

For a moment I was uncertain whether his tone was mocking or haughty, and I looked to Dervila, whose great pride made her pick up the slightest slur or insult. Yet Dartry's queen seemed greatly flattered by the rider's greeting, and she addressed him cheerily.

'It is my honour to be received by such a worthy host!' she replied. Then Geraldine took her hand and fell to one knee, allowing her to rest her foot on his raised knee so that she could clamber atop her mount.

'Were we not expecting an armed escort?' I asked with some suspicion, carefully eyeing the defenceless envoy who walked back to his own steed.

Geraldine shrugged.

'This is a land which still holds its peace with the Sassanas,' he replied. 'The envoy said he will also guide us through lesser-used paths, on which the enemy is never seen. One of Maguire's requests was that we do everything possible to avoid the notice of his people wherever possible.'

The seasoned Anglo-Norman's comfort with the arrangement was enough to appease me, and we rode after the lone horseman deeper into the woods which spread to our right. Before long we were back among trees and growing shadows, since the dense cover of the boughs overhead was such that the sunlight was greatly reduced. The envoy proceeded at a gentle canter, never once hastening the pace of his mount as he calmly led us further and further downhill. At last we found ourselves within a gorge that might once have been a flowing river, riding in pairs along the dry banks as the chieftain's wife rode to my left, observing our new surrounds.

'This would be the perfect place for an ambush,' she observed drily, to which I grunted my agreement without thinking much more of it.

We had hardly covered another furlong when our guide suddenly broke into a gallop that left us staring after him in bewilderment. Geraldine had barely turned towards me when we found ourselves the object of all manner of missiles that flew from the trees scattered about us. I turned in alarm as Dartry's queen snatched the very tip of my sleeve, then collapsed from atop her steed.

'Spaniard!' she gasped.

'The bugle!' cried Geraldine ahead of me. 'The bugle!'

They were his last words on horseback as blood burst from his back. He fell over, holding the end of a crossbow bolt which had passed through his breastplate. I stared about me in fright, seeing mostly empty saddles as the O'Rourke riders thrashed about on the ground, writhing upon the ends of spears and hafts and mouthing a voiceless pain as they sought to recover their wits. My fingers had reached for the stock of my Marquardt rifle when a halter flew round my neck. As I reached for it I was hauled backwards off my own mount, the wind knocked out of me as I crashed into the leaves underfoot.

I shielded my head with a raised arm, only for my raised elbow to be knocked aside by a heavy cudgel blow. My rifle was lost after my tumble, along with the bandolier. As I struggled against the rope round my neck, I could see that the bugle had also fallen off my shoulder and lay a few feet away from me. Meanwhile a dozen soldiers appeared through the foliage about us, dressed in the English manner and possessed of a grim cast. Their swords were already unsheathed as they hurled themselves onto the dying men in my company, intent on finishing them off.

I reached for the bugle, but I was instantly hauled back by the neck. The pain in my arm was unbearable as a great lump formed at my elbow, yet I raised it again to block yet another swing of the cudgel. My eyes watered from the resulting agony as the trooper brought his boot crashing down upon my shoulder, pinning me hard onto the ground as he scowled at me. In the corner of my eye Old Tom had somehow shoved himself back onto his feet, setting upon our assailants with his drawn blade, which he swung repeatedly over his head.

One by one, the ambushers fell before him. Others hopped away from him with drawn blades while they issued low curses. Two of our wounded riders somehow dragged themselves towards the Anglo-Norman, then forced themselves back on their feet with gritted teeth as they held their blades out before them. There followed a hopeless defence against four times their number, as some of the enemy swordsmen toyed with them and the rest fitted more bolts to their crossbows.

'The bugle, Spaniard! Blow on the bugle!'

I turned my head in the direction of Dervila's cries. My blood boiled as I saw her fending off the blows of a staff, which was swung by yet another vile trooper who had sprung out of the wood. My hand fell to Geraldine's *skene* dagger at my waist, and I swung it upwards just as the cudgel swung down on me again. The dagger slid through the forearm of my assailant, who had been taken unawares, and who yelped like a dog as I grabbed his wrist with my other hand, ignoring the agony in my injured arm as I wrenched my blade free.

His cries only added to my alertness, and I plunged the bloodied blade into the man's throat, which caused him to fall over like a sack of sods. I removed the cord from around my neck and was about to snatch up the bugle when I suddenly recalled the ring in the bandolier. Dervila's cries still rang in my ears, and they were soon joined by Geraldine, who had been quick to notice our sudden small chance of survival.

'The bugle, Spaniard!' he roared. 'The bugle!'

I turned back towards the bandolier like some vile, self-serving animal, scattering the dead leaves at my feet. I did not stop until I had grabbed the last ampoule.

'What are you doing?' screeched Geraldine. One of his comrades fell before him, having been overcome by two of the troopers.

Yet I was suddenly overcome by a desperation to rescue the ring. I emptied the contents of the ampoule into my hand and swallowed a handful of powder together with the bauble. I was left coughing and spluttering as I heard the sounds of clashing steel in the direction of the Anglo-Norman, the clamour of Dervila hurling every insult under the sun in my direction. As I turned back towards the trumpet and seized it off the ground, I attempted to blow deeply into it, yet I could not produce a single sound due to the powder that scratched at my throat.

I spat out a mouthful of black phlegm and had returned the mouthpiece to my lips when an onrushing trooper punched me across the face, sending me flying back upon the ground as the bugle rolled over the leaves. I heard the cry of a fallen O'Rourke rider as I pushed myself back onto my knees. I was trying to find the bugle when the boot of my latest assailant sent me rolling over the ground, and a dislodged tooth fell out of my fast-swelling mouth.

The fiend slammed his heel upon my chest, and I groaned while I tried in vain to push his foot away as he glared down at me defiantly. Yet his mocking glance did not last for long. The weight on my breast eased when his head was sliced clean off his shoulders, courtesy of a deadly sword stroke from the Geraldine. The elderly Anglo-Norman staggered towards me and stared at me hatefully.

'Traitor,' he hissed as he tightened his grip on the pommel of his double-hander.

The bloodied patch about his stomach darkened as he raised his great sword over me, fully intending to cut me in half. I drew my breath in sharply at the sight of the raised blade, but the end of another crossbow bolt sprouted just above Old Tom's navel, turning the front of his tunic scarlet as a low groan left his lips. His blade fell from his hands as he collapsed alongside me, his wide eyes as blue as robin's eggs as they beheld me in confused disappointment. I somehow rose onto my knees and cradled his head in my arms.

'Why?' he gasped. 'Why?' Then he soiled his breeches as his awful death throes began.

A loud hiss left him, which cankered my soul to its core. It provoked low laughter from the approaching ring of troopers, who gathered about me with reddened swords and crossbows. As Old Tom died in my arms, I could not help thinking how many dangers he had survived, and might yet have survived, were it not for my moment of acute selfishness, which had cut him as badly as the bolts which ended him. I was so taken up by my shame and sorrow that I never paid any mind to the groans of Dervila behind me, nor noticed the trooper loading his crossbow again with yet another bolt, which quickly tore through Geraldine's breast.

'Whoreson!' I cried after the shaft struck my friend.

I struggled back onto my feet, hell-bent on murder, seizing up Old Tom's sword and racing towards the crossbowman. Deep intakes of breath were heard at my approach, yet my enemies sidestepped my clumsy sword strokes until one of their number kicked my legs from beneath me. Once more I fell into a heap, as the countless swings of our ambushers' boots beat me unconscious.

A nasty throbbing in my arm caused me to stir, and my ribs and other limbs were also consumed by a piercing agony. I slowly raised my head with a groan, my swollen eye barely opening and my nostrils filled with dried blood.

'Where am I?' I rasped.

The cover of trees had only grown since the ambush, and as I raised my hands, I realised that my wrists were bound tightly together.

'We are in hell, Spaniard.'

Despite sounding low and muffled, the unmistakable voice of Dervila was a relief in the shadows. One of my swollen eyes strained towards Dartry's queen to my right. The gut cord bit into my wrists when I tried to move my hands, and I soon found my ankles were bound in the same manner. As I lifted myself off the ground, I shifted my weight onto my knees and tried to stand, only to find that a halter had me bound by the neck to a tree trunk.

'Are you well?' I whispered to her in the scant light which was afforded to us.

'Why did they spare you?' she demanded in return.

'I know not,' I lied after a few moments, 'although I already envy the dead.'

'Yes,' she replied in a subdued tone.

I was unsettled by the dampening of her fiery spirit, and as my eyesight improved in the dimness, the sight of her filled me with dismay. She lay alongside me with a halter also binding her to the same tree. Her dress was torn open at the neckline, and the turned-back cuffs of both her sleeves were torn almost to the shoulder. Dried blood crusted the side of her mouth. Both her eyes were also swollen, and a great welt sprouted from the side of her forehead.

I spat over my shoulder, until my throat had cleared enough for me to be able to speak more audibly.

'We must escape.'

'How?' she replied almost mockingly. 'We have naught with which to sever these bonds. And even if we could, we are still too wounded to flee them.'

'We must at least try.'

My neck ached as I jerked my head from left to right, attempting to locate a stone shard or broken trunk or anything which might sever the evil gut which ate into our flesh. When my hands fell below my navel, I discovered to my dismay that Geraldine's dagger had been taken away from me. Despair started to gnaw away at my resolve, but then I thought to scrape the ligature against the root of the oak to which we were hitched. A sharp sound was produced by the scraping of the cord against the wood, yet after some minutes my bonds felt as tight as before.

'Holy host of the Madonna,' I hissed in anger.

'We are doomed, Spaniard,' Lady Bourke whispered to me wearily from the ground. 'Gather what strength you still have so that we can meet our fate with honour.'

I fell back upon the ground and groaned aloud. A low laugh was heard ahead of us from alongside another large oak tree. It was then that I realised we had been watched all along, our every word and gesture observed by our captors.

'What do you want, whoresons?' I snarled at them, yet no reply beyond further chuckling was heard.

Our watchers spoke in a low murmur among themselves, completely ignoring us. It occurred to me that I should try and draw one of them towards us in the faint hope of pilfering a blade off their person. Since a quick death was the best that I expected from my captors, I thought nothing of seeking to get them to approach us. Curses left my tongue in every language I had encountered during my time in Flanders, a place where men of many nations had converged to seek employment in the deathly trade of battle.

A few English words were also known to me, yet my attempts to insult the men only provoked further laughter, so I abandoned the exercise. The queen and I were battered and bound as we lay upon the forest floor, our heads barely two handspans apart as we stared up at the dark branches and chinks of sky above our heads.

'They are Sassanas, aren't they?' she asked.

'Yes, my lady. Hard troopers which they only get on the Continent. They are also seasoned skirmishers who are often despatched behind enemy lines.'

'What are they doing here?'

There was a shakiness in her voice as she asked this, which betrayed a dread I had never heard from her. Air rasped through my nostrils, which were still blocked with dried blood, and a quiver of pain ran through my battered ribs as I drew as deep a breath as I could manage.

'I know not, my lady, but the portents are not healthy. Clearly word of our approach had long preceded us.'

Dervila did not reply as she stared up at the sky, and we lay a while longer in silence until the sound of low voices among the trees ahead made me stir slightly, enough so that I could strain my good ear as far forward as the cord about my neck would allow.

'You were not meant to harm him, but to bring him to me in good health!'

The voice sounded strangely familiar, albeit indistinguishable by distance. No sooner was it heard than a harsh reply was heard from another speaker, in an accent that was distinctly foreign.

'Since when should I heed the instructions of a rebel Judas? You wanted him alive, and he still draws breath.'

'The sheriff also wanted him alive, cur,' hissed the voice I had first heard, 'and you should know better than to cross him!'

'Why?' sneered the other. 'Has he fetched us all the way from England to hang us for roughing up a Spanish castaway?'

A loud sigh of frustration was heard from the other speaker, and a few moments passed until he had calmed himself enough to speak up again.

'Is that them?'

'Of course,' rasped the other. 'Did the pox also blind you, apart from scarring your face?'

'I swear by all the saints,' said the first after a few moments of silence, 'that the sheriff shall learn of your insolence.'

'I am sure he prefers the crooning voice of his whore,' replied the foreigner with no shortage of mockery in his voice.

Then a rustle of branches was heard as the survivor of the pox hobbled towards us, his sword dangling by his right side. My jaw hung open at the all too recognisable sight of the approaching man, a mass of black hair sprouting above his face.

'Cathal,' whispered Dervila at my side. She rolled onto her side and then raised herself onto her knees with the slowness of a wary cat. 'Then all that I feared of you was worse than I thought.'

As the tanist stood before us with a contemptuous stare, I stared back at him in disbelief. I could not help wondering whether this was the same honourable man who had risked so much to protect the Armada survivors who had appeared in Dartry.

'What is the meaning of this, Cathal?' asked the outraged queen at my side.

The tanist ignored her; his stare was fixed upon me.

'You know why you were spared, Spaniard. The sheriff has ordered me to fetch what you stole from Sligo.'

'I know not of what you speak,' I replied as Lady Bourke turned her head towards me with an unmistakable look of confusion.

A hateful smile spread across the tanist's twisted lips as his eyes widened in disbelief.

'Even now you would lie to me,' he said at last, 'after all the misery you have caused my people. A people whose only fault was to offer you protection and kindness.'

My stare was averted from the tanist as Dervila staggered to her feet behind him.

'Of what do you speak?' she snapped.

The leaves in her dishevelled hair made her a forlorn yet awesome sight, one which reminded me of her long-lost son, Aengus, just before he was despatched by Gilson. Cathal ignored her, staring at me intently from the shadows, his scarred face more worn than a gravestone.

'Give it up, Spaniard. Give it up, and I might yet spare your life.'

My expression must have appeared doubtful at his offer, and although I was sure he lied, his voice grew as he took a step closer towards me.

'I do not speak idly, Spaniard. I bear you no love due to your treacherous nature, yet even a betrayer such as yourself might be of more use to me alive. Especially given your martial talents.'

'Betrayer?' I stammered, trying to hold his stare. The slightest smirk returned to his face since he was sure he had all but snared his prize.

'What are you talking about?' yelled Dervila as she stepped between us.

A blow from the back of Cathal's hand sent her sprawling upon the ground, her hands held to her mouth and blood streaming down her nose as she screamed in outrage.

'How dare you strike your queen, cur! You will answer for this with your whole herd!'

A low growl left the tanist as he whipped his sword from its scabbard, then used the flat of it to hit the stunned woman in the head.

'Silence, bitch,' he spat. 'Do you think I've endured years of your torment to have you abuse me when you are but my captive?'

The blade was already slick with blood when I leapt forward and seized it, only for the tanist to pull it out of my grasp, which sliced my palms open.

'Holy host!' I cursed, then shoved my stinging hands beneath my arms and pressed them down tightly to dull the pain.

'You have yourself to blame, Spaniard,' snapped Cathal. 'Never get between me and my quarry!'

'But you cannot manhandle her further!' I cried. 'She is your hostage and cannot defend herself!'

'I will treat the old whore as I please,' he replied before he leant over and wiped the end of his blade against her tunic, 'and now you should give up what you took if you value your life.'

'You should also value my life, if you value what I took.'

My reply left him speechless, and he stared back at me in bewilderment.

The whimpering Dervila rose from the ground again. 'What betrayal, Spaniard? How could you have betrayed us?'

'I did not!' I cried, as Cathal turned about and kicked Dartry's queen in the back, just above her buttocks.

Her scream caused huge, rustling sounds in the leaves overhead, and shadows flickered against the trees.

'Silence, whore!' screamed the tanist, having abandoned any semblance of restraint or decency. 'You do not rule over this small glen in Fermanagh! Another word from you and I'll break your back!'

For a while nothing could be heard from Dervila except the lowest of groans, which were interrupted by the heavy stamping of feet as a burly trooper approached us. I rolled onto my back and raised my arms and legs, fully expecting more blows.

'Hey, pox-face, what are you doing? Bingham wants the hostage alive.'

'Stay out of it,' hissed Cathal. He whirled towards the trooper, who stopped dead in his tracks. 'Your master also wants me to conduct other business.'

'What business?' asked the other in his heavily accented Gaelic, raising a cynical eyebrow.

'Business that is not for your ears,' said Cathal, raising his blade, 'and which you would do well not to discover.'

The trooper swallowed his outrage at the sight of the sword, then swiftly flicked his eyes from left to right.

'Be that as it may,' he said at last, 'you would do well to perform this business swiftly and in silence. Maguire has troops on patrol not far from here, and who knows who else might have heard that scream. We must move on soon.'

So saying, the trooper returned from whence he had come. Cathal stared after him.

'Soon?' he exclaimed in annoyance.

'Soon,' replied the other, then disappeared from view.

The tanist returned his attention to us, quietly surmising how to make the best of the little time that was left to him. His features were a horror to behold as his head swung from left to right, his eyes wide with desperation. In those moments I could already tell that he was capable of anything, so I shuffled away from him when he sheathed his sword and approached me with a drawn dagger.

'No!' I groaned, yet he seized my foot when I aimed a kick at him, then shoved me aside and cut off more than a quarter of my mantle.

The length of linen fluttered in his hand as he made his way towards the slowly stirring queen, then shoved it hard into her mouth so that she could not produce a sound. He then sat on her side and pinned her wrists to his knee with one hand, using the other to hold the dagger blade against her smallest fingernail. Then he beckoned to me.

'Give it up, Spaniard,' he said. 'Give it up now.'

'What?' I asked, hoping to buy enough time and not realising the extent of his malice.

'What you stole from Sligo.'

'But the O'Malley witness is dead and buried.'

Dervila's eyes widened, and her legs kicked the air as Cathal dug his blade beneath her nail. He twisted upwards until it was torn away from her finger. Phlegm flooded my throat at the sight of his cruelty, so that I fell forward and retched. I would have been sick had I not also been starving. As I retched in silence, the ring made its way up my belly and nearly fell out of my mouth, only for me to quickly swallow it down again.

'Surrender it, Spaniard,' said Cathal, fixing me with a hard stare and leaving me stunned by his ruthlessness, 'or at this rate it will be all of her talons. I will cut fingers off next; you better believe it.'

Dervila attempted to wrest her hands away, only for him to rest his weight upon her more heavily and pull her hands towards him again. The queen piteously kicked her feet as the whoreson tore out yet another nail, and her reddened eyes bulged with agonised fury.

'Very well! Very well!' I cried. 'I swear by the Black Virgin of Montserrat that I'll give it to you. But leave her be! My secret dies with me if you touch her again!'

I was flooded with relief when he finally got off Dartry's queen and left her writhing in agony upon the ground. He ran up to me and seized my throat, holding the point of his dagger close to my eyes.

'Where is it then, cur? Speak!'

I suddenly hesitated, fearing that he might plunge his blade through my belly and cut me open if I told him the truth. At the sight of my hesitation, the tanist's worn face assumed a hideous contortion. He growled with frustration and shook his gnarled fist in my face. My blood ran cold as he turned on his heel and made his way back towards Dervila, who groaned like a branded calf. Her eyes widened as she wriggled away from him, holding her injured hand.

'Wait!' I cried as he grabbed her by the hair. 'I will tell you all, if you but let me regain my breath.'

'Then speak!' he snapped as he whirled towards me with a murderous glance, still holding his queen by the hair.

'It is hidden,' I lied on the spur of the moment, 'hidden in Dartry.'

Dervila fell forward as he released his grip on her and approached me with bared teeth.

'You lie,' he hissed, his blade held towards me once more.

'I do not,' I insisted. 'It is in Dartry. I would never have brought it with me on this errand. It was too perilous.'

His stare bored into me until I looked away. Then he grabbed me by the chin and shoved his face into mine. The thinned flesh about his eye sockets and mouth were even more discomfiting from so close a distance, but his grip and stare never wavered as he examined my face.

'Liar! You swallowed it. I should cut you open now and be done with your falsehood!'

'Then draw your blade and be done with me!' I cried, finding myself lurching from fear to anger, given the danger of my situation.

I tore my shirt apart like some biblical Pharisee, my hands shaking with rage as I pointed to the space beneath my ribs.

'There!' I cried. 'Plunge it in there! Then cut down and up!'

Cathal snorted at my gesture. 'I have cut enough cows to do so without your instruction.'

'On with it then!' I snapped, assuming a furious glare as I cajoled the tanist. 'I will be dead not long thereafter, content that the bauble will be lost to you forever!'

At my goading the tanist stepped forward and buried his fist into my belly.

'Where is it?' he rasped as I sank to my knees. I fell over sideways holding my stomach, feeling an agonising pain above the navel.

'The glade,' I gasped, as I suddenly thought of the serene place where I would have much rather have found myself. I then fended off a kick to my head.

'Which glade, cur?'

'The secret one with the dye plants! And the hives!'

'You mean the *ollamh's* den of lechery?'

His words left me stunned.

'So you knew all along that it was not rape?' I asked.

'Banish that pained look from your cuckold face,' he scoffed. 'Did you think I would act to protect an adulterer who lay with my wife-to-be?' Cathal seized me by the collar and pinned me to the ground. 'Where in the glade did you hide it? Tell me or I'll flay her hands next.'

'In the skeps,' I lied, fearing for Dervila's well-being, for Lady Bourke had not yet stirred after the terrible torment which had been inflicted upon her.

'Which one?'

The question had hardly been asked when the crunching of twigs was heard behind us. The Irish trooper peered at us in the poor light.

'We are off, pox-face,' he called to Cathal. 'You can remain here and play with the Spaniard or else ride with us to Breifne O'Reilly.'

With a low grunt of annoyance, the tanist flung me away and shot to his feet, hurling a grimace in the direction of the trooper.

'You shall do no such thing. Our course has changed.'

'Changed?' said the other with raised brows of concern. 'Changed to where?'

'To Dartry MacGlannagh. We travel by night.'

'Dartry MacGlannagh?' replied the other with a frown of disgust, mouthing the words as if they were an obscenity. 'That is certain death.'

'We have no choice. We need to find the thing that the sheriff wants.'

'*You* have to find something the sheriff wants,' snapped the trooper. 'We have done all that was ordered of us to help you find it.'

Cathal the Black sighed impatiently. 'I would not suggest that you return empty-handed. If the sheriff discovers that we let this opportunity vanish, then his fury shall know no bounds. There were three things he wanted from us, and we have only two of them.'

The other's lips curled in annoyance, revealing hideously broken teeth. 'But you said we would have all three in hand with the ambush.'

'I erred. Yet I know the secret ways through Dartry Mac-Glannagh. We need only hide along its borders, then enter and leave at first light.'

The trooper stared back at him while biting his lip, due to his frustration and deep concern.

'This is a trap,' he said at last, as his hand fell upon his sword pommel. 'You mean to buy your way back into your lord's favour.'

My heartbeat grew faster as the trooper's blade slowly left its scabbard, only for Cathal to laugh aloud.

'Look at how I have reduced Dartry's queen. Is that also a way of winning my lord's favour?'

The trooper's jaw dropped as he turned to behold the stricken state of Lady Bourke, who still drew uneasy breaths as she lay upon her side, clutching the fingers which had been so cruelly damaged. Her glistening cheeks betrayed silent tears as she stared ahead of her in stunned disbelief.

'You Dartrymen are animals,' said the trooper at last with a shudder. He bit his lip once more and slid his sword back into its scabbard.

'We do as you say,' he said at last, as he turned to walk back to his men. 'You shall lead us. But know that you will have a primed pistol aimed at your back at all times. The slightest whiff of treachery and you will not see out the day.'

It was not long thereafter that rough hands seized us and harsh halters were secured tightly about our necks. Dervila and I were led out of the clearing towards where the ambushers had set up camp. A score of grizzled skirmishers busied themselves with wrapping their blankets and adjusting their packs, greeting us with hateful glances as we were brought before Cathal and the band's leader.

'A dozen should suffice,' said the tanist, 'for we shall rely on stealth and speed, not strength.'

'And am I meant to attempt the journey south with the other half?' asked the trooper. 'The party can move quietly enough together without fear of being seen or heard.'

'It is not the noise that I fear, Verdon,' replied the tanist, 'but our numbers. The fewer men, the less likely for us to be seen.'

The man called Verdon smirked dismissively as he turned to pick up his pack and bandoliers, which he slung over his shoulders.

'I trust my men to cover ground more silently than the slightest breeze. We were not assigned to sheriff's service for no reason. You have yourself seen how we slipped past the border guards of Maguire. Together we will fetch this prize that your Spaniard has hidden, with not a trooper lost. For to a man, we are the very same band that took up arms on the Continent a decade ago.'

At the copperhead's insistence, Lady Bourke and I were blindfolded and gagged, and so my breath could only be drawn with difficulty through my blood-clogged nostrils. With my sight denied to me, my progress was awkward, spurred on as I was by heavy shoves upon the shoulder and sharp jerks of the rope round my neck. All the while my bound wrists flailed against the air as I stumbled again and again, uphill and downhill.

Verdon's claim that his party could move in perfect silence proved truthful rather than boastful, for my ears could not pick up the sound of a single man. Dervila's and my awkward shuffling were the only sounds that could be heard from our band. We proceeded at a slow yet unwavering pace, pausing only once for the tanist to whisper at length to Verdon.

After an hour of steady progress, my thoughts soon turned from my captors and Lady Bourke to the hidden glade and what I was to do if we got there. My only hope of survival appeared to be that of removing the ring from my stomach before our destination was reached, for I dreaded to think what might befall me if the tanist discovered my lie. As unlikely as it appeared to me then, it seemed that my only hope of being spared was to pretend that I had recovered the ring from one of the skeps.

Desperate thoughts of escape also assaulted my mind, only to be dulled by the savage tugs of the rope about my neck, which started to chafe badly as mile after westward mile was covered in silence. At least two hours must have passed in which Dervila and I ambled on helplessly in our blindness, fearing the worst when we were brought to a halt and shoved to our knees, then finding a strange relief in being driven on mercilessly whenever our captors resumed their progress.

With each passing moment the suspicion grew in mind, from the years I had spent skirmishing in Flanders, that Cathal was using his knowledge of Dartry to scout ahead. He did this whenever we closed in on a path that was watched or patrolled so as to ensure that the way ahead was clear. These thoughts were confirmed towards the end of yet another forced halt, when I overheard a snatch of discourse between him and Verdon. The Irish trooper sounded warier with each mile we covered.

'What took you so long, pox-face? It took you and six men a half hour to kill a single watcher?'

'His location had changed,' gasped the tanist, 'yet we found him in the end, for I know of all the hideouts. And now the path towards our end is cleared, and any random wanderers shall be picked off with ease.'

My blood ran cold at the tanist's words, which betrayed a ruthlessness and indifference towards his people that I had never once detected during the whole of my time in Ireland. I wondered if his seditious intentions had long been held closely to his chest, or whether the string of hurts caused to him by the Spanish castaways, together with the constant hostility of Dervila and MacCabe, had finally flung him over the edge.

'So we press on?' asked Verdon excitedly, with a voice suddenly possessed of greater purpose and far less reluctance.

A low groan left me as I readied to get back onto my feet, but a kick was planted in my backside, and the tanist's reply provided an unexpected relief.

'We shall not travel far at night, so we should retire to a hilltop hut which lies north of the lake. The MacGiollas defend that territory but use it sparingly, so we should rest there for the night before recovering the prize at first light. We can then strike a path north towards the garrison towns.'

Verdon had no objections to this proposed course of action. Another lesser-used path was taken up, the crunching beneath our feet and the rustle of leaves above our heads betraying the presence of a deep wood. We eventually scaled a sharp incline, and the end of our march was finally announced by the creaking of a wooden door. Our sight was also returned to us as the rags about our eyes were whipped off, as well as the gags.

Dusk had not claimed our world, yet after hours of blindness both Dervila and I blinked furiously at our surrounds. As suspected, we had been cast into a corner of a mud-and-wattle abode, one of above-average proportions. Verdon's score of skirmishers sat cross-legged in a circle as the night's watch was planned by their leader.

'My lady?' I whispered to Dervila, yet Dartry's queen was in a worse state than before.

My shaking of her arm and shoulders did not draw a response from her as she beheld the roof of the hut with low, rasping gasps and an overwhelmed stare. For at least an hour thereafter she remained silent, long after the four appointed sentinels had silently emerged from our lodging to keep watch on our surrounds.

Then Cathal the Black appeared out of the growing darkness, a couple of tallow candles used by Verdon's men playing upon his jagged features. A bladder was passed to us, from which I drank greedily before the water was snatched away from me and given to Dervila. Dartry's queen also helped herself to deep gulps, yet after a few instants the waterskin was cruelly torn away from her.

'Return it to me, witch,' snapped the tanist as he twisted the bladder free of her desperate grasp.

Dervila had until then endured all verbal and physical abuse without lament, yet she surprised us both when she found the strength to rise back onto her feet and snarl at his back.

'You'll not dare call me a whore again, you shallow, deformed, double-dealing hound.'

'What did you call me?' snapped the tanist, his dreaded dagger drawn from its scabbard.

I feared the worst as I hurled myself into his path, only to be shoved aside as he stepped up and seized her by the collar.

'You heard me well, cur,' she spat in his face, wholly non-plussed by his rough handling of her, leaving me to marvel at her deep reserves of courage.

'Do you want to lose your whole hand?' he asked angrily.

'I should have had you hurled into the bog,' was her immediate reply, 'the moment I laid eyes on such a worthless pup. I was already resolved to do so until that idiot bishop intervened on your behalf. He claimed that you were but a newborn and The Wolf's blood.'

Cathal's jaw dropped as she spoke, and his hand trembled upon her collar.

'You knew me as a child?' he gasped. Of what wolf blood do you speak?'

'Of *An Faolchù*, the wolf who turned my love for Dartry into seething venom. He who was the lawless scourge of our kingdom for four terrible years. He whose name you now bear – and whose looks you also shared, at least until the pox rid us of them.'

Cathal took a step back, wholly aghast at Dervila's revelations. I squatted in the shadows, watching his confusion as my mind raced to grasp the implications of Dervila's words. At the sight of his turmoil, Lady Bourke assumed a hateful smirk and took a step forward, waiting for his next question like a hawk poised for the kill.

'My – my father told you to be rid of me?' managed Cathal at last.

'No, fool,' spat Dervila, 'although there was neither love nor affection in your conception. For it was a loveless union that begat the monstrosity that you are, a vile act of rape of which

*An Faolchù* alone was capable – inflicted upon the new bride of his own brother!'

One of Cathal's knees buckled before he managed to resume his footing, and his eyes throbbed as he served Dervila with a stare so piteous that for a moment I felt for him.

'His brother, you mean Tadhg *Óg* –'

'Who else, fool?' cried the queen of Dartry.

Dervila's eyes smouldered with loathing as she glared at her son. Cathal stared back at her in disbelief.

'So the Spanish concubine . . .'

'There was no Spanish concubine! You have no Spanish blood! I had not even spent the whole of my first week in Dartry when your beast of a father accosted me in the woods! Tadhg *Óg* later discovered me bloodied, bruised and half naked, and I refused the touch of man for years thereafter. When it was discovered that I was with child, I was sent back to my father's lands to deliver it in secret. It was two years until I returned to Dartry again, only after my father had received countless assurances and pledges from Duncarbery that I would never be brought into the presence or vicinity of the beast again.'

'So Aengus was my brother,' whispered Cathal at last.

'Yes,' replied Dervila, 'although not a foul MacGlannagh like yourself. Did you betray him too?'

'Never!' cried the tanist. 'I live only to serve Dartry!'

'By turning against your lord?' scoffed Lady Bourke, delighting in his distress. 'Know you not that he who draws his sword against his lord may as well throw away the scabbard?'

Cathal was about to mouth a spirited defence of his actions, but his shoulder was seized by Verdon, who had slipped up behind him in the growing dark.

'Keep silent, pox-face!' snapped the trooper in a low voice that bristled with annoyance. 'This is meant to be a hideout, not a country fair. We are deep in hostile territory, remember?'

The tanist tore himself away from his accuser and took a few steps away from us, having been rattled by Dervila's revelations. He frowned as he struggled to compose himself, then turned to quietly address Verdon.

'We make for the clearing at first light, then head back to Fermanagh an hour thereafter.'

The trooper issued a grunt of acknowledgement as Cathal trudged towards the other Sassanas. They were already wrapped in their blankets and lying upon the ground as the tanist retired to a corner of the hut which was obscured by nightfall. In the wan light of the tallow candles we could make out Verdon studying us with a creased brow and a dark stare.

'What was your quarrel over?' he asked.

'Loyalty,' was Dervila's instant reply.

Lady Bourke cast me a silent glare of smouldering resentment, leaving me feeling ill at ease as I looked back at the trooper, who displayed a flash of broken teeth in the candlelight.

'Dirty secrets surface when least you would expect them,' he said without ever looking away from me. 'Tomorrow you shall see what your fine Spanish friend has hidden from you for all of these months, causing all manner of misery to your people.'

A pathetic rasp issued from my throat, and Dervila served me with a look of disgust. I stared at the ground and the cabin walls until one of the troopers fetched Verdon two lengths of linen with which to gag us. The Sassanas also bound us hand and foot, then shoved us upon the ground. Verdon's low chuckles filled my good ear as he trudged off to sleep, and as Dervila glared at me, I passed into a dreamless slumber.

A sharp tug upon my collar stirred me before dawn, and soon the tanist was hauling Dervila and me towards the cabin entrance. He had bound a halter to each of our necks, pulling us behind him with a vigour which was as strong as it was disturbing. His face was the picture of rage as he hauled us past the still slumbering troopers and into the forest, drawing his dagger as he grabbed us by the shoulders and flung us both onto the ground.

'Have you seen reason?' whispered Dartry's queen as soon as the linen gags were whipped from our faces. 'Then cut my bonds and let us away to Rosclogher.'

Cathal drew himself to his full height as he observed the kneeling form of his mother, and in the wan light of the moon I could see that he had a deranged look about him. His eyes were bright red from a lack of sleep – and possibly from tears.

'What of Rossinver?' he croaked.

Dervila's eyelids twitched at the question, like those of a card player whose sleight of hand had just been discovered. 'What of it?'

The tanist drew a deep breath, as if broaching a subject too painful for recollection as he held his blade out in front of her face. I could already tell from his stare that he was overcome by rage, so I braced myself for the worst.

'I was but a boy when I was taken to that village, when rumours had already reached Rosclogher that it was plagued by the pox. I have always asked myself what a young prince was doing, being left in a place that most were seeking to flee. None were allowed to leave it until the sickness had run through it, leaving more than half dead. I only survived by a miracle when Tadhg *Óg* learned of my location and had me secretly taken out of the town. Were it not for his kindness, I might have perished from hunger, for even his best surgeons could not save me from the disease that devoured my body.'

'Most unfortunate,' remarked Dervila spitefully. 'It is a lovely village, situated as it is upon the edge of the lake.'

'And you had me sent there.'

'Me?' she protested, though she broke her stare from him. 'What part did I have to play in your misfortune? You should thank the Lord that you were delivered from so terrible a scourge.'

A low growl was heard as Cathal snatched her by the collar and held his dagger close to her face. I rose to defend my fellow prisoner yet received a kick in the stomach, which nearly had me throw up the ring once more.

'Do not mock me,' he snarled at the queen in his grasp, 'for I will cut your head off and hang it from this tree as a warning to all slanderers.'

'Do your worst!' she snarled at him. 'See how your fine new friends treat you if you damage their hostage.'

In the growing light I could see that Cathal's face had turned a hue of crimson, and he slightly relinquished his grasp on the queen of Dartry as she smirked back at him.

'You are a whore,' he said at last, shoving her away, 'a whore who has been the scourge of my life. The pox was nothing compared to the misfortunes you have cast my way from your throne despite my years of loyalty to your husband and son.'

Dervila wobbled slightly as she rose to her feet, then fixed her son with a hard stare.

'You never deceived me, you vainglorious whelp, hungry only for power. With one hand you always feigned to emulate Aengus' grace, yet it was but a pale imitation of his brilliance. You always stood in his shadows, for you were nothing when compared to him except a sallow, sickly reminder of your whoreson father, whose presence was lifted from our lands like an evil fog.'

Cathal breathed deeply as her words cut into him like a volley of shafts, and I wondered what an evil man the previous chieftain of Dartry must have been to have elicited so much hatred from a mother for her own son. As Dervila grinned at the object of her scorn, the tanist finally managed a few words that were whispered below his breath.

'And yet it might all have been so different. I could have been as a son to you, both devoted and loyal. Instead ... instead of thinking myself the son of a Spanish concubine for all these years.'

When he raised his head his cheeks glistened with tears, and my own heart was pierced with sadness at his lot, which appeared a path riddled with grief and anguish. Yet no pity was stirred in Dervila's breast. Her hard stare never wavered as she hurled her last insults at the broken man who stood in front of her.

'Devoted and loyal? A traitorous whelp with the face of a hen-pecked plum who lusts for power? Even that devil father of yours never brokered a deal with the enemy! You should perish of shame rather than stand in front of me claiming devotion and loyalty. For I may be your mother, yet a pox-faced cur you will always remain. I curse my barren husband for the pity he extended to his nephew, and I curse God for having my fine son perish only to spare you!'

'Barren husband,' I muttered, thinking of Aengus and Lochlain. 'Then who –'

Yet she had already spoken her last. Cathal roared aloud as he drew his blade from its sheath, and the queen's eyes bulged as its edge flashed past her throat. She coughed up blood as I flung myself upon the tanist, who had already fallen upon his mother with a raised blade.

'No!' I cried. 'No! Stop!'

Cathal elbowed me in the face as his dagger fell upon her. My head reeled from the blows of the tanist's arm, and when at last I raised it again, I saw Dervila's glazed stare. Her yellow tunic was reddened from the dagger blows which had pierced her breast. A shuffling sound behind us had me turning my head towards the hut. Half-dressed troopers were gathered in the doorway, their faces taut with concern. Verdon was pushing his way through them when a bloodied hand fell upon my shoulder; my eyes met Cathal's bloodied face as he stared at me intently and snatched up my halter.

'Run.'

I pushed myself to my feet and hurried after him, crashing through the trees ahead. We tore through the forest together as if we were joined at the hip, the troopers' cries of rage behind us soon dying away as we scurried down one tree-cloaked hillside, then up and then down another. My lungs were ablaze at our exertions, and tears streaked down my cheeks at the thought of Dervila's passing. Yet I was determined to elude the troopers behind me, and the tanist's blade was reddened with his own mother's blood, so that I never once thought of trying to delay him.

We were soon close to those heights which bordered Lough Melvin when Cathal hauled me by the neck ever closer to the hidden glade. As we drew nearer to our end, I feared that my deceit might soon be discovered, and I was already thinking of how I might attempt an unlikely escape. Yet as we made our way towards the hill where the hidden glade was to be found, Cathal shoved me towards the foot of a tree.

'The witch is finally dead, Spaniard,' he gasped, as I stared at the low-hanging boughs above me. 'She is dead.'

No sooner had I opened my mouth to speak than he stunned me by breaking into a fit of sobs that went unabated for some time. In those instants it was hard to resist the urge to flee his side, and I wondered whether his grief might have slackened his grip on the halter around my neck. Although I was still shocked by Dervila's murder, a suspicion had formed in my mind that the tanist might feel overcome by solitude after fleeing Verdon's men.

'She drove you to it,' I said at last, 'after all she did to you. All considered she got off lightly.'

In the first light of dawn, Cathal's bedraggled hair and grotesque face were not pleasant to behold, yet I met his forlorn stare when he looked at me with the expression of one who had entered a game that he suddenly feared he might lose. He was of a sudden at his most dangerous but also at his most desperate, a fact confirmed almost instantly by his next question.

'Then you understand?' he exclaimed, grabbing me by the shoulder. 'You understand me?'

He burst into a furious sobbing once more, pinching his eyes as he attempted in vain to stem the flood and shaking all the while. I quietly examined our surrounds from the corner of my eye, wondering if I could flee down the craggy, tree-strewn hill which lay below us before he could catch up with me. I thought better of it, realising that I had best play for time and await a better opportunity in which to attempt flight, given that he was upset and quick to commit murder.

So I instead gently touched his shoulder in a display of cautious empathy. His distress seemed to ease and his shoulders throbbed less, and my thoughts turned to how I was to provide him with the ring that was still inside me. I tried to come up with a location where I might pretend that the trinket was hidden. I was instantly dismayed by the thought of the bee skeps, whose winged occupants were swift to fury during the fall. It was then that an idea formed in my mind, which I could fall back on if all else failed.

'You have known only sadness in these lands, my lord MacGlannagh,' I began. 'They have served you a terrible hand, and yet you are a good man of many virtues. When we have recovered the ring, let us away back to Spain together. Between your knowledge of this land and my friends in Seville, we could both start a new life in the Indies.'

My offer was not lost on the tanist, who regarded me in silence for a few moments.

'Think of it,' I urged him. 'We can abandon all torment and battle and live as lords in a new land. Masters of our own fate, free from the vagaries of all these shifting loyalties.'

He shocked me by breaking into a scowl as the cold, hard edge of his dagger bit into the flesh upon my throat. 'You think

I would betray my people as readily as you did? I, who am their last hope of survival?'

I stared back at the tanist, dumbfounded, and he slightly withdrew the blade as he noticed my confusion.

'It is all over, Spaniard. Even now Sheriff George Bingham secretly readies a powerful force with which to invade Dartry.'

'It would not be over if Dervila had been allowed to reach Dublin!'

Cathal snorted. 'That trial shall soon be disbanded. It was but a mere distraction, a ruse which allowed the enemy to make its preparations against O'Rourke.'

'Then why did they kill the witness and capture Dervila?'

'The Binghams did indeed take every precaution to defend themselves against the viceroy, but their allies in London have since ensured that the trial is but a parody of justice.' He smirked as he leant closely towards me. 'You of all people should know, grey wolf, of the flaws of the law. That it is solely a tool of the powerful. The Brehon law of the Irish is fairer than most, yet even you were unjustly accused of rape. I watched you suffer a punishment you should never have incurred.'

I looked away from him as he continued.

'Yes, Spaniard, you do well to turn your stare away from me. Yet you need have no shame. I know that the *ollamh* is drawn to you. I have paid for enough women to know that love for my face cannot even be feigned. But the point remains that the trial in Dublin was ever a fool's hope.'

My voice broke when I met his stare once more, feeling torn by the realisation that in the whole of my life I had never met a better or more selfless man.

'How can you be so sure?'

The tanist fell silent for a few moments, seemingly revisiting a detested memory. At last he replied.

'When the O'Reillys captured me,' he whispered, 'I feared for my life.'

'What did they do to you?'

'I was led to the governor of Connacht, Richard Bingham. He is short in stature, yet when you look in his eyes, you know that you are in the presence of the devil himself. He had the guards cut my bonds and treat me like his honoured guest, never showing the slightest fear that I might attempt to do him harm. He showed me the troops and arms which he has mustered from the Continent. Afterwards he read me letters which bore the seal of Walsingham himself. We then struck a bargain which might yet save our people.'

I shook my head in disbelief, but Cathal pressed on with his story.

'His was not the behaviour of a man who fears a trial's outcome, Juan. His eye is firmly fixed on Breifne and its allies; he knows everything that is decided among us. He knows of Ramos, and how the supply train and the bawn at Sligo were raided. I alone can rescue the tribe and save Dartry from being razed to the ground. I have only to return this trinket to him and we shall be spared.'

'Broken promises have proved more useful to your enemy's cause than their silver,' I replied wearily.

'What do you know of our impending fate, Spaniard?' snapped the tanist. 'Strutting about Connacht with that fool Ramos, thinking that you were about to start an imperial army on the enemy's doorstep! And to what end? To further the cause of a band of so-called allied tribes, fools who flee to protect their own borders at the first setback? No, Spaniard, we cannot prevail against the Sassenach, especially not with allies like Spain. Even Scotland no longer dares to take up arms against Elizabeth. The time has come to embrace the inevitable. It is our only way forward.'

'And what is the inevitable?'

'Peace, Spaniard. No longer shall rivals like MacCabe and me use innocent pawns like you. My offspring shall rule by the authority of the Crown; there shall be no more feuds among aspiring pretenders to the chieftaincy.'

I beheld him in disbelief, though his defiant stare was not enough to silence me. 'You should know that – whatever they have promised you – the Binghams do not intend to share power.'

'Are you deaf?' hissed the tanist in a tone verging on the hysterical. 'What choice do we have? If we keep up the fight they shall wipe us out. Do you not see the burden I carry? Every day I agonise over whether or not I have done the right thing.'

'You have not,' I told him, 'yet it is not too late.'

For an instant I caught in his glance a glimmer of the tanist I had known in the past, a flicker of the old rebel. Yet before I could speak his brashness returned anew.

'If I do not do the Binghams' bidding, God's fury shall be unleashed upon us. Even now they strike deals with minor lords of Connacht like Throckmorton and Clanrickdale. Richard Bingham is not afraid of this trial. I did O'Malley a favour; she would never have made it to Dublin.'

'And Geraldine? Put him out of his misery too?'

'He was an alien; he had no part in our fight. Men like him are as bad as Fearghal the Bard. All they do is give my people false hope without any regard for their suffering.'

The tanist's eyes shot up towards the dells behind me.

'Verdon,' he whispered, suddenly fearful and alert. 'We must make haste.'

We pressed on deeper into the trees ahead of us. The tanist did not waver until we stepped into the thicker foliage ahead. Our surrounds were at once familiar, so that it was evident the tanist was well aware of the location of the hidden dell. When we were almost upon it, he bade me to lie down in the grass, and I watched him draw a bolt in his crossbow which he then used to fell the watcher who passed silently through the trees. No sooner had the guard fallen than Cathal was racing over towards him, still hauling me by the rope around my neck. I stumbled along foolishly until I was sent sprawling over the grass. The tanist plunged his dagger into the groaning guard's throat.

'There, Spaniard,' he said, as he rose back to his feet with a newly blooded tunic and ragged breaths. 'The gates are finally clear for you to render me your trinket. Where is it?'

'In the skeps,' I replied, 'yet the bees are unruly at this time of year.'

'Which one?' he growled, as he trudged over and lifted me to my feet. 'Make haste and give it to me, for we find ourselves trapped between the twin fires of Beltane.'

The tanist's head jerked from left to right as he spoke, and I could tell that he was fearful of being apprehended at any moment. He fitted another bolt to his crossbow and released the rope around my neck. I pretended to do his bidding, walking over to the furthest skep and gently prodding its roof, though I tensed immediately as a low rumbling was heard from within.

'Make haste,' he hissed as he trudged over towards me with his blade held at his side. 'What are you waiting for?'

A low sigh left me at the inevitable pain which was to follow; then I gritted my teeth and seized the roof and flung it towards the approaching tanist, who leapt backwards as it flew towards him. A black cloud grew before my eyes as my hand shot through it and I wrapped my fingers tightly around the honeycomb. My skin crawled as my whole arm was blackened by the insects within. My sight was blurred by their number.

It took a couple of tugs for the honeycomb to be freed, and my arm was already ablaze from stings as the tanist stepped expectantly towards me.

When Cathal took another step I hauled out the honeycomb and flung it into his face. It hit him straight between the eyes and was followed by a black cloud of angry bees which flew from it to assault him. He screamed out just as a trooper entered the clearing with a cocked pistol, but I was already tearing through the dye plants towards the trees ahead, howling as loudly as I could to alert any tribesman within the vicinity of the presence of the intruders.

I looked back but once, spotting the screaming tanist thrashing and rolling across the green as yet more befuddled troopers appeared. Then it was downhill for me, and I ignored the jabbing rocks and sharp sticks that tore at my feet as I jumped past trees, fell over and got up again, resolved to never be captured by the enemy while Cathal's cries rang in my ears.

# XLIX

## ROSCLOGHER TO GLENIFF HORSESHOE VALLEY, DARTRY, COUNTY LEITRIM

### 11 August – 14 September 1589

'You have been a prettier sight, Spaniard,' said Nial, 'that is for certain.'

I grimaced at the bondsman as he plucked yet another bee sting out of my left cheek. I had been found but an hour earlier upon the banks of Lough Melvin, reduced to a shrieking, throbbing mess when two MacGiolla sentries rushed to my side and turned me over. They were startled by the number of bruises, gashes and stings on my body. At my repeated cries of 'Sassana' and my mad gesturing at the trees behind me, they instantly raised the alarm. A score of MacGiolla spears were rounded up and sent back the way I had come, and a bugle blast signalled trouble to the guards stationed at the Rosclogher tower-house across the lake.

I was swiftly put on a skiff and sent across the water towards Manglana's town, and I shivered violently in the stern, where I was wrapped in a blanket. Upon reaching the opposite bank, a few of the townsfolk hurried me upon an unfurled mantle towards the infirmary, where I lay upon a bench until the Jesuit O'Ronayne was summoned. I took deep, ragged breaths while I rubbed my many bruises, trying to ignore the stings in my face, arms and legs. I stared at the mud-and-wattle ceiling above me, realising that I lay in the precise same place where I had first stirred in Manglana's town almost a year earlier.

'What happened?' exclaimed the Jesuit the moment he appeared in the doorway, practically falling over himself as he hurried to my side.

My arm shook violently as my weight was shifted sideways, and I struggled to raise my head to meet his stare. Upon noticing my battered appearance and torn clothes, the Jesuit's jaw slackened. His brows were raised at my single-worded reply.

'Ambush.'

'And Lady Bourke?'

The question was uttered slowly, for he was suddenly overcome by fear. I broke my stare away from him, and there followed a deep, low moan as he sagged sideways, clutching the table in front of him.

'May the Lord deliver her,' he whispered at last, then fell to one knee and held his hands to his face, sobbing silently as his shoulder throbbed against a table leg.

My heart was already all too weary of grief, so I fell back upon my bed, breathing slowly due to my aching ribs until other footsteps were heard in the doorway. I turned my head and saw the bondsman stepping into the hut.

'What is astir?' he asked as O'Ronayne wiped his eyes and returned to his feet.

'Tend to him until my return,' was all the Jesuit managed to say. Then he left the infirmary.

The bondsman removed what stings he could and brought me wine. He listened to my story carefully without ever interrupting me.

'So the tanist has also turned. Did he make mention of any accomplices?'

'None,' I replied, then dropped my head back once more.

I drew deep breaths, quietly disbelieving that I still lived.

'The Geraldine shall prove a great loss,' said Nial. 'He was a valiant man.'

A deep shame ran through me at these words, upon recalling my part in the events which had led to the Anglo-Norman's death. His face was still vivid in my mind when at last I passed out from sheer exhaustion, only to be stirred an hour later by the Jesuit who had returned. I also glimpsed Ramos grinning behind him, limping with Dario through the door. As I again struggled to lift myself, the chieftain himself brushed past my comrades and stood at my shoulder. At his back there appeared his bards Fearghal and Muireann, each of whom openly frowned at me.

'What happened, Spaniard?' asked Manglana. I struggled not to wrinkle my nose at his reeking dragon breath. 'Tell me everything; leave nothing out.'

Tadhg *Óg* listened to my account without interruption, except when I implied that Dervila had made claims about the truth of Cathal's parentage, which had led to her death at the hands of the tanist. Upon learning this, the chieftain's grizzled face turned bloodless and his knuckles whitened. He grabbed the edge of my bed and bared his yellowed teeth.

'The Wolf even hounds me from beyond the grave,' he growled. 'May his soul burn in hell for all eternity.'

'Why were you spared?' asked Muireann almost instantly thereafter, with no attempt to mask the suspicion in her voice.

'Cathal wanted Lord Manglana killed,' I replied. 'He promised to spare me if I shot him with the Marquardt.'

My lie had been prepared well in advance, so that I produced it without a stutter. I had also prepared myself for her next question.

'Then what were you doing in the secret clearing?'

'Hiding,' I said, keeping as straight a face as I could manage. 'After Cathal slew Lady Bourke, he thought to hide in the clearing while conceiving of the best way for me to slay his lord. I fled him after flinging the honeycomb into his face.'

No sooner did I mention Dervila's murder than I instantly regretted it, as large tears appeared in Muireann's eyes at the mention of her dead queen. O'Ronayne shifted awkwardly from one foot to the other and held his contorted face in his hands, yet the chieftain's gaze never once softened as he studied me carefully.

'And would you have shot me, Spaniard?'

'Only you can answer that, my lord, yet I did not tarry long enough to find out.'

The chieftain could not resist a wry smile when I said this, though it swiftly vanished when he turned away from me and left the cabin, his retainers hastening after him. I issued a sigh of relief as they made their exit, but then I made out Ramos, staring at me with a broad grin on his face.

'A pretty yarn you spun, Abelito,' he said, then winked at me before he, too, was gone.

Slumber instantly returned to me, a dreamless sleep as black as pitch, from which I stirred with a shudder. O'Ronayne's pudgy face was barely a few inches from mine, and a literal draught of stale mead struck me when he shook my shoulder again and spoke.

'Can you walk?'

When I nodded back at him, he fetched me my boots. I pulled them onto my calloused feet with great effort, then hobbled after him out into the town, where the wailing of women could already be heard as the retrieved bodies of the dead were brought back to Rosclogher for burial. The cloud-filled sky made for a grey light which hung over the town, so that everything from the clothes of the villagers to the sod-and-wattle huts possessed an obscure cast. Townsfolk thronged about me and the Jesuit as we hurried towards the line of corpses being borne towards the green.

As the bodies were laid out upon the grass, tribesmen gathered alongside them in silence. The Jesuit held me by the shoulder when I fell to one knee at the sight of Geraldine. In their haste, Verdon's men had not severed any heads of the slain, and in death the Anglo-Norman's stare was as fierce as it had been in life. His mention of the great Desmond rebellions sprung to mind when I bent over to kiss his forehead, yet I recoiled at the icy touch.

I wondered if I would one day also meet his end, a thought which left my knees buckling as I climbed back onto my feet. With my hands to my face, I turned my back on the corpse of the aged warrior, his huge sword laid upon his body. Riders appeared out of the mist, having been despatched from Breifne to bear their deceased countrymen back home. The bodies of Old Tom and Riona, the slain witness, were hauled off the ground and flung over the backs of riderless horses. The horsemen then disappeared back into the trees, so that only Dervila's body was left behind on the greensward.

The queen's corpse was placed in a mantle borne by eight bluejackets, and a grim procession of Dartrymen followed them through the ring of the bog and along the path through the heights which lay before us. All throughout I was held in the firmest grip of shame, my eyes firmly fixed on the track we had struck, so that I hardly realised who was who among the shadowy shapes in our company. The shrieking of the keeners did not abate until we had reached one of the heights upon the mountainside, where Dervila was to be committed beneath the rocks of the cairn.

Manglana and his closest retainers were already gathered about the corpse of his wife, and Muireann's cheeks glistened with sorrow. Lochlain stood at her side, appearing as forlorn as the rest of his company, yet the grim, troubled look on the chieftain's face surprised me. When O'Ronayne administered Dervila's last rites, her body was buried beneath the rocks.

At last Manglana turned away, his eyebrows knitted closely together while he was devoured by an inner rage. After taking a few steps before his subjects, he turned back towards Muireann and held her by the shoulder, serving her with the slightest nod. At this sign, the ollave turned back to face the windswept land which rippled far beneath us, lifting her head to the sky as she raised her reddened face and shrieked aloud.

'Cathal *Dubh*! I dismiss you!'

As we left the pile of rubble behind us, it was a quiet gathering which returned down the mountain towards Rosclogher. Ramos held his *brat* mantle tightly about him as he trudged behind me with Dario at his shoulder, only grunting a few words beneath his breath when we finally crossed the bog.

'The tanist an Iscariot. Who could have imagined it? Ah well, at least we have discovered the traitor.'

We used what daylight remained to wander about the town in silence before returning to the sergeant's tent to spend the night. As we crept inside, I was surprised to find the Marquardt rifle alongside my mattress.

'How did it get here?' I asked in surprise as I snatched it up and stared at its bore.

'The chieftain's men gave it to us,' replied Ramos as he drew his mantle across his body. 'They found it with other abandoned goods in the hut where Dervila's body was discovered.'

The following day had hardly dawned when the sergeant barked at me to re-join the militia, which was gathered upon the green. Ramos gestured to me after we had trained and he had disbanded his men.

'Any thoughts?' he asked, removing his helmet and hanging it by the hook of his tin arm, before reaching for the skin at his shoulder.

'There is certainly better movement. But have the men grown in number?'

'Yes, we are turning back conscripts these days. Many a houseboy and churl have sought us out since you left. But never fear, Abelito, for your place at my side is always safe!'

The sergeant issued a bark of hoarse laughter and punched me in the shoulder when he said this, just as Dario walked over to us.

'One of the men spoke to a bluejacket,' he said. 'The sheriff has been sighted at Ben Bulben.'

'How many men accompany him?' asked Ramos, whirling upon the Croat.

"Tis not yet known for certain, yet they say it is one troop of men and one of horse.'

'Has Manglana given the word?' I asked.

Ramos sighed deeply as his brow furrowed in thought. 'Not yet, although I cannot see how he will allow a Sassana rooster to strut around his domains.'

'In any event,' added the Croat, 'we are men of O'Rourke, and this would not be a quarrel of ours.'

'That remains to be seen,' said Ramos with a hint of worry in his voice. He stroked his beard as he silently returned to his tent.

The next day the heavens were thick with cloud, and rain lashed the town as Ramos lined us up and barked orders at us for most of the morning. Yet we were hardly two hours into our manoeuvres when a page appeared from the tower-house to speak to the sergeant. I had staggered away towards the tent, hopeful of stealing some rest, when a cry was heard from the other end of the greensward.

'By the Virgin, Abelito! Where in God's name are you going? We have been summoned by Manglana!'

After the usual crossing of the lake and climbing of the steps, we found the hall resounding with loud voices as the freemen in the assembly turned to regard us with fearful faces

– though only for a moment. They soon returned to sharing their concerns with their chieftain.

'Lord Maguire has borne us compensation for your loss,' declared the wizened figure of Malachy, the chieftain's steward, from the foot of the dais.

'Twenty heads of cattle,' said Manglana to his steward, 'yet will he finally join in our struggle?'

'Alas, he shall not.'

Manglana sighed wearily as an aged tribesman stood forward.

'And what of the trial, my lord? Has another witness been found?'

While the question was asked, we followed a page, who led us through the mass of tightly bunched freemen towards Dervila's empty throne.

'No,' replied O'Ronayne in his lord's stead, 'none have the heart of our valiant queen.'

'And what of the traitor, Cathal? Has he been found?'

'No trace of him was found,' replied O'Ronayne once more. He snorted in indignation as he shook his head in disgust. 'He is most likely already dead, put to the sword by his new friends.'

Manglana regarded his priest solemnly, then spoke again. 'You may well speak truth, friend Redmond. Our enemy never came to share, which is ever the root of our quarrel. Even now the Sassanas rape the land as they constantly seek to divide and exploit us.'

The chieftain sighed and stared at the shadows of the flames that flickered upon his wall. A pained smile spread across his lips.

'Cathal's treachery has cut me deeper than any sword thrust, yet he would not imagine how welcome he is to my seat. Anyone who thinks that to supplant me is to end our people's suffering is nothing but a fool.'

A younger tribesman in the assembly bunched his fists and shook one of them in front of his face. 'How could he have betrayed his own kin? For a tanist to rebel is one thing, but to go over to the enemy?'

'It is not unheard of, Ruaidrí Óg,' sighed Fearghal the Bard. 'Indeed the enemy has long harnessed the practice of using tanists to foment revolt.'

Manglana's brow darkened when he heard this, and his knuckles whitened as he gripped the sides of his throne. 'The days of the chieftains grow dark indeed when we cannot even secure the loyalty of our own tanists! Let us hope that I can at least depend upon the fealty of my subjects.'

'Our swords are yours!' shouted the men gathered before him, and when at last their cries died down, O'Ronayne declared a sobering fact.

'Cathal was popular among the *tuatha*, so word of his treachery must not spread.'

The chieftain nodded his grudging acceptance of the Jesuit's words.

'Indeed,' he said. 'Too many heads have been turned by Saxon silver. We must increase our vigil amongst ourselves, for the most dangerous enemies lie within.'

So saying he turned his head from left to right until he located Ramos alongside a window, then fixed his gaze upon me. 'For how many pieces did Cathal the Black sell me, friend Juan?'

His unexpected address had heads in all directions turning towards me, so that I fumbled for a reply.

'He thought he did what was best for his people. It was not silver that turned him, but despair.'

Manglana did not appear pleased by my reply, as he cast his eyes upon his feet.

'Coward!' he snorted at last. 'For how easy would it be to bend to the Saxon yoke! The enemy serenades us with talk of holding land in full ownership forever and of guaranteeing its passing to our firstborn. Yet how many more shall live as churls if I surrender our struggle?'

Another long sigh left him as he stood up and raised his fist in the air.

'Fool of a tanist! The enemy only wants our strength to be broken and for us to bow to their law, that our swords may not serve their rivals. Yet it is Philip of Spain who is our rightful king, as proclaimed by the pope in Rome! He shall secure for all eternity whoever perishes in the service of the Catholic king. Yet you will prevail in this life, for as long as you remain faithful subjects of the sheriff-slayer and lawgiver of Dartry!'

'Sheriff-slayer! Lawgiver!' howled the saffron tunics before him, behaving no differently to a baying mob of commoners.

Amid their cries, Manglana appeared to only grow in stature. He drew a deep breath, and his right hand fell upon his sword. He suddenly seemed possessed of all the indomitable strut and confidence of a prized fighting rooster.

'For too long have we looked to our enemies to bring justice to their own. But mark my words, one and all, that the time of waiting is now over! I shall deal with these Bingham devils as I dealt with their kind before them!'

His sword rang as he lifted it from its scabbard towards the ceiling.

'I know of one place where traitors cannot hide, and that is the field of battle! Our fathers paid in blood to secure the bounds of our land. They bequeathed us the green valleys in which to fatten our heads and the mountains to serve as an eternal refuge against any army sent to claim us. For there is no fairer land than Dartry, and here we have everything! Thus, let us hasten forth and despatch these invaders with fire and cold steel!'

The freemen roared their support until Fearghal the Bard raised his arms and shrieked his own strident war cry. He cut a fearsome figure in his jacket of bright scarlet.

*'MacGlannagh Abù! MacGlannagh Abuuuuuuuù!* To tarry is to lose the moment! We must attack forthwith!'

The cries of approval only grew louder until Manglana's raised sword was finally lowered and returned to its scabbard. He disbanded the freemen with a final instruction. 'I have rid my lands of one sheriff and will do so again. Sharpen your blades and ready your hafts, for in the following days I shall give the word.'

There followed a swift council of war after the last of the saffron-clad tribesman left the hall. It was attended by the chieftain's closest circle, which comprised of his two bards and his steward Malachy, as well as O'Ronayne, the Brehon judge Echna and the bondsman Nial Ne Dourough. At Manglana's request Ramos had also tarried behind, silently shouldered by me and Dario, as we were privy to the deliberations of Dartry's finest.

'The *tuatha* must be roused at once,' said Manglana, 'for Bingham has already been sighted near Keeloges. What is the latest account of his numbers?'

'Forty riders, my lord,' replied Nial, 'almost twice as many on foot.'

'Then we are well matched in numbers,' replied Manglana, 'if we can manage that many horse.'

'What we lack in numbers we can make up for in stealth and surprise,' observed Muireann.

Manglana fell back upon his throne as he considered the ollave's words, and the fingers of both his hands were locked against each other as he closed his eyes in thought.

'What tidings of MacCabe?' he suddenly asked.

'He has repaired to the coastland bordering Banagh, sire,' replied Nial, 'and it is also said that he shall winter there with his men.'

'No doubt awaiting my forgiveness or other employment,' muttered Manglana, and I noticed a regretful look briefly soften his stare before his scowl returned.

'Despatch runners to watch his movements,' said the chieftain at last, 'and let us pray that word of his son's passing has not yet reached him. The last thing we want is a band of incensed Scots on our tail.'

'Should we not seek to make terms with him, my lord?' asked Fearghal the Bard. 'His men have all too often proved the difference in battle.'

'Especially when they have betrayed us to the enemy,' growled Nial angrily, just as the regretful look returned to Manglana's worn features. It lingered a moment longer before being replaced by an open grin of defiance.

'Why seek terms with a proven traitor when we have Spanish spears? We can now fight and win in the Continental fashion.'

A sheer delight overcame me at the chieftain's words, though Fearghal's features creased in an ill-disguised frown. Ramos did not appear moved by Manglana's open appreciation of his trained militia and did not hesitate to make his thoughts known.

'My men are not yet ready to take to the open field, my lord. Nor are they allowed to engage in combat without the express command of Lord O'Rourke.'

Manglana appeared taken aback by the sergeant's words, which left him shifting awkwardly on his throne as he sought to suppress his growing outrage.

'I am the lord O'Rourke's first lieutenant,' he finally snapped, 'and my own express command to you can be taken to come directly from him.'

Ramos turned a hue of scarlet as he made to reply, then held his tongue and bowed his head to the king of Dartry. 'As you command, my lord Manglana.'

'On your knee and louder, Spaniard,' snarled the chieftain. 'Do not forget in whose domain you find yourself.'

Ramos stiffened upon hearing the order and appeared to struggle momentarily with the command. Then he fell to one knee as Dario and I followed his lead, and together we declared our obedience to the throne before us: 'As you command, my lord Manglana.'

The chieftain eyed us warily when we returned to our feet, then addressed Ramos again. 'Are you afraid of the sheriff, Sergeant?'

'No, my lord,' replied Ramos. 'He leads a force unable to secure your lands or storm any keep. His is but a cheap act of provocation, as he evidently wants to draw you out into the field.'

'And there we shall have his head.'

''Tis an unnecessary risk, sire.'

'What would you have me do instead?'

'What you have always done. Winter behind your stout walls and take in what people you can. Order the rest to take to the heights and islands, and to leave nothing behind that the enemy may use. Bingham shall not linger here, and you will have saved lives that can be spared. Think about your overlord's wrath if you encounter a setback and waste lives better spared –'

'That is enough,' cut in the chieftain angrily. 'Your view has been considered. My people have long been unruly, with many questioning my protection. The hosting of the Scots and the endless raids of the enemy have spared none of the *tuatha*, and I can ill afford any more dishonour to be cast on my name if I hide behind my walls again. The sheriff's is a force that we can defeat, and our victory shall assure all Dartrymen of my protection, a protection that they have dearly paid for. Bingham shall regret his entering so heedlessly into the wolf's lair. Make ready to march with me, and we shall return with his head on a spike.'

Ramos bowed grudgingly as the chieftain next addressed Muireann and Nial.

'My daughter and faithful bondsman, you are two servants whose loyalty I can still call upon – a boon both rare and great in these days of fast-growing darkness. Rally forth and call a rising out of the *tuatha*! Tell them to flock to the banner of their lord, as is required of them yearly! Tell them to send even the whiskerless lads and any maidens that would fight, and to march to Glencar, where my runners will guide them to my force!'

No sooner had his commands left his lips than Muireann and Nial bowed to him and hastened out of the hall. My eyes briefly met those of the ollave as she turned, and amid all the talk of raids and fighting I felt a twinge of helplessness as she vanished through the doors with my friend the bondsman. After some further discussion about arms, Manglana asked that we leave him alone with Fearghal the Bard to intone an aged ode to war.

As the first notes of the bard's instrument reached our ears, Dario muttered beneath his breath in Spanish. 'It seems to me that these Irish chieftains are but brutes who surround themselves with the learned to sweeten their brutality.'

'Be quiet,' snapped the sergeant ahead of me, 'or the priest will hear you.'

We did not utter another word throughout the boat crossing. When we climbed out of the boat, O'Ronayne scurried off into the town to rally men to battle while the sergeant drew us aside.

'All this calling to arms has left me flustered,' he said. 'I need a walk to clear my head. Walk with me along the lake.'

We followed him at a brisk pace, keeping close to Lough Melvin's muddy banks, sometimes slipping upon the soggy soil underfoot. Before long, our eastbound progress led us into deeper foliage. Ramos and Dario never once looked back as they walked through the trees, though they ofttimes jerked their heads from left to right, almost as if we were on a skirmishing mission behind enemy lines.

I wondered whether the hidden apothecary of Lady Bourke stood close at hand. I was haunted by the memory of her beating during the ambush, when I had foregone the bugle and the safety of my friends for the ring. The thought of what I had done left me feeling disgusted with myself, only to find that Ramos and Dario had stopped in their tracks and turned to face me with sly grins on their wicked faces.

I stared back at them askance as I stopped to regain my breath. Meanwhile Ramos walked around us with his good hand rested behind his back.

"'Tis indeed most fortunate,' he said, 'that you are back among us.'

'Indeed,' I replied, sensing that something was astir. "Twas a greater miracle than that of the loaves and the fish.'

Ramos raised a suspicious eyebrow at me whilst Dario's grin widened.

'The numbers of this miracle, however,' noted Ramos, after a few moments spent biting his lip, 'are certainly less bountiful. For while our Lord fed the multitude with only six loaves and two fish, it was over a score of riders that set off for Enniskillen and yet you returned alone.'

'It was five loaves,' I replied nervously, having always had a good memory for both scripture and writing.

Ramos' one eye pierced all before it as a deathly, grim cast overcame his features.

'Five or six matters not to me, Abelito. All that matters is that you made it back alive. For as we both well know, yours is the most valuable quarry of all, which might draw a troop of *tercios* to the O'Rourke's banner. Indeed it can be the only reason why you are still among us.'

I stared at the ground. 'I know not of what you speak.'

A blow to my stomach left me gasping for breath upon my knees, and Dario pulled my head back by my hair and rested his *skene* dagger along my throat.

'Do not breathe.'

My body stiffened at the low growl of the forest Croat, for fear that his blade would leave me wearing the grin of death from ear to ear. Meanwhile Ramos snatched up the lowest powder charge on my bandolier, emptying its contents upon the ground and examining them with his forefinger. I was dismayed by the sight of this, for after fleeing Cathal I had taken great care to secretly return the ring to the ampoule.

'You think you are so crafty,' snapped Ramos, 'with your stupid stories of Cathal telling you to assassinate Manglana, while thinking that you are safe from prying eyes whenever you defecate.'

His inevitable discovery cut him short, and he whistled aloud as he raised the ring before him. I shook once in outrage, but the edge of cold steel against my gullet rendered me immobile once more.

'My word, Abelito,' whispered the sergeant. 'Not for nothing have I endured your whining for all these years. You have done well, brother.'

He flipped the ring into the air and then snatched it, chuckling once in disbelief as he held it closely to his one eye. 'Now that is plunder indeed. A king's ransom, by God.'

So saying, he thrust it into his jacket and trudged back towards the lake. I was left almost whimpering in fear of losing my miserable life, but then the Croat's dagger vanished and I was shoved into the gold-brown leaves underfoot.

'Do not tarry, Abelito,' called the sergeant behind me, 'for these woods are choked with wolves at night. Including that big, black one – the one these savages think is Cathal's father.'

I rose cursing to my feet, then cut a pathetic figure as I stumbled after the shadowy pair, crushed by anger and disappointment despite the fact that I yet lived. All the way down the hill I cursed myself for my carelessness, fixing my stare on the figure of the sergeant and feeling the old embers of fury being stoked up again into a blazing hatred. If my face betrayed these sentiments they were utterly ignored by Ramos, who barked at me to form square with the rest of the men who came running from the tents the moment he beckoned to them.

'Any day now we shall take the field again,' he warned us, 'yet this time the enemy will be expecting us. Our training must be harder and longer than ever before.'

Ramos proved as good as his word, taking us through our paces mercilessly for an added couple of hours a day and demanding greater speed throughout all of our manoeuvres. Any bitterness I held towards him swiftly vanished from my mind, for as soon as we took to the greensward we engaged in forming squares and hand-to-hand combat. Many of the townsfolk often appeared to gawk at us, for a great stirring had also overcome the town, what with the ringing of anvils and men hurrying to prepare their weapons and sharpen their fighting skills.

The bluejackets performed their own sparring outside the ringfort while also training the other kerns and tribesmen who were to join the chieftain's force. Manglana himself could be seen hurling spears with his score of freemen until he rode off with them to Duncarbery to summon more men to his banner. The air was taut as a bowstring as each able man went about his duties in silence, knowing that we might be ordered towards the enemy on a day which might prove to be our last.

No amount of training would ever prove enough for the impending fateful encounter, and I threw myself heartily into the sergeant's gruelling manoeuvres. At the end of each day, I barely had the strength to trudge back over to our tent, where I cleaned my gun and passed out on the ground. Yet despite the long hours that were put into our preparation, the sergeant was never appeased, always demanding greater speed of execution and roaring at those men who hesitated to execute his orders.

'You are not ready!' he would bellow in frustration, even though I scarcely shared in his misgivings. 'You must move as one if we are to find and slay the snake in the grass!'

At his express request, large, round, wooden shields were made by the villagers, then given to the men on the sleeves of our square. Ramos spent many hours instructing them to haul the weapons off their backs to protect our front, back and flanks.

"'Tis all a waste of our time,' he once caught me grumbling.

He seized me by the collar then and yelled in my face. 'Do not speak so idly, fool! Do you know if Cathal was Bingham's sole spy?'

My exertions also served to banish any further thoughts of the ring, especially when word of enemy raids reached us. The noose had started to tighten, with Rosclogher becoming a haven for rebels who fled the sheriff's force. None who stood in George Bingham's path were spared as he blazed a deathly trail of ruin through Dartry. Manglana appeared at Rosclogher a day later with forty mounted freemen at his back. The townsfolk retired with their valuables to the keep and the surrounding islands, leaving nothing behind for the enemy.

The steward Malachy was entrusted with the command of the tower-house, which also held the relics from Saint Mel. He was given strict instructions not to grant entry to anyone until the chieftain's return. No word had yet been received from Muireann or Nial as we left the town towards dusk, the Jesuit riding alongside the chieftain and invoking us to battle with the *catach* held over his head. We travelled with the kerns behind Manglana's riders, making for the direction of the enemy. I marched at the square's centre with a heavy heart, finding myself strangely relieved at having lost the trinket yet fearful for the safety of both the ollave and the bondsman.

One horror followed another as we kept to our westward path, and our fears were soon replaced by rage at the sight of each atrocity. One settlement had been rendered a small forest of skewered natives, and the remains of a smoking church were littered with the charred bodies of those believers who had been locked inside it. Any remaining caution was thrown to the wind as Manglana pressed us on in a blind rage. We struck camp in the heights around Truskmore at dusk, where a whiskerless scout with a flushed face stormed into the chieftain's tent.

'They are not a day's ride hence, sire. Camped in the horse-shoe valley beneath the cave of Diarmuid and Gráinne.'

'A fitting slaying ground,' observed Manglana as the shadows of the low fire played upon his face and the canvas. 'How many?'

'A company and squadron.'

'Have none of the *tuatha* arrived?'

'Only a few, sire. Less than half.'

Manglana's face reddened in annoyance. He flung his head back with a horn of brandy held to his lips. 'We will pay the rest a visit when we are done with this sheriff,' he said. 'Let them seek the protection of the sheriff-slayer then.'

At night I retired to the tent I shared with Ramos and the Croat. Pale stars glittered over the great peaks to the south, and a cold wind blew from the side of distant Ben Bulben to our right. All about us the country was wrapped in a growing gloom as we lay on the ground in silence.

'It shall be a fight like any other,' said Dario at last. 'Men better than us shall die, while lesser men will live.'

Ramos grunted his agreement before he turned over and fell asleep.

We were ready for the last stage of our march at the first light of dawn. Within the hour our force came upon Bingham's camp, the rank odour of his men filling our nostrils as we advanced towards him, against the wind. They were soon spotted beyond the knife-edged peak of Ben Weeksen, which rose to the iron-grey canvas of the sky to our right as we stealthily moved towards the great horseshoe-shaped valley.

A great cleft in the mountain wall emerged as we drew closer towards it, like some gap in the bottom row of a monster's teeth. Little did we realise the death trap into which we so readily walked, for word of our advance had already been borne to the sheriff by his own scouts. Yet we waded deeper into the tall grass, Manglana trading plans with Ramos while he scowled at the enemies that were gathered before us.

'This is as far as these butchers go in my kingdom,' he declared at last.

'We shall engage with them to draw out their horse,' said Ramos. 'Have your kerns withdraw to the hills, then get your riders to surprise them from the rightward slope.'

The chieftain did not reply as he donned his helmet, then raised his arm to disband his kerns, who ran off towards the hills while his mounted freemen followed his lead. As they rode away from us, Dario leant over the side of his mount and tapped me upon the head.

'Leave some pickings for us, Abelito.'

'It is not over yet,' I mumbled as I wiped some more sleep from my eyes.

The lanky Croat chuckled at my curt reply. 'Have faith, soldier, for it soon will be.'

He made after the chieftain's riders, who rounded the foot of the slopes to the right of the valley. Ramos waited until the last of the cavalry vanished from view, then ordered us to take up our positions and addressed our ensign and drummer boy.

'Hoist the banner and commence the taps, as loudly as you can manage.'

The beats of the bodhrán filled our ears as Ramos pulled his helmet onto his head. He tightened the strap of his tin arm and raised his sword aloft. 'And now to enter the valley of death. Forward march!'

To a man we made towards the high cleft, the sharp ends of pikes swaying above our heads as musketeers blew on the slow matches that were curled like pet grass snakes about their forearms. The Marquardt was already loaded as I marched in the middle of the square with Ramos, and the stirring of the enemy before us only grew with each blade of grass that we covered.

'Any moment now,' whispered Ramos to me, 'let us pray that the ploy works.'

My reply died on my lips as the slightest of thuds was heard. We neared the slow incline of the slopes, which rose to join the mountain wall ahead, and which hemmed us inside the growing horseshoe valley. The noise grew until it all but masked the beats of our tireless drummer boy, and scores of riders could be seen charging towards us. Behind me a man cursed when the force was barely a hundred yards from us, and the ground reverberated beneath our feet.

'Prime!' snarled the sergeant, and we stopped dead in our tracks to swiftly meet his command. We followed all of our steps from the training ground as the sergeant took us through them, the great wall of mounted steel thundering ever closer towards us. The whites of the riders' eyes soon came into view, which was the prompt for Ramos to bark his final order.

'Fire!'

Rank, white smoke filled the air as the serpentines were jerked back, and amid the din, nothing could be seen or heard for a few moments.

'Draw pikes!'

As the spears were lowered the whole square tensed; we braced ourselves for the usual impact of horses upon spears. Yet there only followed an eerie stillness as shadows wheeled away from us and the enemy horse formed two separate files upon either side of our square. Men fell to their pistol shots and the bolts of their crossbows as they thundered just beyond reach of the spears. The riders sported cruel smiles as Ramos yelled at the men at our flanks.

'Shields! Shields! Draw those shields!'

The command was somewhat late, as a half-dozen of our men lay writhing upon the ground following the fusillade from the mounted troopers.

'Caracole,' I muttered in disbelief.

The mounted Sassanas beat a swift retreat to reload their arms as Ramos swiftly roared his next orders. 'Dead and wounded to the centre! Fill up those gaps! And use those shields, for the love of the Virgin!'

His instructions were no sooner delivered than he jabbed me sharply in the arm with his elbow and uttered a low cackle of delight. 'The bastards think they have gotten away, but just watch this, Abelito.'

So saying, he pointed to the heights to our right, where the mounted figure of Manglana could be seen kicking his mount downhill. Two score freemen followed his standard as they thundered downhill to assault the unsuspecting troopers like a tidal wave. They rode Irish Cobs, which were each lighter than the English horse, and so they swiftly covered the decline. The riders' savage war cries filled us with renewed hope as we hauled the injured to the centre of our square.

*'MacGlannagh Abuuuuuuuuuuuuù! MacGlannagh Abuuuuuuuuuuuù! MacGlannagh Abuuuuuuuuuuuuuuuuu uuuuuuuuuuuù!'*

*Yet our passions were no so*oner stirred than they were doused again. The chieftain's horse suddenly tumbled and rolled, followed by one mount and then another. We stared on in shock at the sight, rocked to our core as all but a handful of the chieftain's mounts foundered, kicking the air but a few feet away from the field of battle. The screeches of fallen horse reached us, together with the cries of some riders.

Ramos was the first to act. 'To the chieftain!' he roared. 'Run!'

Across the field the enemy troopers hastily reloaded their weapons and readied to charge once more, and I grabbed the sergeant by the shoulder.

'But our dead and wounded?'

My jaw was left hanging in surprise as he shoved me away in a rage.

'What would you have me do?' he demanded. 'Manglana's life is at stake!'

The sergeant cried his order again as he raced towards the hills, leaving us to make after him. Our wounded were left groaning behind us as we closed in on the foothills, where the chieftain could be seen holding his arm as he staggered among his riders and tried to rally the fallen. We had hardly reached the foot of his slope when the ominous thud of hooves could be heard behind us again.

'Form square!' howled Ramos between deep breaths. 'Form square!'

The men gathered about their subalterns as they had countless times on the training ground, forming a defensive shield in front of the chieftain who still cut a forlorn figure. The hillside behind him was strewn with the bodies of broken steeds and riders alike.

'Pick your man!' cried Ramos as the mounted troopers drew closer. I took aim at the foremost rider, and our musketeers scrambled to adjust their slow match.

'Fire!'

Most of our shots were true to the mark, and a dozen troopers crashed to the ground. Ramos gave the order again while our enemies wheeled about the lowered pikes. Our shields met most of their volleys until we released another one ourselves. At last, the mounted Sassanas broke away, riding hard towards the wounded we had left behind us on the plain. As they were slain, their cries made me sick to my stomach. Ramos glowered with rage beside me.

'This is bad war,' was all he could say.

Then Dario rode up to us, short of breath, since he was one of the few horsemen who had survived the tumble.

'Thank God you appeared. They would have had us.'

Behind him the wounded steeds were already being put out of their misery. The sound of blades cutting gizzards reached us as we gritted our teeth, saddened by the sight of so many destroyed horses.

'Caltrops?' I asked.

The Croat nodded as he held out a palm, a three-pronged piece of rusted steel held upon it. 'As many raven feet as there are blades of grass.'

Manglana rode before us with a fresh horse. Blood still streamed down his forearm and thigh while another wound darkened the side of his throat.

'How do you fare, sire?' yelled the sergeant.

A scream from the very depths of hell was heard in reply. To our left a column of our men flew into the air and collapsed amid groans and cries, leaving the rest to shiver behind their arms, scared witless by the new devilry which had been unleashed upon us. As we stared ahead of us in disbelief, Dario said the word on everyone's mind.

'Cannon?'

Ramos adjusted his helmet and gritted his teeth.

'We are doomed.'

L

# Gleniff Horseshoe Valley, Dartry, County Leitrim

*14 September 1589*

Ramos wiped the sweat from his eyes and gestured to his subalterns.

'Fill in those gaps and get ready to march. Bear what wounded you can with you.'

'Rats in a trap,' I sighed.

The sergeant ignored me as he stared at the distant plume of cannon smoke, his brow creased in deep thought. He then turned to call out to the chieftain.

'Do we retire, Lord?'

Manglana reined his mount in alongside the square and removed his helmet, revealing flushed cheeks and lips which were curled in frustration.

'Does your courage fail you again, Sergeant?'

Ramos jerked his reddening face away from the chieftain. He muttered darkly beneath his breath until his composure was regained enough for him to address Manglana once more.

'The cannon's precise whereabouts must be located, sire. Methinks the battery is stationed along the waterfall.'

The chieftain galloped off without a reply, with less than half his horsemen on his heels. They were all that remained of his two dozen riders, and we stared after them as one of the Spanish subalterns leant over towards the sergeant.

'If he shall not retreat, then we should charge them. Most of these men have not withstood cannon before; they cannot endure many more of those.'

Ramos grimaced back at him.

'He will not retreat until he or the sheriff are dead. If we break now, we shall all die. You only move at my order.'

A cry was heard ahead of us, and the enemy squadron were seen thundering towards us again. As the sergeant barked new commands, our flash pans were refilled and balls shoved and rammed hard down our guns' muzzles. Amid a blare of trumpets, the enemy horse drew ever closer. The shields at the front of our phalanx were raised as the odd crack of pistol fire came from our foes, yet there was no caracole. Our assailants' lances fell forward, and we could make out the whites of our enemy's eyes.

'Raise pikes!' cried Ramos, instantly guessing the troopers' intentions.

After the torment of the caracole and the cannon fire, the troopers were gambling on our resolve having weakened enough for them to break our square. Our shape was all but lost as the mounted men crashed into the long spears held up before us, but we also served them with a shower of musket shot. The collision was as heavy as their mailed horses, and men were killed on impact amid the pop of knees and shoulders belonging to both man and beast.

A sickening shearing of sinew ensued as blades were drawn in the stinking fog, the faces of the unhorsed troopers roaring in the haze as they assailed us. I despatched at least two of them with the Marquardt until the remaining troopers fell back again, riding towards the sheriff's ground force. Men stood about me panting and coughing as the enemy drew away, for our mettle had been fully tested by the assault.

'Jesus wept,' sighed Dal Verme ahead of me as the howling wounded in the van were hauled to the back of our square.

Their sounds of agony were drowned out when the distant cannon belched fire a third time. To a man we fell silent; the din was followed by the screech of the missile aimed at us. All orders and weapons were instantly rendered useless, and we were blinded with soil and gore as yet another file of men was riven by the cannonball.

Ramos was first to recover his wits, roaring above the ensuing groan of the newly wounded. 'Drag them to the centre! Let us get moving. You at the front, prime your muskets!'

By the time we had abandoned our position along the rightward slopes, another booming sound was heard. Men ducked and made themselves small, and the hair rose upon the back of my neck. Grass rippled along the back of our square, the cannonball missing a sleeve of musketeers by a couple of paces. We breathed a deep sigh of relief as Dal Verme uttered the very thought on my mind.

'Bastards have a good gunner.'

Ramos wiped his forehead as he jerked his head from left to right, attempting to identify the chieftain's whereabouts.

'Where in hell is he?'

He had barely asked the question when a small band of horsemen could be seen charging across the plain. A stiff jerk on the reins had the chieftain halting his mount alongside us. Manglana's face was more flushed than before.

'It is left of the waterfall!'

'Within a musket shot of any trees?' cried Ramos.

'Yes,' replied the chieftain after a few moments of ill-concealed bafflement.

Ramos chewed at a knuckle as he did whenever he was thinking hard. To a man we shuddered when a distant thunderclap was heard, so unnerved were we from the cannon blasts.

'Get your rifle ready, Abelito!' Ramos finally declared.

'What?' I replied in surprise, but he grabbed me by the shoulder and next yelled at the chieftain.

'Fetch him a horse and get him within sight of the battery. And assign half your riders to Dario's command.'

'The battery is well guarded,' replied Manglana after yet another peal of thunder.

Ramos shoved me through the men ahead of us and towards the mounted freemen. 'It matters not,' he yelled as the first raindrops reached our faces. 'They need only be distracted. 'Tis our only hope against the iron beast.'

I slung the Marquardt onto my back and hurried towards the mounted freemen, feeling relieved to be free of the square. My gun had been swiftly wrapped in leathers at the first sign of rain, so I feared not for the slight drizzle as I hauled myself upon the horse surrendered to me by a freeman. Meanwhile Ramos' square moved once more.

'Make haste!' yelled the sergeant. 'We shall keep to the field to distract them.'

Manglana ordered six of his riders to be assigned to Dario's command, then rode off towards the hillside with his remaining horsemen. I rode after the Croat, who was making a westward arc, intent on fooling the enemy into thinking that we were abandoning the field. When we were almost outside of the valley, we wheeled back eastwards, charging in the direction of the waterfall.

As we drew closer, the whereabouts of the battery were revealed to us by a canvas awning which was being erected over it and which explained the delay in any further fire. A tell-tale plume of smoke could be made out as we wiped the rain from our faces, and thunder was once more replaced by cannon fire as another shot was directed towards Ramos' square.

I jerked my head to the right and cupped a hand to my forehead, feeling a tinge of concern for Dal Verme and the Canarians. To my relief I could see that Ramos had shrewdly egged his men on towards lower ground, so that only the ends of raised pikes and Manglana's standard were visible. They swiftly vanished when the ball tore past them.

'Almost there!' called Dario through the rain. He had reached for his sword just as the ground gave way beneath a freeman who had nosed ahead of him. Both rider and horse collapsed into a ditch which had been dug by the enemy. Amid fevered jerks of his reins, Dario called a frantic halt, but his horse buckled against the edge of another plashing. We followed his lead as one more freeman flew headfirst into a third ditch. We dismounted and ran to the aid of our companions, coming upon man-made pits which were also filled with stakes; both freemen had been fatally impaled through the chest.

'Bastards,' said Dario as the rainfall grew amid the firing of another cannon shot, 'and yet we are so close.'

We walked across the remaining ground towards the small copse, leading our mounts behind us. Our cautious gait revealed two more ditches, each of which we were carefully avoiding when a dozen troopers suddenly burst through the trees towards us, causing our company to haul itself back onto our mounts.

'Not you, Spaniard!' Dario cried out. 'Make for the trees while we distract them.'

So saying, he charged with his riders towards the slopes, swiftly chased by the twelve troopers. I abandoned my horse and raced towards the sparse foliage ahead. I stopped short at the last tree, ducking behind it as its bark was showered with enemy fire.

'Holy host of the Madonna!' I cursed, then peered out cautiously from behind the tree trunk.

Cries were heard in the distance, where the Croat and his men engaged with the troopers, and the makeshift battery also came into view. Beneath the awning, a bald master gunner and his team sweated like pigs, killing the embers down the nozzle of a saker, which rested upon a limber and a caisson. The gun looked both rusted and Spanish, yet another Armada survivor which had been dragged off a beach to be employed by the heretics.

About six pounds of shot had been laid about the gun, which was shielded by rough-hewn boards. The chief gunner was less than a hundred yards away as his aides cleaned the cannon with a swab and readied another powder charge. Behind the usual sight of the ramp and swingletrees, I could make out holes in the ground which contained stocks of gunpowder. Six more pounds of shot were laid about them.

The tree's boughs offered protection from the rain, so I slid the Marquardt out of its leathers while I studied the snipers positioned about the battery in their dull-coloured uniforms and unpolished armour. Since I had held their role in bygone years, I knew their ears would be stuffed with wax to dull the cannon's roar.

Their guns were already reloaded as two of the snipers abandoned their post and slowly made their way towards me. I emptied a powder charge down the Marquardt's bore and rammed wadding and ball after it, then primed the flash pan and gave the wheel a quarter turn. My eyes never left the chief gunner, who used a quadrant to adjust the height of his weapon. My usual utterance was whispered beneath my breath, as I sought to steady my hand after more shots were taken at me.

*This day will the Lord deliver thee into mine hand;*
*and I will smite thee,*
*and take thy head from thee.*

My rifle almost fell from my grasp, though, when across the field the infantry square led by Sheriff George Bingham made ready to advance amid the crashing of kettledrums and bugle blasts. The shoulder pieces and helmets of his men gleamed upon their canvas doublets. Another howl of anguish was heard from the mounted engagement behind me, and another two shots struck the bark of a tree but a handspan from my eyes.

As I peered out from the other side of the tree, I could see the artillerymen turning a screw to train the cannon on Ramos' square. As the gunner reached for the touch hole with his long priming stick, I caught the glistening pate of his head in my silver sights, then lowered the dogshead on my rifle and took aim at the space just above his ear. A plume of smoke rose past my forehead as the Marquardt's stock kicked my shoulder at my touch of the serpentine.

The gunner whirled about after I caught him in the crown, the linstock falling from his hands and tipping towards the open sacks on the ground. My eyes were showered with bark as the snipers aimed another shot at my head. My last image of the battery was that of a diving Sassana getting a finger to the end of the falling match.

I was blinded for a few instants, and I crawled away from the tree on my hands and knees. No sooner had I climbed to my feet than the very earth beneath me quivered. A withering blast spun me around like a top, sending me crashing into another tree. After a few moments I regained some form of consciousness, enough for me to glimpse the boughs and the iron-grey sky overhead.

For a short while I lay in a daze as I regained my breath, entirely shaken by the force of the eruption which I had inadvertently caused. As I looked behind me in the direction of the battery, an immense, grey cloud could be seen beyond the trees. It climbed towards the heavens like the smoke from the pyre of a pagan giant, spreading out across the horseshoe valley with the end of its black fingers reaching towards the peaks.

My ears were still ringing from the resultant blast, and for a while I could hear nothing else. When at last I climbed to my feet, I spotted Dario on horseback, howling his head off at me. His arm must have been broken by a pistol shot during the skirmish on horseback, since it lay limply upon his thigh. At last, he dismounted and led his horse over towards me. After shoving me towards his saddle, he used his good arm to haul me over it. So doing, he climbed atop his mount and lashed its withers with his reins, so that we were soon thundering back towards the valley.

As we wended our way past the plashings, everything seemed surreal. I bounced upon the back of the horse, so lightheaded that I felt as if I was borne by a winged mount of Greek myth. Dario pulled my rifle off my shoulder as I bobbed before him, taking in the sight of the growing field of battle to my left. The distant sight of the sheriff could easily be made out by his feathered hat and red doublet, and he gestured madly at the huge cloud of smoke where his battery once lay.

Bingham's forces of foot and horse had been overwhelmed by the explosion, and the grass was littered with the corpses of men and dying mounts, some of which kicked the air in a frenzy. As we rode deeper into the valley, my good ear cleared enough to pick up the cry of Ramos' men to my right, who raced towards the heretic host with all their tactics and discipline cast aside. Behind them Manglana led his remaining riders and the *tuatha* down the hillside, with all the Dartrymen waving their spears above their heads and yelling their war cry, which caused the hair to rise upon the back of my neck.

'*MacGlannagh Abuuuuuuuuuuuuuuù! MacGlannagh Abuuuuuuuuuuuuuuù!*'

Across the field George Bingham frantically rallied his remaining footmen to his standard just as Ramos and his militia attacked what was left of the stunned cavalry. Riders were hauled from their mounts and stabbed to death, made to pay in full for the caracoles which had slain close to a dozen men. Dario kicked our mount harder at the sight of the growing rout, so that our hobby was wholly blown by the time we reached Manglana's furious kerns and freemen.

Less than two score troopers were left to defend Bingham after the MacGlannaghs' spears had been flung. The sheriff drew his sword as he howled at his men. They fought like cornered rats, and desperate hand-to-hand combat ensued. For a few moments the air was filled with a glitter of blades, though they were soon darkened by blood. The Sassanas resisted a few instants longer until the sheriff was sighted turning and fleeing with his bodyguards. Ramos' men killed the last of the mounted troopers, then rushed to join the chieftain's part of the skirmish.

'Victory!' cried Pedro, his face flushed with excitement.

As I slipped off the horse, I grabbed Dario by the shoulder before he could run off and join the militia.

'Who are they?' I asked, pointing towards the horsemen who fast approached us from the direction of Benwiskin. The Croat's face turned pale as the men drew nearer, and our dismay was complete when we heard the war cry of the O'Reillys. Dario threw me the Marquardt, then tore off towards the direction of Ramos.

'O'Reillys!' he called to the sergeant above the clash of arms. 'Form square! Form squ –'

His last cry was cut off as a spear was rammed through his throat by a wounded trooper, leaving the Croat to twist and turn upon the ground like a twig flung into a fire. My horror was doubled when the swollen features of Cathal the Black thundered into view, leading a score of the O'Reilly riders. The kerns from Dartry's *tuatha* ran behind them, having decided to aid their tanist in supplanting Manglana. The horsemen swiftly split into two files as they gained upon us and curled about our force like deathly pincers. I stood rooted to the ground and uncovered my rifle.

Barely a score of the sheriff's men were left, yet their resolve was regained at the sight of the unexpected force which struck their assailants down. Cathal's swollen eyes glowered with hate as he thundered upon me with a raised sword, which swiped the Marquardt from my grasp before I could take aim. The blow hurled me onto my back as the priceless rifle flew into the air, spiralling above my head until it disappeared into the fierce melee.

The tanist had already wheeled his mount about and charged straight back towards me, seeking to trample my body beneath his horse. I somehow rolled away from the onrushing charger just as its front hoof pinched the flesh off the edge of my shoulder. With a groan I clutched the wound while forcing myself onto my feet, then turned to find Cathal rising in his saddle with his spear aimed at me. My body tensed at the sight, and I noticed that his grotesque face was swollen to near twice its size because of his recent bee stings.

As he was about to deliver his mortal blow, he was thrown off the back of his mount, which shrieked in agony. For Gorman had rammed his spear through the beast's side. The elderly herdsman grimaced as his weapon was torn out of his hands, the dying horse whinnying and rising on its hind legs to kick the air before it charged into the bodies locked in fatal combat.

As Gorman drew his skene dagger, Cathal was swift to recover from his tumble. The disgraced tanist quickly dodged a thrust of the herdsman's blade, then rolled onto his feet.

I raised myself onto one knee and drew the pistol from beneath my shirt, shielding it from the downpour and aiming it at the tanist's back as he seized Gorman's wrists. The two were locked in a deathly struggle, though the elderly herdsman more than held his own. In their frantic back and forth, it was hard for me to get a clear shot at Cathal, so I returned the gun to my belt and raced towards them with my sword drawn.

A spear flashed past my face as I approached them, and a fierce-looking kern slipped in the growing rain just as he aimed a stab at me. Spotting my approach, Cathal released Gorman and gained an instant on my startled rescuer, then buried his fist into the herdsman's throat. As the old man fell choking into the mud, I crashed into the tanist with a roar, finding the wrist of my sword arm caught in his slimy grip as we slipped and struggled in the squelching filth underfoot.

In instants Cathal had the better of me, leaving me pinned beneath his knees as he shoved my own sword blade down towards my throat. The edge of the weapon had been dulled by a lack of care, and I thanked the Lord for its neglect as its blade cut into my fingers, which were all that kept it from reaching my throat. The horror of Cathal's features almost made me gag; the reddish swellings about his dark eyes contrasted sharply with the nicked, pale flesh that clung to his skull.

Then a loud crack was heard. The end of a spear butt met Cathal's temple and sent him flying to my left. Amid my deep breaths, I saw Gorman's broad son Finn glaring down at me in disgust before sauntering off towards the tanist, who lay in a dazed heap, clutching his bleeding head. With a howl of fury, the younger herdsman raised his spear again, then stabbed him repeatedly through the back so that Manglana's nephew soon breathed his last.

The great struggle had gathered us up into its bosom, and we found ourselves in the very thick of a spirited fight which raged around Manglana. The chieftain stood with bloodied blade as he traded blows with the O'Reillys and the traitors from his own land. He felled many of his own subjects as a deadly crescent of bluejackets and Spaniards rallied around his standard. In my countless years of skirmishing I had never seen a fight turn so swiftly. One could not tell friend from foe as Dartry warred with itself, leaving me to strike out at any kern whose face I could not recall.

The defence of Dartry's colours was spirited, yet our chances were grim, reduced as they were by the mounted O'Reillys who cantered just out of our reach and picked us off at will with their bows. By this time the sheriff had returned to the fray with his bodyguard, his stomach for a fight returning at the sight of Cathal's reinforcements.

As our own were shot and cut down, we were reduced to around forty men. We gathered in a desperate ring around Manglana, madly parrying yet another spear thrust. Amid the wave of assailants I saw Dal Verme collapsing onto his knees, clutching a bolt which had caught him in the midriff.

Despite his fatal wound, the Milanese still swung his long blade over his head, catching two kerns unawares as they tumbled into the dirt. Yet his valour was short-lived as a spear was thrust through the Lombard's breastplate, flinging him onto his fast-whitening face. With a cry, the Canarian twins engaged in a spirited defence of the adventurer's body, though it stranded them from our desperate defenders. They were also cut down without mercy by our assailants.

Two more spear thrusts were deflected, although one grazed my skinned shoulder. As I howled in agony, I was suddenly filled with a blind fury which startled me as I resolved to die as costly a death as I could manage. As our enemies closed in, I struck out with my blade at faces, elbows, ankles and any other defenceless part of our assailants' bodies which were closest at hand. At least five kerns were disabled in this way until a younger herdsman thrust his spear at my legs.

I hopped back in time to prevent its point from going through my foot, but the kern bundled into me so that we were left to wrestle in the mud underfoot. With a gasp of desperation, I whisked my dagger from my belt, then sank it into the youth's throat.

I hurled the hissing cur away and climbed back onto my knees, attempting to pull my knife out of the writhing body, then snatching the pistol back out of my belt and firing it in the face of another onrushing herdsman. A hand grabbed my collar and hoisted me to my feet, and I turned to find O'Ronayne, who stood behind me, holding his own crimson blade.

'It is all over, Father,' I muttered, 'in a bloodbath of fratricide.'

The Jesuit did not meet my stare. He instead gaped at the hills to our right, his pudgy face drawn in horror. I turned to view the sight as a bugle blast resounded across the valley and a fresh force of footmen charged towards us with almost merry abandon.

'Gallowglasses,' I gasped, and my heart instantly sank. 'MacCabe's men.'

The battle standard of the constable could be seen, with gold birds embroidered in its sewing. Bugle blasts ripped again and again through the air, while behind us the chieftain was heard crying out in awe.

'The ollave rides with them! The ollave rides with them!'

'Does she?' asked the Jesuit in disbelief. Then we made out the slight figure of Muireann riding atop a blown hobby, which was being outpaced by the running Scots.

Ramos was already calling out to his men to hold firm, and our enemies stared over their shoulders in bafflement as the approaching redshanks waved their battle axes and howled their own war cry.

*'MacCabe Abuuuuuuuuuuuuuuuuù!'*

Scottish horseboys ran ahead of their masters, then halted a few feet in front of the mounted O'Reillys and flung their spears at them. The shower of javelins toppled many enemies on foot and horseback just as MacCabe's men charged into the fray, cutting men down with the blades of their great Loch-abers, which had been dipped in snake poison. Their long shirts of chainmail glittered like the scales of a growing sea monster as they did their deathly work, with wild swings of their axes rending steel and bone.

Amid the ensuing slaughter, I glimpsed Ramos running away from the chieftain's men, back towards the hills along-side the still smoking battery. It quickly occurred to me that having lost most of his men, the sergeant had decided to flee the field and take his chances in the country. He had, after all, found himself in possession of a ring worth a king's ransom.

I instantly ran after him, fleeing the scenes of bloodshed as I crested the hill. Ahead of me the back of the sergeant's helmet bobbed madly from left to right, and the distance between us grew shorter.

I fell upon the grass whenever he looked over his shoulder, only to resume my chase when he staggered on towards the thickening woods ahead. Ramos had all but achieved his escape when two troopers appeared out of the foliage to his right, deserters from the sheriff's force. As I drew nearer I could see that they were the usual lean, gaunt types, men who had been pressed into military service after languishing in some dank English gaol cell.

Ramos toppled to the ground with something resembling a yelp as a crossbow bolt got him through the calf. No sooner had they felled their prey than the two Sassanas were running towards him with their daggers drawn. My stomach roiled at the sight for fear that they would strip him for booty and discover my ring. I tore up clumps of grass as I sped up the steep hill, met by the sight of the sergeant shielding his face and neck while clumsy knife thrusts rained down upon his shoulders and breastplate.

I despatched the first trooper with an almighty sword stroke to the back of his head, which sent him tottering off in a daze until he collapsed. His fellow took a swipe at me, which I swiftly dodged, then fled back to the cover of forest after I sent his blade flying into the air with a skyward thrust of my sword. Ramos grunted in pain as he rolled over to face me, his displaced eye flap revealing his empty socket. Blood flowed freely from a bad wound at the side of his neck, and a pained smile spread across his lips when he saw me standing over him.

'Abelito . . . my guardian angel . . .'

I wordlessly planted my foot upon his good arm, then bent over towards him and relieved him of his sword, dagger and pistol, which I then hurled beyond his reach. I sank upon one knee and searched his jacket and trews for the ring; he observed me with what seemed a passing interest before heaving a deep sigh.

'The eighth ampoule, Abelito.'

I was flushed by embarrassment as I reached for the last charge on his belt, then felt elated as the trinket fell into my hand from within it. A hoarse whisper reached my ears, and I turned to find Ramos serving me with an ironic grin.

'Do not take it,' he said.

'Why?' I snapped angrily. 'Why should you have it and not me?'

'Because you don't know what it means. Yet I learned of its significance in Breifne. From O'Rourke's spies.'

I stared back at him defiantly. 'What does it mean? Is it not but a gift from the prince of Ascoli's mother to her fop son?'

Ramos sighed. 'More than that. Much more.'

'So Ascoli is the king's bastard son. What of it?'

Ramos was somewhat taken aback by the revelation, then resumed his explanation.

'Do you not know that the king has only one son? And a weak one, like his three, late brothers? If the king's son dies, then that ring is proof of Ascoli's royal paternity and of his claim to the throne!'

'He has no claim to the throne,' I replied, 'for he is illegitimate...the law forbids it!'

'Indeed,' replied Ramos. 'But needs must, and the law can be easily changed or a bastard legitimated, rather than allow the king to die heirless. All that is required is royal or papal dispensation.'

I was suddenly stunned by the enormity of the revelation and the true significance of the trinket, so that I felt it weighing heavily in my hand when Ramos spoke up again.

'Furthermore, the English queen has learned of it. She desperately wants it. It will fetch her an enormous ransom from Ascoli's backers, *and* it is proof of our king's infidelity! The ring would be both a trophy of her victory against the Armada and an embarrassment to Spanish envoys!'

The ground seemed to rise and fall around me at the revelation, so that I almost dropped the ring. Then I was overcome by a grim resolve, to use it to secure the future of Elsien's brother, not hand it to her killer.

'I shall heed your warnings,' I said, 'yet it remains mine.'

Ramos grinned more widely as my fingers closed around the ring. 'We are not as different as you might think.'

With a low growl I seized him by the collar and hauled him close to me, hissing in his face. 'Never more different were two men than you and me! Never more different!'

His sideways glance was accompanied by a furtive yet amused grin. I felt further angered by his mocking stare, and I raised my blade towards him, rasping 'for Elsien' beneath my breath, though I hesitated when he rolled his eye.

'Even now you would err over that Flemish girl? Against one who fought alongside you like a brother? We were family, Santiago; the five of us were family. You and I are all that are left of it . . . don't you understand?'

'I do not understand!' I replied angrily. 'I do not understand a family that readily abandoned me for plunder meant to be shared by all, less one which murdered my wife!'

'"Twas not murder, you fool!' he fumed, his face turning crimson. 'It was not her we meant to kill; I swear it upon all the saints! Kill me if you must, but do not level that false accusation at me again!'

'Then what of Reynier?' I retorted, shaking the knife in his face. 'Did you have to burn a sickly man down in his own home?'

Ramos fell silent as his head fell back upon the ground. A few moments of silence passed between us, broken only by muffled cries from the battlefield.

'The damn cur owed us money, but I knew not that he was within. We left the town in haste, burning those houses that owed us as we left. No one ensured that they were empty, but everyone knew the price for not paying us protection.'

His explanation was a poor one, yet it was the closest thing to an apology which I had ever heard from him. Although his words were clumsy, they served to finally quell my rage as I fell alongside him. I realised that the man I so desperately wanted dead was all I truly had left in the world. Tears of sadness welled up in my eyes as Elsien's face appeared to me in the grey sky, and another memory left me sobbing.

'She was with child,' I whispered, almost by way of explaining the murders of Salva, Gabri and Cristó.

I momentarily refrained from my weeping then, for I was startled to hear the sergeant crying alongside me.

'Lord forgive me,' he blubbered. 'I slew my own child.'

For a few moments more we wept together until the meaning of what he said finally struck me. I lay still, rocked by disbelief as I suddenly recalled the bruises and cuts on Elsien's face which she had suffered at Christmastide. She had claimed that the injuries had been caused by her tumble on the ice, and she had suddenly urged me to lie with her in the days thereafter. I also remembered the unmasked hatred that she demonstrated whenever she stood up to Ramos.

I slowly rose onto my knees with bared teeth, as I realised then that she had not spoken of her violation to me for fear of my life.

'Slew your own child?'

It was then that I noted the fleeting look of guilt in his eye, which had always betrayed him whenever he hotly denied cuckolding an angry soldier. I was overwhelmed by fury as my dagger was raised, and tears still flowed from his eyes when my blade fell. Just as quickly it was raised again, and I roared my rage and grief at his misdeed.

'Rapist!'

His severed throat gurgled and spurted blood into my eyes. It dripped off the end of my nose and my ears. His hand reached for my face too late as I delivered countless blows, and the fight in the valley may well have been taking place in Peru for all it mattered to me then. I saw nothing but red as thoughts of Elsien being deflowered at the hands of the brute below me raged in my head. A light rainfall began and ended long before the rain of my own knife blows ceased, and all rage and pain abruptly ended when at last I collapsed sideways and passed out from weariness.

# LI

## GLENIFF HORSESHOE VALLEY TO ROSCLOGHER, DARTRY, COUNTY LEITRIM

*14 September – 1 November 1589*

I spat on the sergeant's corpse, then turned away from his butchered body, which had been rendered a shredded, faceless mess. As I picked the reddened ring out of a small pool of blood, I walked away from the cadaver, which would become a wolf feast at night. It seemed a fitting end to Ramos' life as I made off in the direction of the battlefield, where the desperate din of war had subsided.

The palm of my hand still burned from my attack on the sergeant, my deep breaths burning my breast and my nostrils as I hobbled down the hill, my throat still raw from breathing rifle smoke. Dusk was deepening in the valley as I reached the field, my nose already full of the stench of pierced stomachs and severed entrails. Like a deathly shadow, I made my way through the dead and wounded men who lay upon the grass, my good ear full of moans as I made out the figure of Manglana.

A blazing fire raged behind the chieftain, lending him the shadowy cast of a haggard wolf. His tunic was crimsoned with blood as he stepped towards me and seized me in a furious bear hug, rasping his foul breath into my face, which was buried against his swollen breast.

'We won, but at what cost? Still, we won!'

His bard, Fearghal, stood behind him with his mouth hanging open, one eye so swollen that it seemed to take up half his face.

'Will he not sing for you now?' I asked as Manglana released me, jerking my head towards Fearghal.

'He shall be fortunate to speak before the month is out,' replied the chieftain, then walked away from the fire after gesturing for me to follow him.

A dozen bluejackets and fourteen Spaniards formed a defensive ring about us as we made our way towards a row of tents which had been erected a few feet away from the fire.

'Where is Ramos?' asked Manglana.

'I last saw him alongside you,' I lied after a moment's hesitation.

The chieftain nodded solemnly. 'I hope he has not perished, for he is a formidable fellow. He commanded his square with great skill; we have need of more like him.'

He took a deep breath and then slapped me upon the back. 'You did well with the battery. It turned the fight.'

'For a while,' I replied, for we both knew that it was the appearance of the gallowglasses which had in truth saved the day.

He ducked beneath one of the flaps of hide as we entered the tent to find it choked with wounded Dartrymen and Scots. O'Ronayne was bent over the bristling figure of Donal Mac-Cabe. The gallowglass constable still clutched his bloodstained axe as two of his men tried to stop his violent throbbing by holding him down. The Jesuit finished stitching the constable's chest wound, which I recognised as having been caused by a pistol shot.

As the gallowglasses released their grip from their master, Donal raised his head towards us, still shaking madly as he regarded us with a hateful stare.

'Will he live?' asked Manglana.

'The wound is mortal,' replied the Jesuit in a low whisper. 'You should leave before you unsettle him any further.'

'We fought bravely, MacCabe,' the chieftain declared suddenly. 'Your people shall be welcome to winter in Dartry.'

The constable gritted his teeth in reply, the loathing on his face only growing at the chieftain's words. 'My son,' he hissed furiously, then fell back and wheezed horribly.

I looked away and was met by the sight of Finn.

Gorman's son also lay upon the ground, his eyes closed and one of his arms half severed at the shoulder.

'Is he alive?' I croaked, pointing at the young man.

O'Ronayne quietly rested his hands upon our shoulders and escorted us out of the haphazard infirmary. 'You should rest now,' he said. 'There is much to do in the morning.'

'Why did he fight for us?' said Manglana as he stepped out the tent.

'Muireann sought out his camp,' whispered the Jesuit. 'She promised him her hand if he joined her.'

Both the chieftain and I were speechless as the Jesuit let the flap fall, leaving us out in the darkness. For a few moments neither of us could talk. Then the chieftain managed to break the silence.

'And where is she now?' he said.

'In her tent, my lord MacGlannagh,' said one of his blue-jackets, 'where she withdrew not long after the battle was over, after issuing strict instructions that none should disturb her.'

'She must be tired from her hard riding,' said the chieftain.

'Indeed, my lord MacGlannagh,' said the same guard. 'It is said she rode a horse to death to find reinforcements.'

Manglana sighed and then wished me a peaceful slumber, sending two of his kerns to fetch me food from the great cooking fire as he stumbled off with his guards towards his own bed.

I ate some of the cooked meat which was served to me, yet memories of me slaying Ramos seemed to rise out of the flames to haunt me, and a relentless guilt gnawed at my soul amid the groans of the dying behind me.

'Plundereeeeeeer,' the voice of the dead sergeant seemed to whisper upon the wind that wailed gently in the night. It was not long until I was soon asleep upon the ground, warmly wrapped in a mantle handed to me by a kern. After the day's events, my slumber was of the very best kind, being both black and dreamless and leaving me revived when my eyelids flicked in the first light of morning.

I saw the *brat* mantle of the Jesuit as he placed his stained knives and forceps upon the ashes of the glowing peat. With a groan I rose upon one arm and observed him as he next picked his tools off the hearth and returned them to a wooden dish which he drew from his mantle.

'You are up late, Spaniard,' he said, 'and there is much still to be done.'

I kicked off my mantle and rose to my feet, then stepped over towards him and took the jug of water which he held out to me. I drank half of it, then poured the other half over my head. The sleep and grime were rubbed from my eyes, which still felt reddened from the previous day. Then I joined a guard of kerns across the field as we slew the enemy wounded who still lived, then searched dead bodies for booty.

O'Ronayne also partook of our exercise, searching instead for souls he thought he might still administer last rites to. Those kerns who had joined in Cathal's treachery were glad for his presence at their side, as were the dying O'Reillys of Breifne. Yet many of the troopers who had formed part of the sheriff's force cursed him and held their hands out to him, refusing until the last to receive a sacrament from a papist. One of these men did not even give the Jesuit the courtesy of a stare as he groaned aloud and pointed his finger at me.

'That man! The Spaniard! He has something the sheriff wants!'

I turned in fright at the familiar voice, then felt rooted to the spot by terror as I recognised Verdon, the skirmisher whose party had ambushed Dervila's party in Maguire's lands.

'Spare my life and I shall tell all!' he cried as he clutched at his severed stomach. 'He has a precious stone, a trinket, that Bingham covets!'

No sooner had he delivered his cry than I was already upon him. I drew my sword in a rage and held it by the pommel, then delivered a downward thrust so that the point of its blade tore through the flesh behind the trooper's collarbone and the organs in his breast. A loud wheeze was followed by a burst of blood from his mouth, and he sagged forward upon his face.

After I kicked him off my blade, I stepped away from him, still trembling with anger and panic. The Jesuit and the other kerns stared on at me in disbelief, then slowly returned to their pursuits as I trudged off towards the tents. I was overcome by shame and anguish at what had just passed.

Then I was met by the sight of Dal Verme's corpse.

I looked away from the grisly sight of the slain Lombard, only to be met by the sight of the dead Canarian brothers, Pedro and Franco, who lay at the feet of their Italian comrade. I sighed aloud as I trudged away from the corpses, making a quick sign of the cross just as I found myself walking towards the corpses of both Dario and Gorman.

Their death stares were almost accusatory as I collapsed to one knee in shock, realising how many had perished because of the ring which I still hid like a thief. I told myself that the sheriff would have attacked Dartry anyway, yet it did little to ease the guilt that weighed down heavily upon my shoulders. As I returned to my feet, the hair rose on the back of my neck when a shrill voice rose from the grass behind me.

'I know you! You are the Spaniard who fled with the sheriff's prize from Sligo!'

For a moment I hoped that I might be about to stir from a bad dream, yet the high-pitched accusations continued.

'Surrender the ring, thief! You shan't make it out of Ireland alive!'

As I turned upon my heel I stared at the ground in disbelief, recognising the Irish traitor Killian, who had betrayed my trust to the sheriff of Sligo a year earlier. As his lips parted to deliver yet another accusation, I hurled myself upon him with a drawn dagger, ignoring his moan of agony as I slashed his gullet open with one deft motion.

His blood splashed across my already scarlet shirt as his head fell sideways. I stumbled back onto my feet and turned about, rocked by my second killing of a wounded man when I caught sight of Cathal *Dubh's* severed head mounted upon a spike. The tanist's nicked face was still grotesquely swollen and twisted in agony as his eyes were turned up towards the heavens, almost as if he was repulsed by the sight of me.

I fell on all fours as I felt a spasm in my stomach, then threw up what remained of the cowflesh which I had devoured the previous day. After returning to my feet, I was met by the sight of Manglana and Muireann, both of whom served me with severe frowns as they stood but a few feet away.

As they turned away I cursed beneath my breath, knowing full well that Killian's cries risked uncovering my secret at a time when the chieftain's tolerance for hidden motives was likely to be at its lowest ebb. The sight of other dead comrades had also shaken me, and I returned to my tent. Two hours later I heard the rustle of a pike dragged by a Basque bastard named Eneko, which prompted me to stick my head through the flaps and beckon to him.

'Are we leaving yet?'

'Hey, Abel,' said Eneko, 'you also made it? Terrible fight, eh?'

'Indeed. Yet I asked you: are we leaving?'

'The chieftain refuses to abandon the field until Ramos is found.'

'What?' I exclaimed, having hardly expected this turn of events.

Eneko stared back at me askance as I tore through the tent, fearful that Ramos' body might be discovered before I got to it first. My mind raced to remember whether I had stripped the sergeant's body after killing him, hoping that some enemy survivor might have finished what I had foolishly forgotten to do. Yet already cries of despair were heard from the hillside where I had abandoned Ramos' body the previous evening, and I feigned a look of the highest concern as I hurried over the heather towards the chieftain's search party.

To my despair, I could see that both Manglana and Muireann had already reached the kerns who had found Ramos' mangled corpse, which had been shredded by wolf fangs. Beneath their watchful stare, I assumed an air of distraught silence, finding it impossible to feign any further grief for the corpse of the disfigured whoreson. As I fell to my knee beside the carrion and touched an exposed shoulder bone, it seemed almost comical that the daring Ramos had perished so far from the Low Countries, where he had survived so many worse theatres of battle. The thought also struck me that Ramos might still be alive had he not tried to flee the fight like some petty thief.

'He must have chased down the enemy,' I whispered, nodding towards the body of the trooper I had also slain the day previous, which had also been ripped apart by curs.

'There were other men about,' replied Muireann curtly as she avoided my stare, then wandered over towards two impressions alongside the sergeant's body. I froze as she knelt alongside one of them, then raised her head as she observed the other prints that led down towards the valley. She next glanced at my feet.

'Those are the marks of a shoe,' she observed, then traded glances with the chieftain who watched me in silence.

No more was said of the matter, and Manglana ordered his men to dig a grave for Ramos. No sooner was the order given than a group of Spaniards and natives hacked at the ground with their spear ends and sword points, digging up a jagged burial pit. In my attempts to avoid further scrutiny I offered what help I could, even cutting a breastplate off a dead trooper and using it to scoop dirt out of the growing grave.

In less than an hour a hole had been dug beyond knee height, and we dragged what remained of Ramos' corpse towards it. Under the watchful stare of the chieftain, I hauled so hard at an ankle that the entire leg came away from the body, causing me to tumble upon the grass. I rose to my feet and flung the limb into the pit, then pulled the corpse from the sergeant's torn trews instead. We had almost flung the whoreson into the hole when the observant ollave spoke again.

'The bandolier . . . bring it to me.'

A kern hauled the belt off the chewed torso and handed it to Muireann, who held it up in both hands as she examined the powder charges.

'The last powder charge,' remarked the chieftain at her shoulder, 'it is missing.'

They both observed it in puzzlement, then returned to staring at me again. I feigned not to notice them as I snatched up the breastplate and started shoving mud back onto the sergeant's body. When at last the body was consigned to the ground, the Jesuit was summoned from his makeshift infirmary. As O'Ronayne administered a last blessing, I realised that although I had loathed the sergeant, his death marked the end of what had formed almost a third of my life.

It was shortly past midday when we readied to make away from the horseshoe valley, after other bodies had been buried or consigned beneath mounds of rocks. My distress was hardly allayed by the behaviour of Manglana, Muireann and the Jesuit, each of whom ignored me as I marched alongside them. Following the burial of Ramos and Dario, none had asked me to assume leadership of the remaining militia, who marched in disbanded formation with a dozen gallowglasses behind the kerns and the handful of surviving riders.

Less than half the force which left Manglana's town returned, a disconsolate and ragged gathering which bore almost as many wounded as there were men still fit for fighting. All throughout our return journey the injured bard had never once uttered a word, nor had the drums been tapped following the fall of the drummer boy the day previous. Yet upon our arrival, a great wailing was soon heard in the town as mothers and children learned of the passing of their relatives.

With a sigh I staggered off towards the green with what was left of Ramos' force. As the men set about pitching their tents, I cast a lonely and forlorn figure until Eneko called out to me, inviting me to share his lodging. When his tent was pitched we crawled inside, and the Basque soon passed into a deep slumber. Despite my own fatigue, I tossed and turned late into the night, wondering if I should steal off with the ring before slumber overtook me too.

Dawn found me chewing at a scrap of dried meat, thinking of making my escape within the hour, when Nial shoved his smiling face through the tent flaps. The appearance of the bondsman was as unexpected as it was welcome, for we had not seen him since the day he had been despatched with Muireann to rouse out the kerns.

'Nial,' I remarked, 'when did you return here?'

'Mine has been a wearisome and fruitless last two days,' he answered, 'for most of the *tuatha* had already marched off with the traitor Cathal, who had promised them everything short of the chieftain's seat. Yet you may hear my full account in the hall of Rosclogher, where you have also been summoned by my lord MacGlannagh.'

A deep unease filled me at news of the invitation, as did the feet of the bluejackets I observed standing outside the tent.

'Very well,' I replied. 'I shall wash my face and clean the blood off my clothes to make myself ready for the audience.'

'No, Juan,' replied Nial, shaking his head, 'for my lord MacGlannagh has said that his summons is immediate.'

My distress only grew upon hearing this instruction and grew even further when I stepped out of the tent to find myself instantly surrounded by the bondsman's kerns.

'Am I a prisoner?' I asked as the men closed in around me.

'Not entirely,' Nial replied, then turned away, 'yet my lord MacGlannagh also requested that you be guarded from hereon at all times.'

'Did Lord Manglana issue any further instructions that concerned me?'

The bondsman chuckled but once, then led us through the town, where some of the tribesmen watched on in silence; then onto the jetty wherefrom the usual ferry ride to the tower was undertaken. In the hall of the tower house, Manglana appeared to be in too sombre a mood for one who had returned victorious from battle. None of his closest retainers appeared cheerful either, and no one greeted us when we entered. The Jesuit and Muireann raised expectant eyebrows at the chieftain, who cleared his throat and fixed his eyes on the wall over our heads.

'The wailing of the keeners has sickened me,' he sighed. 'We have turned back the sheriff, and yet never did a victory seem so pointless.'

'It was not in vain, my lord,' said Muireann, after some garbled mumblings had left Fearghal's broken jaw. 'You could not have retired before the enemy host again. You are the protector of these lands and the defender of its people.'

'You have done God's work, Lord,' declared O'Ronayne in a firm voice. 'The heretics have been despatched, and these lands are safe once more.'

'Yet for how much longer?' the chieftain asked as his eyes fell upon me. 'What say you, Spaniard?'

My fingers fidgeted awkwardly as I tried to keep my legs from shaking before the solemnity of his stare.

'The mountains and tower-houses are easily defensible,' I replied. 'The whole garrison of Dublin could not take this keep.'

'Indeed,' exclaimed the chieftain fervidly. 'Indeed, you speak truth, Spaniard! For both you and de Cuéllar demonstrated that this time last year!"

'Yes, my lord,' I replied, somewhat taken aback by the sudden vigour in his tone. 'With but twelve men we fended off hundreds of troopers.'

'There were so many of them!' yelled Manglana as his eyes widened and he rose to his feet, madly gesturing in all directions. 'The banks of the lake were black from their bodies! For a time it seemed that an entire host of biblical locusts had been despatched against us!'

'Indeed,' I replied, perturbed by his erratic movements as he suddenly descended the steps of his dais and placed his hand upon his sword pommel.

'Yes, thousands!' he replied as he pushed through the guard of bluejackets that stood before him and walked over towards me. 'And even now I ask myself: why were so many sent here?'

His sword was drawn from its scabbard when he said this, and there was a murderous glint in his eye. As Nial silently stepped away from me, I could only look on in horror as Dartry's king stopped and held his sword above our heads, before bringing it down. In that instant I closed my eyes, fully expecting my skull to be split open. Yet Manglana's sword butt crashed into my shoulder and dropped me to my knees; the point of his blade kissed my throat and drew blood when I looked up at him.

'Tell me, grey wolf,' he growled, his lips drawn back to reveal two rows of yellowed, irregular teeth, 'why would Dublin's garrison make its way towards Rosclogher in winter? Why not stop in Breifne? Why not march on to Duncarbery?'

After a few moments I made to speak, only to hesitate when the point of the chieftain's blade bit further into the flesh beneath my chin.

'Any lie that you utter,' he hissed, 'will be your last.'

I hesitated for a moment, then reached for the last ampoule on my bandolier, pulled open the powder charge and turned it over into my hand. When the ampoule was pulled away, the ring sat in my palm upon a small handful of gunpowder, glistening in the light which streamed through a window. The chieftain drew away from the sight with a sharp intake of breath, scarcely able to believe the value of the treasure which I held. His sword clanged upon the ground.

His retainers also gathered about us as he stood in stunned disbelief, each of them visibly overcome by bafflement when they saw the ring. Fearghal the Bard's eyes became almost as wide as his mouth while the half smile was entirely wiped off Nial's face. Muireann appeared more surprised than she had been when MacCabe's men had interrupted our tryst in the woods, and O'Ronayne struggled to mouth an exclamation, though he was finally the first to break the silence.

'So that is what you meant by the Sassana stone!'

No sooner did he say this than the looks of surprise turned to ones of fury, and I feared the worst as I turned my face away from the Dartrymen. Then the chieftain issued a high-pitched laugh, which possessed a shrillness which verged on lunacy.

'To think how easily you could have paid off your fine.'

So saying he surprised me by reaching for the golden ring and pulling it out of my hand, holding it up to the light and marvelling at the gem encased in it.

'A king's ransom,' he said at last, as his fingers closed about the trinket as he shook his head. 'A king's ransom.'

'Why did you not tell us?' whispered Muireann in a trembling voice.

'I couldn't,' I said. 'I promised its owner I would return it –'

The hollowness of my excuse made me fall silent, and another scrape was heard as the chieftain raised his sword and held it before my face again.

'Did you have it when first we found you?'

'Yes.'

'And you took it back from Ramos by force?'

'Yes,' I said, meeting his stare in the hope that my honesty might grant me some reprieve.

He stared back at me as a look of outrage appeared on his face.

'This man is a murderer,' he bellowed, stepping away from me and raising his arm protectively before the ollave as his retainers also drew away. 'Fetch the guard! He is a danger to the tribe!'

A half-dozen bluejackets stepped out of the shadows, seizing me by the arms. I found myself being dragged away towards the staircase.

'Where are you taking me?' I exclaimed, yet none spoke as the household kerns dragged me down the steps and ladder to the skiff, which was secured to the edge of the crannog.

Rough hands shoved me into it, and any chance at escape was blocked by spear ends until the water was crossed and I was led to the ringfort along the side of the town. To my disbelief I found myself clapped into the same chains which had bound Gilson until his poisoning.

'You shall be held hostage until Lord O'Rourke decides your fate,' said the leader of the bluejackets.

He handed me a pail of water and a scrap of brick-hard pork, then departed from the fort with his fellows, leaving me under the watch of the other kerns who occupied the defence.

Some of my guards cast me curious looks of puzzlement while others entirely ignored me, busying themselves with sharpening the ends of their weapons or engaging in idle chatter and the odd game of dice.

My sudden turn in fortune, coupled with the accusations hurled at me in the keep, left me feeling entirely drained as I slumped against the wall of the ringfort. With a weary exhalation I fell to my side and closed my eyes, feeling almost grateful for the peace and relative solitude of my captivity. Before I knew it I found myself entirely overcome by sleep, which was crudely broken two hours later by a sharp shake of my sore shoulder. As my eyes opened I was greeted by the sight of the ollave, her fine features having been rendered a furious scarlet.

'Why did you not tell me?' she snapped angrily. 'Could you not trust me?'

'I tried,' I protested meekly.

She seemed taken aback by my feeble response, rising off her knee and glaring at me as I cowered against the wall, too ashamed to meet her stare for long.

'I promised I would return it to its rightful owners,' I said at last, hoping to appease her with my half-reasoned response.

'Liar. You wanted to keep it to yourself. All so that you could pursue your dream of the Indies.'

Her face turned a dark hue of violet as a vein throbbed at the centre of her forehead. 'The truth is that you used us to serve your own ends. Just like de Cuéllar. MacCabe was right to mistrust you. Yet we shared everything with you –'

Her voice broke at the end of her last accusation. I was stung by sorrow and reached out for her arm, only for her to recoil from me.

'You are no different from the tanist,' she spat. 'Do not come within a handspan of me.'

She drew away from my shaking, outstretched hand, then ran out of the fort with her brown hair fluttering above her whirling, saffron tunic. I sagged against the wall with a low curse, thinking that it had been a day of far too much change. Before long I was asleep again, though I awoke towards dusk with an aching bladder.

'Hey!' I called out to a kern walking past me. 'Are prisoners left to piss themselves?'

'Ask your guard,' he said, nodding towards another blue-jacket who sat hunched over his crossed legs against a wall but a few feet away from us.

After overhearing our exchange, the burly guard rose reluctantly to his feet, then reached for a key which hung from his belt. As he approached me with his spear held out before him, a low growl was heard from beneath the edge of his mantle, which furled around his head like a hood.

'Any fast ones and I'll gorge you.'

The rusted irons were removed, and I gratefully rubbed my chafed wrists as he seized me by the arm and hauled me to my feet.

'Do not expect me to do this again tonight.'

He next shoved me ahead of him and followed closely behind, reminding me of his closeness by the odd jab of his spear point in my buttocks. The pain spurred me forward until we were outside the fort and halfway towards the midden. I snatched a quick glimpse of the village over my shoulder, where folk had already retired for the evening and where there was barely a soul to be seen. As I stood over the rubbish pit and relieved myself, my thoughts instinctively turned towards the location of the ring, though I remembered that it was in the keep of the chieftain.

A curious sense of irritation and relief ran through me on my way back to the fort, and I asked myself whether I had been foolish when heeding the jabs of my conscience and surrendering the ring to Manglana so easily. The thought of what might have befallen me if I had not done so served to temper my annoyance, together with the lightness I suddenly felt at having been relieved of so valuable a burden.

In the following weeks my pangs of loss were instead replaced by fear, and I wondered whether I would spend the remainder of the year chained inside the ringfort awaiting the overlord. After the first few weeks of my imprisonment I lost all track of time, until yet another walk to the midden revealed large pyres erected along the green in preparation for the feast of Samhain.

'Already November,' sighed my guard, as he stopped a few feet away from me as I squatted over the rubbish pit.

'The reign of the Cailleach is at hand,' I whispered with an ominous tone, which left him glaring at me uneasily.

'God forbid the next winter is as bad as the last,' replied my guard as we made our way back towards the ringfort.

The following day the first heads of cattle could be heard lowing as men returned from the mountains to lock them in the byre. As always, they led the cattle through crackling fires before the festivities began. Only a handful of guards remained behind to man the ringfort since the rest had left to join in the tribe's feasting. I fidgeted with a pork rind, which had proved too hard to eat, as I leant back against the wall with my legs crossed.

My imprisonment had already lasted for two weeks, in which time I had barely had a decent meal. I had also come to realise that the absence of my friends among the tribe had proved harder to bear than the chains round my arms, with the lack of Nial's company being the most keenly felt. My thoughts were crudely interrupted by a low rustle against the wall, and my back became as straight as a ramrod when I saw the shadow which accompanied the sound.

'Shh, it is I,' hissed a familiar voice, just as my lips parted to summon the guards who sat upon the other side of the wall, their faces sulkily buried in mead.

In the scant light of a torch I made out the auburn locks of Lochlain, who crept up to me with a grin as he handed me some cuttings of cowflesh.

'Why?' I asked, then buried my face in the food as he gestured for me to help myself.

'You must be lonely and bored,' he whispered as he stared from left to right and took in my surrounds. 'This is a bleak place.'

'Can you get me out of here?' I replied between mouthfuls, a question to which his youthful eyes gleamed slyly.

'That I could,' he said, 'yet I could not get you beyond my lord grandfather's border guards.'

'Could you get me a book then?' I blurted whilst licking my fingers, still craving the taste of the fine beef I had just scoffed.

The young prince gave the question some thought.

'I will mention it to Father O'Ronayne,' he said at last.

I nodded to him gratefully, and the young prince surprised me by sitting alongside me as if I was no more dangerous than one of his highborn peers.

'Why did you hide it?' he asked at last.

'Why do you think?'

'I do not know, which is why I ask. Mother says it was your dreams of the Indies.'

'Perhaps it was,' I sighed, 'or maybe I am indeed a most evil and dangerous man.'

The slight chuckle at my shoulder left me feeling irritated and belittled, and after days spent bound to the wall of the fort, I wondered if the prince took me for some sort of fool. His laughter swiftly ended when I grabbed him by the shoulder and bared my teeth in his face, leaving him in no doubt that I was not to be mocked despite my vulnerable state.

'Who do you take me to be?' I growled as he drew away from me in bewilderment. 'Are you sure that you know me so well, young prince? Do your betters not have a right to their suspicions, to have me chained to this wall like a beast? Get away from me forthwith, for I am not your fop to be laughed at and ridiculed!'

'But I meant no –' he muttered, as his face became flushed at my outburst.

'Get out of my sight and take your empty promises with you!' I hissed. 'You are one who must live up to his father's honour! You should not visit a lowly, thieving soldier who would consign the whole tribe to the grave only to line his purse!'

'But I thought you were one of us?'

'One of you? I was never one of you! The whole of Dartry could be razed to the ground, and I would not blink an eyelid! For your people were only but a means to an end for me – just as the Spanish army was before you! I am no one and one who belongs nowhere, a godless cur who serves only himself! I have no use for faith or country so long as it meets my own ends!'

By this time tears had appeared in the prince's eyes, and one of the drunken guards called out to us from the wall as I delivered my last broadside at Muireann's son.

'Begone from my sight, you fatherless cur. Repeat not the error of your betters by offering me the hand of friendship. Do not take me for some soft-hearted zealot who would risk his life for Rome, Madrid or any self-serving Irish lord.'

With a gasp he turned and hurried off into the night, still stunned by my tirade as I collapsed back against the wall. I felt wholly wretched and disgusted at myself, and I scratched at the lengthy stubble which gnawed at the flesh behind my chin. In the days that followed, I felt increasingly ashamed by how I had treated the boy.

'It was for his own good,' I whispered to myself. 'No good will come of his visiting you.'

My next visitor found me slumped upon the dirt on my back and snoring aloud with my hands spread out alongside me. A nudge of his foot woke me with a start so that I made out the Jesuit standing over me in the growing dusk, holding a heavy tome in one hand.

'Father,' I croaked as I sat up.

The stern features of O'Ronayne bore into me as he fell to one knee and grasped me by the shoulder.

'I hope you shall treat me with more kindness than Lochlain,' he said as I noticed the book in his hands.

'Is that Erasmus?' I asked, then gratefully drained a cup of goat's milk which he held out to me.

'All in good time,' he replied. 'I would first hear your confession.'

'Confession?' I gasped, staring at him as if he were a madman.

'All of the sacraments are the Lord's gifts to us,' he replied as his eyes narrowed, 'and what greater relief could be served to you than to unburden your soul in full to me? Do so, that you may gain even greater relief than when you surrendered your prize in the chieftain's hall.'

'Gift,' I said, trying not to laugh in his face, since I could not recall the last time I had confessed to a priest.

'Am I to be executed?' I asked at last, to which he issued a low chuckle.

'No, no, Spaniard; at least, not that I know of. Your fate is to be decided by the overlord, who often visits us at this time of the year. My visit is solely to be of service to a wretched hostage, and your confession is long overdue.'

I regarded him suspiciously, wondering whether anything I told him would really not go any further. There had been many men of the cloth in Flanders who had proved less scrupulous than the lowest-born soldier; men who were known to trade secrets learned during their duties as readily as they would cheat a dying soldier of his earnings meant to be passed on to his family back home. I then decided to use the priest for my own amusement rather than to give up anything which might further compromise my position amongst the tribe.

'Very well,' I said. 'Where shall I begin?'

'Wherever you please.'

I rubbed my eyes for a few moments before I spoke. 'It has been years since I left home. When I look back on my life, it has been an incredible journey.'

'Where were you raised?'

'In a foundling home in the victorious city.'

O'Ronayne's eyes fill with wonder. 'The legendary town of the Crusader order?'

'Yes, was sired by one of their number too.'

The man's breath quickened at my mention of the Hospitallers, and I suddenly remembered that being born a bastard was of no concern to the Irish.

'Juan de los Hospitalarios,' he said, as if hearing it for the first time. 'I should have known.'

'Yes. But I abandoned that name long ago.'

He seemed taken aback while I explained myself further. 'I am commonly known as Abelardo de Santiago.'

'Is Juan not your Christian name?'

'It is,' I replied, 'but with my background names mean nothing unless you invent them.'

The Jesuit frowned when I continued.

'It was always my wish to become one of the order, a proud warrior of Christ. Yet that path was not open to me. Fair enough for them to father me, I suppose, but not to accept me among their number. I was only allowed to serve their fleet.'

'You were indeed fortunate,' he proclaimed. 'It is said to be one of the best in the world.'

I told him how I distinguished myself as a powder monkey before mastering the firearms of those I served.

'One of the more foresighted among them – de Bragança, I think his name was – was impressed by my skill. He enlisted me as a harquebusier. It was the proudest day of my life. Long before Lepanto, the Spanish crown offered a good pay to musketeers. Eventually I abandoned the household of my uncle in Spain and joined the army, yet I did not intend to be derided for being one of the order's bastards. Thus was born the monster Abel de Santiago, a name chosen before I enlisted.'

'Monster?'

'Assassin and sharpshooter,' I added, 'which brought me good money in times of both war and peace. It made my fortune. I also served Spain as a bombardier. Life in the army was hard, but I always loved gunpowder. Whilst in the Low Countries my skill was noted by none other than Alba himself, who took me into his service as a sharpshooter.'

'The Iron Duke,' said the Jesuit.

'Yes, the devil himself. Men like me are greatly rewarded when the going is good, but are as soon forgotten when things turn sour. Anyway, Alba promoted me and took me into his confidence. The Duke wanted men he could trust, but his peers always looked down at me. They said I only earned favour because I used the tools of the devil.'

I smiled faintly, my stare fixed on the wall ahead of us. The events which I described seemed a lifetime away.

'My name gained a certain notoriety amongst the heretics, which is why I have refrained from using it here. What we did to the Protestants is not even worthy of confession, and Ireland has shown me what we put them through.'

The ensuing silence was only broken by the crackle of fire in the ringfort; after a time O'Ronayne spoke again.

'Perhaps you are beyond redemption, Juan, but I do not think so. In the face of this enemy we must resort to all means.'

I beheld him bitterly and took the book from his hands, curiously examining its binding while I replied to him thoughtlessly. 'In their place we might be as bad, if not worse.'

O'Ronayne served me a withering gaze, which I only noticed when he growled at me between bared teeth. 'What do you mean? Heretics work for the devil. If you are not with the church, then you are for Satan.'

I beheld him defiantly and slowly repeated my words. 'In their place we might be as bad as them. If not worse.'

The Jesuit snorted. 'You do not only behave like a thief and a murderer, but you also speak like a heretic – one that is wholly unrepentant! May the O'Rourke serve you with the justice that you deserve, for you have earned no forgiveness from me.'

My dismissive glare was met by a furious look of disgust, yet I was taken aback when the Jesuit bent over to snatch the book from my hands, then made his way out of the ringfort.

# LII

## ROSCLOGHER, DARTRY, COUNTY LEITRIM

*8 – 16 November 1589*

The week after Samhain was lean of both meat and companionship, and my diet of pork rinds ensured that I had become more haggard in appearance than a skeleton. One day I snatched up the wooden plate and hurled it at my guard's head.

'Shove that up your arse! I am done with eating your leftovers!'

'Then starve to death!' he replied as he rubbed his sore head, turning to aim an angry kick at mine.

His foot caught my elbow and instantly numbed my arm. I fell over and clutched it as a loud grumble erupted from my stomach.

'Spanish whoreson!' snorted the bluejacket as he planted another kick between my shoulders, leaving me to writhe in my clanking chains as he walked off back to his post.

When my pain had in part subsided, I rose onto my knees, rubbing the growing welts on my arm while the small of my back still throbbed. I felt the first drops of rain on my nose, and had just decided that things could hardly get worse when the blare of a trumpet was heard outside the fort. Many cries were heard outside and within the fort, and the bluejackets ran to the walls and doorway to stare at whatever it was that had started the whole stir.

'What is it?' I called out to the kerns who ran past me. In response I heard great cries of wonder.

'The overlord! The overlord! *na Múrtha* is here!'

'O'Rourke is here?' I gasped as yet another blare of bugles sounded, followed by the loud throb of bodhráns as the host made its way towards the town.

I slumped back against the wall, somewhat disappointed at having missed the sight. My disappointment soon turned into anxiety, since I feared what the lord of Breifne's arrival might mean for me. The commotion had long subsided by the afternoon. My worries had long since abandoned me as I cut a downcast figure on the ground, not even stirring when the sound of heavy footsteps were heard behind me.

'I'm warning you,' I hissed, 'not to place that filth in front of me again.'

'It is me, Juan,' replied a deep, familiar voice, and I turned in disbelief to find the bondsman with a wide grin on his face. Two bluejackets stood at his shoulders. I had not seen Nial in well over a fortnight, and the last days had not appeared to have been very kind to him either. Grey pouches had grown beneath his twinkling eyes. His face was worn from fatigue, and his blond hair looked greatly dishevelled.

'What brings you here, Nial?' I replied.

He winced at my injured tone. 'The overlord has requested that you appear before him.'

I sighed as I rose to my knees, holding my chained wrists out before him. 'I might as well stretch my legs with you.'

The bondsman led me through the village towards the banks of the lake, where we boarded the boat which bore us to Rosclogher. Nial insisted on removing my manacles so that, for the first time in half a month, I found myself revelling in the freedom of being able to sway my arms past my hips as I walked.

'What news from the east?' I asked him as the great punts of the boatman drew us closer to the crannog.

'It is poor for the most part,' he replied, his constant grin vanishing from his face, 'for it is said that the Binghams are to be acquitted by the lord governor. The bishops have also given up on us rebels, since no witness has been forthcoming.'

The tidings struck me like a knife through the heart, as his reference to the trial in Dublin reminded me of the passing of both Old Tom and Dervila, and of the riding party which had been ambushed in Fermanagh by Verdon's troopers.

'That is indeed bad news,' I whispered at last. 'I expect the Binghams will seek to exact further vengeance upon us.'

'Of a certainty they will. O'Rourke's spies have said that the Anglo-Norman lords of Clanricard and Thomond plan on throwing their lot in behind them, as do other loyalist clans. They also say that Richard Bingham will order all rebels to surrender by mid-January, the moment he is officially acquitted.'

'A grim winter beckons.'

Nial nodded once by way of reply, yet said nothing more until the keep was reached and we climbed to the chieftain's hall. A swarm of retainers appeared before the blazing hearth, Dartry's highborn mixing freely with the aristocrats of Breifne as they spoke of the events of the previous year.

Ahead of us the O'Rourke occupied the throne of Manglana, the king of Dartry having taken up his late wife's lower throne as a mark of his sub-king status. As we approached them, *na Múrtha*'s head turned towards us like that of a hawk, his piercing eyes fixing themselves upon me as we fell to our knees before him and Manglana.

'So here is our thief,' he declared, then proceeded to stun me by holding up the ring with a growing scowl on his face.

'So sayeth the enemy,' I replied wearily, 'yet whatever I may be, I am certainly not in league with them.'

O'Rourke was attired in black like the last time I had seen him, yet his shock-white beard flowed from features which had become lined and worn from the struggles of previous months. He stroked the end of it pensively as I knelt before him, as the chieftain's closest retainers glared at me.

'Did you kill Ramos?' he asked at last.

'Yes, that I did,' I replied after barely a moment's hesitation, 'and I make no apology for it, for it was no less than he deserved.'

'And what did he do to deserve to die at your hands?'

'Raped and murdered my betrothed,' I replied, 'and was directly responsible for the death of her father and brother. Which is not to mention all the vile acts of misery he inflicted on countless wretches over the years, all of which went unpunished. The sergeant was one of the best fighters I have met, yet he was profoundly wicked.'

'And of great value to our cause,' sighed the overlord as his celeste eyes bore into me angrily.

'But no more, my lord,' I replied wearily, 'for I accosted him as he was fleeing the battlefield with the ring he had stolen from me in days previous.'

'Is it true?' asked O'Rourke. He swiftly sat up in his seat and traded a look of concern with Manglana.

Dartry's king had barely parted his lips to speak when I interrupted him. 'His body was found in the hillsides, my lord. Do you think I had the strength or time following battle to drag him there myself?'

The hall fell silent at my question, and the chieftains stared back at me for a few moments until the overlord spoke again.

'Where did you come by the ring?'

'When my ship was wrecked upon the coast, I was captured by the enemy shortly afterwards and led to Sligo. It was there that I was dealt with the mark of the spider, whilst being tortured in the dungeons of the sheriff, George Bingham.'

I tore my tunic open with my hands as I said this, and great intakes of breath were heard throughout the hall as I showed the horrified gathering the burns upon my breast which had been inflicted by Treasach Burke.

'It was there that the renegade sergeant, Treasach Burke, tormented me and lamed an elderly Spaniard by the name of Hurtado. Yet we somehow contrived to overpower our torturers, and Hurtado made me swear to return the ring to its owner, the prince of Ascoli.'

Upon hearing my embellished account, O'Rourke nodded once before falling back on his chair and holding the ring up before his face again. He next surprised me with a question of his own.

'A noble act, friend Spaniard. And do you still hold to your pledge?'

To my right I could see that Muireann's face had turned a hue of scarlet, yet I ignored her as I bowed my head to the overlord.

'That I do, my lord. Yet I am accused of being a murderer and a thief, and I cannot achieve it without your authority.'

'My authority is my own to concede, Spaniard,' replied *na Múrtha*, returning the ring to his finger, 'and this trinket could do much to rescue the fortunes of those that bled to protect you. Yet an oath should not be easily broken, and I must devote some thought as to how this bauble can be returned to its rightful owners.'

'God bless you, my lord,' I stuttered, awed by his deep sense of honour and wondering whether his words hinted at my eventual release.

'I have made no decision yet,' he warned me, 'and the murder of an officer in my army is no small crime. You shall remain a hostage in Rosclogher until my decision is made. You shall learn of it in coming days. Until then I suggest that you seek the Lord's pardon and pray hard for your soul.'

He turned to engage in discussion with Manglana once more, entirely disregarding me as if I were one of the hounds which lay on the floor. O'Ronayne and Lochlain paid me little regard as Nial hoisted me back upon my feet, then escorted me out of the hall.

'We can share the outhouse again,' said the bondsman.

I could scarcely believe the suddenness with which I had been freed from the ringfort. Indeed, the thought of being able to come and go about the town as I pleased left me almost reeling after we had left the tower-house and crossed the lake.

When we reached the town I immediately made my way to the bondsman's lodgings, where I was met by the sight of my old palliasse. Before collapsing upon it, I drained half a beaker of Nial's brandy, feeling a warm glow inside me as I fell to the ground. The bondsman cleared his throat as he strode in behind me, although I had already noted the clatter of his two scabbards.

'Make yourself comfortable whilst you can,' he said as he raised his beaker to his lips and took a long swig. 'We might soon be on the move again.'

'Where to now?' I replied with a tone of resignation, as I wondered whether I would ever be able to reside in a place for more than a couple of months.

'The mountains, most likely,' he replied, 'although the battle at the horseshoe valley might have won us a brief respite during the winter.'

'So the trial of the Binghams is definitely over?' I asked, vainly hoping that the rumours he had heard would prove nothing more than such.

'The trial was a farce,' he scoffed, 'merely a way to pacify us while the English launched their own armada against the Spanish coast.'

'The English despatched their own armada?'

'Indeed, they despatched a fleet of their own against Spain. Yet by all accounts it met with a catastrophic end.'

'Certainly not as disastrous as the one we sent against them.'

'I hear it was,' said the bondsman.

'Ah,' I replied, 'then Spain is not yet dead at sea. But in any event, how does this concern us?'

'Well for one,' said Nial as he sat alongside me and rested his chin pensively upon his fist, 'now that the English have been kicked away from the Continent, their attentions will be returned to Ireland. I fear the seasoned veterans who ambushed Dervila's party are but the first trickle of a flood which shall drown us.'

'Neither deluge nor flood can reach the mountains,' I replied, although even the jovial bondsman could barely manage a smile.

'I wish I shared your confidence, Spaniard,' he replied, 'yet I fear that even the mountains cannot protect us for long in the upcoming months. The Binghams will descend upon us with a vengeance, and it appears that the reign of the chieftains hangs by a thread. Our plight is indeed desperate.'

We did talk again for long thereafter; then Nial left me to attend to his other duties. I stretched my limbs upon the straw beneath me, which suddenly felt as soft as down cushions when compared to the stony ground of the ringfort.

'Free again,' I whispered to myself, 'but for how much longer?'

Instinctively my hand reached for my bandolier, but then the realisation struck me that the ring was held by the O'Rourke, whose plans for me were still unknown. Any hope I had of discovering the overlord's purpose disappeared the following morning when I learned that he had ridden off to attend to urgent matters in Breifne. I also learned that I was to be kept hostage until he had decided what to do with me.

The following days were among the coldest I had experienced in Dartry, with a freezing westerly assaulting the town and natives serving me with hard stares on every corner. Men whispered 'murderer' in muffled tones behind my back, and mothers hurried their young away at the first sight of me. All this frostiness was largely met with the cold shoulder. I kept to myself, huddled away in Nial's outhouse while I awaited my fate.

I was otherwise free to come and go unhindered, and my days were mainly spent traipsing along the edge of the Melvin like a forgotten ghost. Yet my time was not entirely lonely; any thoughts of flight were kept at bay by a knave who shadowed me whenever I left the hut, keeping a constant watch on me from a distance. He was one of a handful of boys used to watch hostages, since the Gaels rarely chained or imprisoned their captives unless they presented an immediate danger to their fellow men.

In time it seemed like my imprisonment had only been resumed in a larger cell, so that I found myself longing for any sentence to be pronounced by the chieftains. At the very least, it might end my boredom. My prayers were answered when the bondsman shook me awake one night, urging me to get to my feet.

'What is it?' I blurted aloud, blinking at the tallow light.

'Keep your voice down,' hissed Nial sharply, so that I stared at him askance.

'Arise, Spaniard,' uttered another's deep voice, which I instantly recognised as the O'Rourke's.

My arms and legs flailed everywhere as I swiftly rose to my feet, then fell to one knee before Dartry's overlord. A quick glimpse in his direction also revealed the familiar silhouette of Manglana at his shoulder, as well as another score of shadows among whose number I only recognised the Jesuit and Muireann.

My eyes were fixed upon the ground, and I could not resist a shudder when the O'Rourke slowly paced about me.

'The noose tightens, Spaniard,' he said, 'for we approach our darkest hour.'

Nothing further was said for a few moments thereafter, which I mistook for the chieftains expecting a response.

'Use the ring, sire. It should fetch you an army of Scots.'

For a while thereafter there came no reply, so I raised my head to find the overlord staring at me in befuddlement.

'Do you mean that I should just pawn it? What became of your pledge to the nobleman Hurtado?'

The edge in his voice kept me from speaking, and he soon resumed his pacing about the hut, leaving me to fear the worst.

'A pledge to one's allies must be honoured,' he said at last, 'for otherwise we are no better than these brutish colonists who offer us peace in our own lands. Word of their lies has already reached me from the Spanish king's agents, as they accuse us of robbing his subjects and selling them to the enemy.'

A loud scrape of earth was heard as he turned suddenly on his heel and raised his voice in indignation.

'I will show them that the sons of Connacht are neither thieves nor beggars! You are still bound to me, yet I release you and your prize, that you may return it to its lawful owners. All aid shall be provided to you to speed you on to your end.'

My jaw quivered until I finally addressed him. 'My thanks, Lord. I will not fail you.'

O'Rourke cleared his throat awkwardly as he stopped his pacing and met my stare.

'Do not thank me yet, Spaniard, for you do not know of the perils that yet lie ahead of you. They are by far worse than the fine owed to me for Ramos' death.'

So saying, the overlord turned away from me and departed from the hut with his kerns, and it was the last time I saw him. Manglana and his retainers scowled at my kneeling form before also making their way out of the hut, leaving me in the company of Nial and the flickering candlelight.

'When do I leave?' I asked, almost to myself.

'No doubt all will be revealed tomorrow,' replied Nial, as he returned to his bed and fell asleep.

After tossing and turning for a good hour, slumber finally overcame me, yet it was over a week later when the chieftains' designs was at last revealed, when my silent watcher approached me upon the eastern edge of the great lake.

'Hasten you to your hut, Spaniard,' he said with a stern look on his wild, whiskerless face. 'The priest awaits you there.'

I ran back towards the distant belfry of *Doire Mel,* issuing low curses whenever I stumbled over the muddy banks against the water's edge. When I reached the end of the town, I ran past the church towards the outhouse, finding the Jesuit standing outside it with Nial. O'Ronayne's arms were folded, and he was entirely garbed in black. He regarded me with evident distaste and ignored my salutation.

'We must leave this place at once,' he said dryly.

'We?' I asked in astonishment.

'Yes, *we*,' he said almost regretfully. 'The chieftains have ordered me to travel north with their sons.'

'Are you to travel with me to Spain –' I managed just as Nial cut me off.

'We are to escort the boys and Father O'Ronayne to neighbouring Banagh,' he said, 'where they will receive the protection of Lady Mac an Bhaird's brother, Diarmaid. He is a worthy sub-lord of the MacSweeney, who shall host us until we are ready for the next part of our journey.'

'And what of the ring?' I asked, unable to contain my curiosity.

O'Ronayne reached through one of his flowing sleeves and drew a small, iron casket which had a leather shoulder strap attached to it. When he passed it to me, I could hear something rattling within it. My heart leapt as I seized it up in both hands, instantly trying to open the strongbox.

'It is locked for added safekeeping,' said O'Ronayne dryly, as he observed my attempts to obtain the ring with a look of acute disappointment.

'Who has the key?' I replied, instantly regretting the hasty tone of my voice.

'Nial has one,' said the Jesuit, 'and the *ollamh* has the other.'

'The ollave also travels with us?' I asked.

'That she does,' replied O'Ronayne. 'She remains our best guide when travelling abroad, and she wishes to escort her son to the demesne of her brother.'

'Why not retire with the Dartrymen to the mountains?' I asked in bafflement.

'Because even the greatest heights are unsafe,' replied the Jesuit, 'if one cannot even trust his own people.'

So saying he scratched at his beard and cast his eyes from me to the casket in my hands for emphasis.

'Too many heads have been turned by the enemy's false promises,' he went on, 'as was witnessed in the valley of the horseshoe. War spares no children, and the winter ahead shall be full of troubles. You should instead ask how many of the tribe will see out the winter, for even my lord MacGlannagh can no longer vouch for his own safety.'

'We must leave Dartry at once,' added the bondsman, 'for it can no longer guarantee our safety. Once we reach Banagh we shall next press on through the hidden passes of Donegal to Derry, from where we shall journey to Scotland and then venture on to Spain.'

'Scotland?' I asked in surprise. 'Can we not attempt a sea voyage from Ireland instead?'

'At this time of year?' exclaimed Nial. 'You shall be hard pressed to find a captain who shall risk his vessel on such a journey in winter. Which is not to mention the enemy ships which prowl along the coast. No, Spaniard, our best hope is to reach the Spaniards in Scotland, who await the English queen's permission to allow them to return home.'

'Is it likely to be granted?' I asked.

'Her talks with the king of Spain's envoys are said to be reaching some sort of agreeable conclusion. In any event, we can wait until the sailing season there, then board a ship bound for the Continent.'

'And upon reaching Spain you must bear the O'Rourke's letters to Ascoli,' added O'Ronayne with a raised eyebrow as he passed me a handful of sealed folds of vellum.

'You must guard these as closely and jealously as if they were the ring,' he said, 'for it is the overlord's desire that Ascoli's retainers may be our sponsors in Madrid during our time of direst need.'

I took the letters and held them out in front of me, wondering why Ascoli would care for a distant tribe of Irish beggars after being reunited with his father's trinket. I thought of warning the Jesuit against this course, yet refrained from doing so when I realised that it might hinder my return to Spain.

'Are we to travel alone to Derry?' I asked instead.

'A half-dozen kerns will be assigned to us,' replied Nial, 'who shall first escort us to Banagh before we make for Derry.'

'You will find all that you need laid out on your bed,' added the Jesuit, 'so get some rest before we depart at midday.'

O'Ronayne left me standing in stunned silence, scarcely able to believe that my time in Dartry was almost at an end.

'Come in, Spaniard,' said Nial as he placed his hand on my shoulder and gently pushed me towards the hut. 'I will give you your things.'

I found a *skene* dagger and my old bandolier lying on my bed, as well as a musket in half-decent condition. A fresh shirt and trews were also neatly folded and laid upon a new pair of brogues, with a helmet and mail shirt placed before the shoes. My sword and scabbard had also been returned, together with a ball bag, primer and ramrod. I could not help but grunt in amusement when I picked up the black piece of soap which had been placed upon the vestments.

'You might want to use that now,' said Nial, pointing at a bucket of water which had lain unnoticed in the shadows.

'Can you wake me in an hour?' I asked hopefully.

'Of course,' he replied, then turned his back on me and walked out of the hut.

As always, the bondsman was as good as his word, so midday found me thoroughly scrubbed, dressed and armed to the teeth. When we approached the small gathering of men upon the green, I could see the ollave among the party, wearing a coat upon her saffron tunic and scowling openly at the sight of me. The casket hanging about my neck felt like a millstone beneath the crushing accusation of her stare, so I instantly looked away.

It was only her son, Lochlain, who smiled as I stepped in alongside the kerns and the two ponies. A quiet solemnity overtook our party as we observed the chieftain and his steward, Malachy, who both stood a few feet away from us, surrounded by a score of Spanish and Irish bodyguards.

The previous days had not been kind to Manglana, and he appeared both bleary-eyed and unkempt. His hair was an unruly mess, his tangled beard still uncombed since the battle of Gleniff and streaked with matted blotches of blood as it fluttered upon his breast.

'Farewell, friends,' he said, 'and Godspeed on your journey north. Tarry not upon the road, for they say that the guard in the garrisons has doubled . . .'

His voice broke off as he spoke, and my heart was broken at the sight of so proud a man, soon to be rendered a fugitive within his own kingdom.

'My place is at your side, Lord,' declared the Jesuit hotly. 'My mission is to serve the men of Dartry.'

'Begone, priest,' snapped the chieftain. 'You are to be spiritual guide to Lochlain and advance our cause abroad. You are languishing here.'

O'Ronayne grimaced by way of reply but did not object further.

The chieftain addressed us a last time. 'Now begone, and do not look back until you are safely in the lord Mac an Bhaird's keep. May God bless those faithful subjects among you, and remember us in your prayers, that the Lord may yet deliver us from the enemy.'

After he said this I could have sworn that he served me with the swiftest glare. The kerns hauled at the ponies' reins. One of them nickered as we all followed Muireann, who made towards the trees south of the town, alongside the ring of bog. A flood of sadness welled up inside me as I flung my head over my shoulder, taking in my last sight of the town which had hosted me for over a year.

I took in the sight of the chieftain and his men standing before the town, as well as of the ringfort, chapel and the distant tower-house. Then the growing cover of boughs concealed all, as if a curtain had been permanently drawn across a chapter of my life in a place rendered all the more mystical by its sudden disappearance.

I wondered whether it had all been a dream, as I turned my head back towards the muddy path to cross the bog. Muireann took up a westwards path as we hurried after her, and within the hour we reached the village of Kinlough, after which we struck out north. We travelled for well over three hours without a word before pausing for a brief rest and a meal. An hour later we pressed on again, climbing and descending hills for another two hours before the early dusk of winter started to set in.

Before long the odd howl of a wolf was heard, and Muireann stopped in her tracks to gesture at the trees ahead of us.

Seated beneath a great oak was the great, black wolf which had for so long plagued the land of Dartry. I instantly drew my rifle and loaded it, then rested its butt to my shoulder as I took aim at the creature.

'Quick, Spaniard,' hissed O'Ronayne. 'Rid us of that cursed beast.'

As I took in the sight of the wolf, I knew that I could have it clean through the head. Yet something stopped me just as my finger was about to pull back the serpentine. As the beast raised its head and issued a piercing howl, I slowly lowered my rifle and put it away. The creature ran off into the shadows, and the tribesmen proceeded to tell me off.

'Why did you do that?' snapped the Jesuit as Muireann looked away in disgust.

I whispered something about saving our stocks of powder and how the noise of the gun might alert the enemy to our whereabouts. These reasons hardly placated my companions, who trudged on through the forest. Meanwhile I slowly realised that what had stayed my hand was an overwhelming sense of guilt at having hidden the ring for so long, which in my mind made me no better than the one-eyed wolf.

# LIII

# ROSCLOGHER TO BANAGH

*16 – 17 November 1589*

M y days of confinement in the ringfort had left me short of stamina, and I laboured to keep step with my fellow travellers. I often fell behind them, and I found myself snatching a pony's tail on the uphill track. Although the party largely kept silent, the odd exchange could be heard as we progressed towards Donegal. Eventually a great excitement grew among the group as with quickened step the ollave led us through over an upland pass and by strong little waterfalls.

At last we came to the larger waterfall of Eas Doonan; in the growing dusk we could still see Lough Belshade surrounded by cliffs, as well as the highest summits of the Croaghgorm. We sought shelter in the cave above the lake, where two of the kerns fell to their knees to start a small fire. Their task was relieved by Nial, as the bondsman produced a tinderbox which he had brought with him.

'Good thinking, Ne Dourough,' remarked O'Ronayne, as he sat upon the ground and rubbed his hands together.

Lochlain sat in silence as his mother assigned guard duties before the night set in. With a gasp of relief, I collapsed onto the ground on the left side of the cave mouth.

'Fetch firewood,' someone growled behind me. I recognised the voice as Muireann's.

When I raised my head I found myself the object of her withering disapproval. I rose onto my feet with a low grunt, then shuffled off with another kern to pick up any wood and leaves which we could gather. Before long we could hear the howling of Irish wolves against the moon, which cast its radiance upon us.

'Let us hope that cur *An Faolchù* is not amongst them,' muttered my companion to himself as he picked sticks off the forest floor. 'Dim-witted fool should have shot him when he had the chance.'

I pretended not to hear his slur, given that the hour was late and we could ill afford to alert any brigands to our whereabouts by starting a fight. I knew that our journey would turn only more arduous in coming days, and I craved sleep even more than I did the evening dinner. When we made our way back to the glowing cave mouth, we found two kerns standing guard while another busied himself cooking two skinned rabbits. When we finally started to eat, O'Ronayne spoke to Lochlain who sat alongside him, seeking to raise his spirits by telling him of his first travels abroad.

'I was but a mere novice, not a handful of years your senior when I journeyed with Bishop O'Gallagher to Rome to attend the Council of Trent.'

'What was Rome like?' asked Muireann's son as I observed him from the shadows at the cave mouth.

'I felt I had crossed the very gates to Paradise itself!' exclaimed the Jesuit, his voice thick with awe as Lochlain's eyes widened. 'Splendid cupolas like you have never seen, my son! And the statues! Oh, the statues . . .'

'I met someone who travelled to Rome,' said Lochlain, suddenly staring about him. 'Oh! There you are, Spaniard.'

I rolled my eyes and turned away at his words, not wishing to partake of their conversation. The ollave and the bondsman were also within earshot, and the last thing I wanted to do was incur their ire at gloating over far-off places to which I had travelled, when in their minds I had brought ruin to their tribe by hiding my trinket from them for so long.

'Many Spaniards have visited the eternal city,' observed O'Ronayne, as the shadows of the fire played upon his scowling face. 'Indeed 'tis a miracle that the city survived them.'

'If you refer to the sacking of '27,' I replied hotly, 'it is worth noting that it was German mercenaries who performed the sacking while the Spaniards desperately sought to restore order.'

'Indeed,' continued the Jesuit as if he had never heard me, 'it is a wonder that anywhere survives the Spaniards for long.'

Nial could not resist a snort at the barb, and the kerns shared Muireann and O'Ronayne's open scowls of loathing. The whole cave glared at me except for the prince. Lochlain's face was a contortion of conflicted emotions, and with a grunt I turned sideways and gave the tribesmen my back, knowing that there was nothing I could say that would change their attitude towards me.

'So despite the Spanish barbarity which had briefly preceded my visit,' said O'Ronayne, 'the city was still a wonder to behold. At every opportunity I wandered its streets and alleys from morning until night, feasting my eyes on the palaces and churches that were discovered past every corner.'

'Have you returned thither since, Father?' asked Lochlain.

Their exchange continued when more meat was served for our dinner. Nial held out a skewer of braised rabbit for me. My nod of gratitude was not acknowledged by the bondsman, who stepped back towards the flames while I devoured the food. My eyes were shut shortly afterwards, my last memory being that of Irish faces glowing red as rainwater dripped off the edge of the cave mouth behind them.

We stirred from our shelter well before dawn, with the slightest rainfall still hissing as we drew our mantles about our heads and led the ponies back into the open country. In the late moonlight Muireann nimbly pursued a rockier path downhill, until we came to a densely forested lowland area, where we could keep to our path while remaining largely unseen. Two of the kerns were sent to scout ahead, and after an hour's march we came at last upon them. The pair were waiting for us within sight of the distant shimmer of the river Erne.

'Sassenachs,' said the more thickly set of the two. 'Lots of Sassenachs.'

'How many?' asked Muireann as she came to a halt and stared ahead of us.

'Dozens,' was the kern's reply. 'Both banks are crawling with them.'

The ollave fell silent and bit her lip in thought as the rest of us looked about us helplessly, mulling over the meaning of the scout's words.

'We head east,' she said at last, then beat a rightwards track without so much as a look back over her shoulder. We hurried after our fleet-footed guide, though thoughts of the enemy were soon dispelled as we stared at the track ahead of us. After another half hour spent following her brisk steps, we came at last to a part of the forest where the trees began to recede again, and where the soggy leaves underfoot also dwindled.

Muireann fell to one knee and beckoned to us to do the same. We hid behind the roots of a gnarled oak while she quietly ordered the scouts to venture ahead again. The two kerns made off ahead of us, crouching low in the dells as they inched ever closer to the rushing water. Nial had already fitted a bolt to a crossbow when the scouting pair returned, pausing to regain their breath as they were met by our expectant stares.

'Less guards here,' the first one said. 'Just four by our reckoning.'

'Yes,' said the other, 'and the ford is wider but shallower. When a rider crossed it, we could see his horse's knees.'

'Well,' said Muireann to Nial, her raised eyebrow clearly demanding a response.

'The guard is still heavy far from the main crossing,' observed the bondsman, 'but I say we take them. For they are outnumbered and we know the meaning of stealth.'

'Are there no crossings further east?' asked the Jesuit, clearly not appreciating the prospect of a confrontation.

Nial slowly shook his head. 'I do not advise it, for the guard at Ballyshannon will be greater in number, and it is too close to the territory of those loyalist tribesmen who helped the viceroy to reach Dartry.'

'Then we are presented with little choice,' I remarked, only to be openly ignored by the tribesmen, who sat about an oak and proceeded to unroll their blankets and lie down at the foot of the tree.

Upon realising that our attack would consist of a night raid, I followed suit, knowing full well that it also meant a hard night's march after the enemy had been slain. I instantly fell asleep and was shaken awake two hours later to perform guard duty before the evening set in.

'Take this, Spaniard,' said Nial as he passed me a drawn crossbow.

He beckoned to me and the kerns to make after him, and he treaded slowly towards the water. The recent rainfall meant that the leaves did not crunch beneath our feet as we drew closer to the water's edge. We crouched low behind the boughs of the trees, and my blood froze as a mounted trooper slowly trotted past us. He bore a torch aloft in one hand, which revealed his rugged features as his eyes jerked from side to side.

Nial peered out from behind the bark, then drew back alongside me. 'The bastards are indeed out in full force,' he whispered beneath his breath.

'It is too risky,' replied one of the kerns. 'If one of them so much as cries out, we may have another dozen on our hands.'

'I know that,' snapped Nial as he snatched another glimpse from behind our tree.

'If two of us can steal closer to those bushes nearer the water,' he said, as he fell back alongside us again, 'we can seek to slay the four of them at once.'

'Are you certain?' asked the dissenting kern. 'The timing is difficult.'

'We have no choice,' snarled the bondsman. 'The lady Mac an Bhaird has said that there is no other way past the garrison towns. If we can ford the river here, then we can be halfway to safety before our crossing is discovered.'

'Very well then,' grunted the other kern. 'Who goes across? Methinks we are going to find ourselves torn to shreds before the night is out.'

'Damn your eyes, Fergus,' said Nial, barely able to contain the anger in his voice any longer. 'Will you not refrain from your womanly rant? It is not as if we have not done this before. I will take three across with me. Meanwhile, summon the *ollamh*, then get yourselves down to those bushes ahead. At my whistle we must strike as one. Remember: get your hands over their mouths first.'

No sooner had he issued the order than he beckoned to three of the kerns behind us and proceeded to dig his hands into the wet soil beneath us. We followed his lead, smearing our faces with mud and silt before wiping the whole of our hands with it. The clinking of our belts and weapons had already been muffled with strips of cloth.

Nial hurried off to the right, his tall, lanky form bent over the ground as three crouching shadows clung to his footsteps. I saw them vanish into the forest without ever making a sound, just as Fergus ran off to fetch the ollave and returned with her and the remaining kern.

'Cling to me, Spaniard,' said Fergus, 'and make sure you only do what I tell you. If you blow our cover, I shall slash your gizzard before that of the enemy.'

'Keep your voices down,' whispered Muireann, then made away from us with the other kern, keeping low as they slowly crept from one tree to the other. My attentions drifted away from them as Fergus and I crawled over the grass, wincing whenever we felt the end of a twig sticking into our arms or felt a branch beneath our feet. We covered the last length of treeless ground towards the low bushes which grew along the lakeside, and our assigned rider was at least ten feet away from us. At a nod from Fergus I drew my dagger, yet he clutched the hair at the back of my head and drew my ear so closely to his lips that I could feel their touch.

'At the whistle you shoot,' he said. 'I will do the rest.'

We waited for what seemed like the whole of the night as the trooper passed us twice more; my hair rose on end whenever the shadow of his heavily armed presence fell upon us. Meanwhile I looked out for a sign from the bondsman and his men upon the moonlit water. My body became as firm as a ramrod as the horseman approached us once more, and when he passed us, a low, shrill whistle was heard from the opposite bank. I rose to my feet and released the crossbow, planting its bolt between the rider's shoulders as Fergus sprang towards him.

The trooper's head fell backwards. I stiffened as his lips widened to scream, but just then the kern caught him by the face and hauled him over the horse, which issued a low whinny before cantering off. Fergus's incredible leap combined the agility of a deer with the strength of a wolf, and I stared at the tumbling figures in disbelief as I raced towards their struggle. The kern's arm was tightly wrapped around the trooper's neck, and the heretic issued a hissing sound as he struggled to breathe or scream while he fumbled for the pistol at his side.

'Cover his mouth!' hissed the kern.

I met his request until Fergus could produce a dagger. I snatched it up and slashed it across the trooper's throat. After this deathly work was done, I fell away from the kicking Sassana, whose wound showered me with blood. Dropping the blade to the ground, I fell to my knees. The odd scrape and shuffle could be heard around me as our companions rid us of the other three riders.

Within instants all was silent again, save for the low, rushing sound of the Erne. Then the voice of O'Ronayne was heard as he abandoned the cover of trees with Lochlain, having been summoned by one of the kerns.

'Good work, Spaniard,' said Nial as he waded across towards us from the opposite bank, where the two other troopers had been swiftly despatched.

'We must hasten off,' called Muireann from behind me, and I turned to see her cut the saddle off her dead trooper's steed, then whack it across its buttocks with her bow. With a whinny the horse cantered off into the dense brush behind us and, after Fergus had smacked it with the flat of his sword, was soon followed by the other mount.

We tarried along the water's edge just long enough for us to search the bodies of the slain troopers and to fling any weapons that the ponies could not carry into the middle of the river. We then forded the river, re-joining the other kerns on the opposite bank, diving into the cover of the dark foliage which lay behind it. The path was familiar to Muireann, who had often used it to visit the lands of her house.

'Be silent,' whispered O'Ronayne when two kerns exchanged words, 'for we are no longer in our own lands.'

No sooner had he spoken this than the blare of a bugle tore through the night, and we all looked over our shoulders in horror.

'The guard must have changed,' said Nial, 'but at this hour?'

'Move,' snapped Muireann as she resumed her course, leaving us with no choice but to scramble after her. Our swords were loosened in their scabbards as we made our way through the thickening trees, and we heard the distant cries of the enemy behind us. The ponies issued a nervous whinny as we pushed on hard into the night.

Lochlain cast nervous looks over his shoulder, but the Jesuit urged the prince on as I closely followed them, feeling increasingly bothered by the ring's heavy casket bouncing upon my thigh. Nial and his kerns were at our back, a force ready to cut off any danger that followed us, though also able to rush forward at need. After what seemed like a half hour of hurried pace, we were fortunate not to have crossed paths with either wolves or bandits, yet the sounds of the enemy behind us only grew louder and were soon accompanied by the sound of baying hounds.

'Don't fall back,' hissed Muireann ahead of us. 'Stay close.'

At her urging all caution was thrown to the wind, so that our hurried footfalls tore up leaves and twigs as we made our way through the thickening wood. The sounds behind us grew as we pushed on with ragged breath, our legs burning from fatigue as we made after the ollave's quickening step. Our guide never once looked back as she hurried across the ground before us, veering sharply to the left and then the right as the sounds behind us slowly wavered.

'Narrow river ahead,' hissed the ollave. 'Not long now.'

The Irish were no strangers to covering ground at speed, yet the odd gasp could even be heard from the kerns as we ran ahead. The very soles of our feet were aflame. It was a good drop from the bank into the rivulet, which was concealed by high grass and reeds. One of the kerns lost his footing, and the Jesuit fell in headfirst, with me tripping over his leg just as I was about to regain my footing.

'Watch your step!' growled O'Ronayne as I spat out brackish water and cursed him for having soaked my firearm.

We turned our heads to see Muireann swiftly wading through the water, leaving us to scramble after the gleaming ripples she left in her wake as we ventured west. After a few minutes of stumbling through the dark water, we made our way back on land. We hurried after her like a breeze through the strands of tall grass as she clung to the seaward track.

Before long the sound of hounds and men could be heard behind us again, and we turned to see distant flames along the brook we had crossed. Once more the ollave urged us on, until the sounds of the enemy could no longer be heard.

'Lost them,' said Muireann. She raised her hand to call a halt, and we fell upon the ground, wholly winded and weary from our exertions.

We lay on the ground for almost a half hour until the ollave rose from the grass and urged us on, earning herself a low grumble from the reluctant prince.

'Stay your protests,' she snapped at her son, 'for we have only to press on a little further to ensure our safety. Can you not match the vigour of a woman?'

Not another word was heard from Lochlain as we struggled back onto our feet in the growing dawn. Thereafter we marched ahead in silence through open grassland, the odd clump of trees breaking the interminable, verdant sea about us, which was confined by the brightening hills to our right. Another hour was spent on the move in open country, until at last Lochlain pointed to the distant glimmer of a lake to our right.

His mother raised her hand towards us again.

'Stay back here, all of you,' she said. 'I shall venture on with two of the men, to make certain that he is here.'

She crouched low to the ground as she made off with the two kerns at her back, and together they covered the ground ahead of them with the speed of hares, so that they soon vanished from sight. At Nial's command we lay low in the grass. Some of the men fell asleep, only to be stirred by approaching hoofbeats and the jostling figures of a dozen riders, who approached us fast from the direction of the lake. The bondsman sprang to his feet and drew his blades as the riders approached, then returned them to their sheaths as the ollave came into view with her arm raised reassuringly.

'Lower your weapons, for these are my kin.'

'Uncle!' cried Lochlain. He raced from the Jesuit's side towards the tall man clad in a bard's short, scarlet jacket, riding a grey palfrey at Muireann's shoulder.

'Uncle?' I asked no one in particular.

'Nephew.' The bard grinned. 'You have grown.'

O'Ronayne grunted as he shoved himself to his feet and stepped forward. The rest of us followed his footsteps with shared wariness, for the bard's horsemen lowered their spears and formed a circle about us. The gaps between them were soon filled by countless savage-looking kerns who had made after them from along the water. As I looked past the men of Donegal, I was struck by the sight of the bard, wrapping Lochlain in a huge embrace. The man's eyes glistened with repressed joy as he finally withdrew from the young man, grasping him by the shoulder.

'You have filled out splendidly, *mac an ri*. Your father would be proud.'

A smile grew across Lochlain's face as the bard turned towards the rest of us and addressed the Jesuit.

'Father O'Ronayne. It has been many winters since last we met.'

'Too many, my lord Mac an Bhaird. They were fairer days back then.'

At the Jesuit's words the realisation finally struck me that the bard was Muireann's brother, who had succeeded their deceased father as bard to the ruler of the southernmost kingdom of Donegal. As he approached our band, I saw that his yellow tunic was drawn in at the waist by a broad belt, and his wide sleeves were parted above the elbow, falling in large folds to the ground. His hair was the same colour as his sister's, to whom he bore a passing resemblance despite his wind-burned cheeks and the silvering hair at the sides of his head and upon his chin. His expression seemed kindlier as he nodded at Nial, yet darkened as his eyes fell on me.

'Is that the Spaniard?' he asked his sister, who stood behind him.

'Yes,' she replied quietly, averting her eyes from me.

I bowed deeply to Muireann's brother, yet he beheld me with distaste when my head was raised again.

'I should flay the skin from your body for the dishonour you cast upon my sister, then send your hide back to those fools who still protect you.'

His face turned scarlet when he said this, and he gripped his sword pommel and stepped towards me. Yet he was stayed when his sister's hand snatched his forearm.

'No, Diarmaid,' she whispered. 'We have sworn an oath.'

Her brother's lip twitched once as he struggled to withhold his rage, and my companions hung their heads in shame at the sight of his great ire. Then the bard whirled away from me and clasped his sister in a tight embrace, seizing up Lochlain with his other arm as he walked back towards the lake. Muireann's brother took long strides in his untanned boots while a horse-boy led his hobby behind them.

'My heart is filled with joy at your arrival,' he declared. 'You shall be safe here with me, for this is your home. You belong here with your people.'

The sound of his voice became fainter as we followed him at a respectful distance, allowing the family members of a great bardic house to enjoy their reunion in peace.

'Where are we bound?' I asked Nial.

'Diarmaid is to escort his kin to Donegal Castle,' he replied wearily. 'He shall accompany us for part of the way, and after that we are on our own.'

'We? Do you mean you and me?'

'And the band of kerns,' he replied, then turned his head away and would say no more.

Upon reaching the banks of the lake we re-joined the rest of the bard's men, who had taken shelter in a village along its banks. It was a small settlement of straw houses, unremarkable in its similarity to the many other ones I had seen in Connacht, populated by natives of the same cast and dress. Yet by the way they stared at us, one would have thought that we were as exotic in appearance as the Moors of southern Spain.

'Dartrymen,' grunted a guard as we crossed his path, only to be greeted by frowns of suspicion cast at us by both the young and the old.

As always, the fresh-faced features of the younger maidens caught my eye, yet I quickly curbed any attentions I was tempted to direct at them, given the open ire of Muireann's brother towards me. The bard's kerns stood about the centre of the town, where Diarmaid turned to address us.

'You must be weary after your journey and narrow escape. Let us rest here for the day, then venture on towards Donegal Castle at first light.'

No sooner had he said this than he made towards a sizeable hut to his left, beckoning for Muireann and Lochlain to join him. Other tribesmen invited the rest of us into their homes. I found myself escorted by a herdsman's wife to a smaller hut on the edge of the village, where I gratefully lay upon a damp bed of grass inside. The strongbox was wrapped in my mantle and placed beneath my head as a pillow, and I ignored the peering eyes of children in the doorway as I soon passed into a dreamless sleep.

It was the sound of a lyre that stirred me, as well as the sound of snatched whispers and the patter of feet. My eyes were met by the faint daylight that preceded dusk, and I turned to find an old man sitting cross-legged in the corner. He greeted me with a kindly smile. His hair was worn in the manner of all kerns so that his eyes were barely visible beneath his white fringe, and his wooden instrument was clenched between his thighs and caught in the crook of his handless right arm.

'Good evening, stranger,' he observed, as the fingers of his left hand gently plucked again at the harp strings. 'Did I waken you?'

'Perhaps,' I croaked. I used my elbow to jerk myself upright while wiping the sleep from my eyes.

'You are no Dartryman,' he observed upon hearing my accent. 'Are you one of the Spanish castaways?'

'What is happening outside?' I asked, hearing the fevered voices of children that ran past our hut. 'Are we in danger?'

The old man chuckled.

'There is no danger, Spaniard. The lord Mac an Bhaird prepares to regale us with one of his recitals. It is a recent composition about the Battle of the Swilly, which tells of our lord O'Donnell's famous victory against Shane the Proud.'

'Oh,' I replied with some disinterest, for I had tired of bardic poems about the Irish warring among themselves. 'Will you also perform?'

'No, Spaniard,' chuckled the tribesman again, having been obviously flattered by my question. 'I am but an aged rhymer who only picked up the harp after I lost my good hand in a fight. I have myself written a poem on the famous fight. Would you like to hear it?'

The man was obviously keen for company, and his voice turned hopeful as he uttered his last words.

'Maybe tomorrow,' was my heartless reply as I fumbled for the strongbox and put the leather strap over my head.

Not a word was uttered from the maimed rhymer, and I soon abandoned his company for the outdoors. As my head passed through the hut's doorway, the smell of cooking meat reached my nostrils. It drew a grumble from my stomach as I made my way towards the great cooking fire at the centre of the huts.

The evening darkness had already claimed the dim outline of the hillsides, so that the shadowy figures of men were only visible through the light which was cast by the flames between them. Great cuttings of meat sizzled in the great hides erected over the fire, which was surrounded by hands and buttocks held out to it in the growing chill of night. As I drew nearer I was struck by the beauty of Muireann, who sat alongside the *tuath's* leader and his closest hearth-men.

When the sizzling flesh was taken off the fire and shared, a growing silence fell amongst the feasting tribesmen, and the figure of Diarmaid stood above his sister. His chest was swollen like that of a proud rooster, but his face was gaunt and severe as he cast his eyes across his audience. Only the crackle of flames was heard when the bard's lips were parted.

'You shall now hear tell of the valiant victory of our lord's forebears – victory both cunning and glorious, which rescued Tír Chonaill from a vicious, skulking foe.'

His account ensued as he told of Shane O'Neill's invasion of Tír Chonaill with two thousand men, a force that was subsequently destroyed by the O'Donnell with the help of four hundred of his MacSweeney gallowglasses. The poem was recited with calm and precision, with inflections of the voice at the right moments to draw the odd gasp from the assembled listeners. All throughout I sat behind the feasting tribesmen, waiting like a hound for the odd scrap of meat to be shared with me.

When at last a piece of half-cooked flesh did reach me, I sank my teeth into it while watching the handsome face of the ollave, staring in admiration at her brother. When at last Diarmaid's recital was ended, great cheers were heard about the fire. Cries were heard demanding more of the bard's verse, which prompted the *tuath's* leader to quickly rise to his feet.

'My thanks, Lord Mac an Bhaird, for reciting your most accomplished composition to us. You are owed a great many beeves for so great an honour, yet I fear we cannot repay you for more of your delivery.'

'The hospitality of your people has earned it,' replied Diarmaid in his deep voice, 'and your kindness deserves yet another recital, which I shall gladly deliver.'

At his words a fevered anticipation seized the tribesmen. Their many mutterings of excitement died away when the bard raised a hand for silence. He proceeded to recount the events of the great battle. Thereafter the cheering at the end of his poem was even greater than before, so that the bard betrayed a smile as he helped himself to a cup of mead which was held out to him.

The appreciation of the gathering had left him in good cheer, so that he shared another two more compositions to the natives' delight, after which he declared his happiness at the presence of his sister and nephew. At the end of his second poem more meat was cooked on the fire, and more drink was served by the herdsmen until they made their way back to their huts. As I slowly stood to return to my hosts, Diarmaid called out to me.

'Hail, Spaniard! Why do you retire to bed so early? Have you not already slumbered for most of the day?'

His voice possessed a mocking tone, so that I was on my guard as I advanced towards him and his company. My approach was not greeted by a single smile or nod of acknowledgement, with each of the Jesuit, ollave and bondsman regarding me sombrely. Lochlain appeared indifferent to my approach while the members of the *tuath* still regarded me as a foreign, suspicious subject.

'We must talk alone,' said Diarmaid as I stood before him. Everyone except his sister quickly stood up and shuffled off towards their huts for the night.

'Be seated, Spaniard,' said Muireann's brother, gesturing to a log cast along the flames to his right.

I took up his invitation so as not to incur further ire, then took in the hard stares of the Mac an Bhaird siblings, who appeared to bear little love for me.

'I hear that you bear a precious quarry,' said Diarmaid at last. 'Does it weigh heavily on you?'

'Ah yes,' I replied, fumbling for the iron box which rested upon my belly, since I assumed that he wanted to see the ring.

'What are you doing?' he asked suddenly. 'I do not wish to see the object of your greed.'

'I thought you wanted –' I stuttered, then let go of the casket as the bard regarded me in disgust.

'You did not answer my question.'

'Which question?' I asked nervously, fearing that he might lose his temper with me at any moment.

'Your quarry,' said Muireann as her eyes bore into me. 'Does it weigh heavily on you?'

'It always has,' was my reply.

'Has it?' said Diarmaid. 'Did it weigh heavily on you when you hid it away for over a year like a thief?'

The accusation left me feeling on edge.

'Yes,' I replied at last, breathing slowly to steady my nerves. 'It did weigh heavily then too.'

'Then why did you not share your burden?' asked Muireann. 'You had many allies about you.'

'Is this a trial?' I asked, serving her with an accusing stare of my own and hoping it would remind her of the false accusation I had borne on her account in the past.

'A trial?' scoffed Diarmaid, his mocking tone again replacing his aggressive one. 'Why, it is but a discussion among close allies! For is that not what we are, Spaniard?'

'I suppose we are,' I reluctantly conceded, looking away.

'Of course we are!' declared the bard with exaggerated cheer, then gestured to his horseboy who stood in the shadows. 'Let us drink to our close alliance!'

'I am not drinking anything,' declared Muireann, 'and it is too late for you to drink too.'

'Can the Spaniard not drink?' replied Diarmaid with a look of bewilderment that seemed somewhat affected. 'Why, you will gladly drink to our health, Spaniard, will you not?'

'That I gladly will,' I replied, thinking to take him up at his own game, 'and I would eat plenty to your health, too, for I am still hungry.'

'Why, you have only to ask, Spaniard!' declared Muireann's brother heartily, clapping his hands together. 'Indeed there is nothing we would not endure for our close alliance! Would meat please you, sire?'

To spite his mocking salutation I nodded my approval, and in moments his servant had me served with a wooden plate heaped with braised cowflesh and a mazer filled to the brim with wine. I wolfed down all the food within moments, then half-mockingly raised my cup to the bard and his sister before draining it.

'Truly,' I said, barely stifling a burp, 'you are indeed most delightful hosts.'

Diarmaid bristled hatefully, then slowly nodded with a wry smile on his face.

'Eat up, Spaniard; eat up. You will need all your strength for the journey that lies ahead.'

The ominous words were not lost upon me, and I remained silent as I swallowed the remaining meat, then washed it down with what was left of the wine. My manners were forgotten as I wiped my mouth upon my sleeve, then slid off the log onto the ground and stretched my legs out, my arms folded comfortably upon my chest. Suddenly it seemed like I was overcome by the most mellow feeling in the world, and my whole body seemed to loosen as I struggled to keep my eyes open.

'You will be glad to leave us behind, Spaniard,' said Diarmaid, who was still watching me like a wolf in the night.

'Why do you say that?' I replied.

'You can have all you want once you get back to Spain.'

'That's true –' I started, then said, 'Why do you say that?'

'Why? With *your* ring,' exclaimed the bard, 'you can have *anything* you want and more.'

'It is not my ring,' I replied. 'I am but the bearer of someone else's property.'

'Such an honourable man, Spaniard,' crooned Muireann's brother, his voice seeming ever more distant, his hawkish profile seemingly blurring into the darkness. 'If only we Irish beggars showed such loyalty to one another.'

'Indeed,' I slurred, then started as I almost fell asleep. 'That is, you do.'

'I do not want to hear this,' snapped Muireann. She got to her feet and made off towards her hut. 'Good night, brother.'

I felt a jolt of sorrow at her departure, and I shifted my head in her direction as she stamped off past me, my hand slightly raised towards her.

'Muireann . . .'

'Miss my sister already, Spaniard?'

My head felt even lighter as I tried to face Diarmaid, who appeared like a beige blur against the glow of the embers. It took a great effort to part my jaws and reply to him, and what words were uttered I hardly knew. He peppered me with a few more questions that I forgot the moment they were uttered. Any sense of trepidation I had before the bard seemed to melt away from me together with my consciousness.

I was nudged awake the following morning, getting up with a start as I found myself back in the straw hut. For a few moments I wondered if the exchange with Diarmaid and Muireann had been all a dream, and I looked up to find the herdsman's wife kneeling alongside me.

'You must get up, Spaniard,' she said. 'They are waiting for you outside.'

I slowly rose to my knees, then surprised my host by fumbling through the mantle which had been wrapped up beneath my head.

'The casket! Where is it?' I snapped at her, then breathed a sigh of relief as my hand fell upon it. I whisked the box out of the blanket and shook it hard; the rattle within it filled me with relief. I was next aware of a soreness in my head, which left me to wonder if I had drunk as much as I felt I had or whether the discussion with Diarmaid had all been a dream.

'The one-handed rhymer,' I said suddenly. 'He was here last night, was he not?'

'Yes, Spaniard,' replied the young woman. 'He is my father. He was wounded in a battle with the O'Neill's gallowglasses.'

'Ah,' I replied, relieved that I had not yet lost my wits. 'Then I must hasten off.'

I quickly snatched up both my satchel and scabbard, and I bounded out of the hut towards the centre of the camp. Upon reaching it I noticed the mounted figure of Diarmaid, whose proud profile was set against the hills to our right. Muireann and O'Ronayne clambered atop two of the spare hobbies in the party of the bard, whose voice reached me just as I reached Nial's side.

'Here is our worthy ringbearer, he who drinks less wine than a woman before passing out.'

His kerns snickered and giggled at his remark, although I was too shocked to respond, though I also wondered how I had passed out so quickly from so little drink. I pressed the back of my aching head as the bard bade farewell to the leader of the *tuath*, who stood before the band of villagers who had gathered to see us off.

'Until our next meeting, most worthy Conchabar.'

'It shall be our honour to host you again, Lord Mac an Bhaird.'

A wry smile appeared on the face of Muireann's brother. He kicked his horse forward at a gentle trot, and the rest of us followed him closely. A blast of icy wind from over the grasslands ahead crinkled our faces, and I reached out for the mantle on my shoulders and furled it in front of my face to ward off the chill.

We clenched our jaws against the assault of the frosty gale, which rippled the grass about us as we trudged on. Our band veered leftwards from the hills to our right as we kept to a northeasterly direction. The air only grew colder as we travelled on, and before long our mantles were wrapped about our faces until only our eyes were showing. Soon enough, white flakes floated down and landed upon us from the heavens.

'The cursed snow is finally with us,' grunted one of the kerns behind me, yet our step never wavered as we pushed on through thick grassland and heavy forest, in which we were often forced to walk in single file with little view afforded to us of our surrounds. After almost two hours of marching, our verdant surrounds had been powdered white, so that it soon became harder to see what lay beneath our feet. The odd traveller among us cursed aloud whenever he scuffed his toes against an unseen branch. At last, we came to a fork in our path, and Diarmaid called a halt and turned back towards us.

'This is where our shared journey ends, Spaniard. Were it up to me I would slit your throat and abandon you by the roadside, yet our pledge to your master will be upheld in full. I bid you farewell and a safe journey ahead despite your poor manners towards those who have sheltered and protected you. The way ahead is fraught with greater peril with each mile covered.'

Muireann did not turn her head when he spoke, yet O'Ronayne's eyes narrowed at the words of the bard.

'You must make for Derry in all haste,' added the Jesuit, 'for the enemy will be abroad and searching for you. Word of your departure will have already reached Sligo from spies in Dartry and Breifne, which is not to mention the slayings at the ford.'

As they spoke, I shifted awkwardly from one leg to the other, fearing that I was to be abandoned to attempt the remainder of my journey alone. Lochlain's stare seemed sad as he observed me from alongside his mother's horse, and he nodded in a final gesture of farewell after his uncle had addressed me a last time.

'I doubt you shall leave Ireland alive, Spaniard, yet we were never as relieved at the loss of a great burden as we are now. At last, we are freed from your endless days of lies and deceit, and can only hope that our future allies will be less false than you.'

My awkwardness turned to rage as he gave me his back and made off at a canter, his guests and retainers making off after him towards the west. I resisted the urge to hurl insults after the bard as his party were finally lost behind the snow-clad trees to my left. My anger was soon replaced by the pain of Muireann's departure, by her never once turning to bid me farewell. It was some time before I finally regained enough calm to realise that the bondsman and his five kerns had tarried with a single horse, as well as a horseboy from Diarmaid's party, who had been left behind to guide us.

'Are you to accompany me to Derry?' I asked hopefully.

'Let us move on,' said Nial without betraying a whit of sentiment as we made off through the trees to our right.

'Where are we bound?' I asked.

'Na Cruacha Gorma,' replied the bondsman dispassionately, 'and we should not linger here much longer.'

We continued on foot towards the dim outline of peaks that rose ahead of us. Two of the kerns scouted ahead as we ventured on – within a musket shot's distance, as we were all watchful for the first signs of peril. The next two hours passed without incident as we made our way through our fast-whitening surrounds. Our feet crunched the snow-clad ground as we drew nearer to the mighty range of Cruacha Gorma.

'Almost there,' said Fergus, his voice slightly muffled behind his mantle. His face was florid after nearly a full day's march, and his eyes were watery from the frosty blasts.

'Where to from here, boy?' cried Nial to the guide that walked ahead of us.

'The gap!'

'But is it safe?' asked Fergus with a look of alarm.

The question was no sooner asked than our scouts were seen hurrying back towards us, keeping low to the ground until they reached us. Nial waited for them to regain their breath as they panted and wheezed from their exertions. At last one of them could speak half coherently.

'Choked with Sassanas,' he gasped.

'Dozens of them scattered throughout the pass,' the other added.

Nial sighed aloud as he clenched both his sword pommels in frustration.

'Ill tidings indeed, and so close to the end. Now what do we do?'

'There are other passes, master,' replied Diarmaid's horse-boy.

'And what of that?' scoffed Fergus angrily, rubbing his palms against his knees. 'You can be sure that they will also be watched! We must abandon this fool's errand and make for Donegal Castle!'

'We have sworn an oath to the chieftains,' replied Nial quietly.

'To hell with their oath!' roared the kern. 'Why risk our lives for one who has secretly betrayed us?'

'Betrayed you?' I fumed as Nial raised his arms to us to keep calm. He nodded for Fergus to follow him.

'Walk with me, Fergus Corcán,' he said. The broad-chested warrior wandered off after the bondsman, and we awaited their return.

As we sat in silence and puffed up large clouds of mist, I could not help but notice the distant figures of Nial and Fergus from half a musket shot's distance, arguing in hushed tones as they wildly gestured at each other. At times their voices were unwittingly raised and then lowered quickly again, so that nothing could be gleaned from the odd snatch of conversation which reached.

As the icy air entered my nostrils, I marvelled at the sight of the great mountain range which loomed ahead of us, and I wondered if I would ever see the other side of it. The other men ignored me as I stretched my legs out, thankful for the unexpected moment of rest and ignoring the feeling which had gnawed at me ever since we had left Dartry. Although the pain in my head had subsided since the morning, I could not help feeling that it was not slumber alone which had caused me to pass out during my conversation with Diarmaid. This had also led me to suspect that I might form part of some larger game devised by the chieftains.

'Get up,' called Fergus as he walked back towards us behind Nial. The bondsman did not cast us a second glance as we slowly returned to our feet.

'Where are we bound?' asked one of the kerns.

'Croaghgorm,' said Nial as he walked past us towards the mountain range ahead, the horseboy making off after him.

'What?' protested one of the kerns. 'Are we to scale the mountains in this weather? Did you not say that –'

'You heard him!' snapped Fergus as he seized the kern by the shoulder and shoved him ahead of us. 'Get ahead of us and resume your scouting! And take Domhnall with you!'

With low grumbling the man did as he was told, resuming his scouting duties with the other kern and venturing ahead while we made for the growing peaks, our breasts burning as a snow swirl slowly grew. It was still going strong when we reached the western bank of the great body of water, which my companions called the 'lake of the fish'. We kept to the edge of the bank until we spotted a keep surrounded by a town to our left.

Everyone appeared to ignore it as we ventured on along the frost-hardened mud upon the banks of the lake. We found ourselves on a downhill track sheltered by trees, and we trudged along the path until yet another stronghold was spotted to our left. We were pelted by the elements as we approached the growing heights, and the forest about us grew denser. I had quickened my pace to ensure that I did not get stranded when a small exchange of words was heard ahead of us.

'The boy says the Fianna used to hunt in these paths,' whispered one of the kerns to Fergus, who issued a low snort.

'Let us hope that the Sassanas do not do the same.'

A nervous silence resumed at the kern's utterance, yet our path took us along the shore of the majestic lake which stole my breath away. It was speckled with water lilies and islands, and I observed the gentle hills which flanked its rightward bank. We ploughed on through the bulrushes and reeds, clenching our teeth whenever we waded through icy rivulets that flowed into it from the island. Lichens greeted us on the faces of grey rocks as we crossed through a meadow. We then entered the cover of a great wood full of many of the trees I had found common to Ireland.

The view of the lake was soon behind us as we left the cover of forest and struck out to a large mountain range ahead of us. Our step was swifter as we closed in on our end, though there was still not a soul seen in our brown and white surrounds. We soon worked our way up the foot of a steep rise, labouring up it until we came to a sheer ledge and a sharp decline that presented a steep path to the gorge below.

'The heights of Na Cruacha Gorma,' whispered a kern in wonder as he stared at the belt of northern rises which spread across the horizon before us. He then gestured ahead at what he called the cliffs of Lough Belshade.

I stared in wonder at all the valleys and mountains about me, wondering how I would have ever made it through them without the guidance of the natives. Fergus drew a length of sheep gut from his pack and tied an end of it about his waist before thrusting the length of it along the length of the rocky descent before us.

'You first, Spaniard,' he called to me, shaking the cord which ran down the hillside.

I quickly seized it and thrust myself over the edge. With heavy breaths I slowly clambered down the rope; the gut cord burned my icy palms until my feet met the ground. As I released the rope I took a few clumsy steps away from it, seeking not to slip upon the heather while I waited for the next Dartryman to slide down after me. After a few moments my head was raised towards the precipice, where I saw Nial and the four kerns staring back at me solemnly.

'What is the matter?' I asked. In response, Fergus bent over and swiftly pulled the end of the rope away from me.

'What are you doing?' I called out to them, overcome by disbelief.

'We have held to our oath, Spaniard,' declared the bondsman, his gaze never wavering as he stared down at me. 'We have brought you to the borders of Donegal.'

So saying, he turned away with the rest of our party as the faces vanished one by one behind the ridge from which I had climbed down.

'And what of Derry?' I called out, suddenly overcome by fear as I found myself about to be abandoned in the unfamiliar wilds. 'What of the ring?'

The face of Fergus briefly reappeared as he scowled at me from on high, snarling his last address with gusto.

'Take your damn ring and shove it where the sun does not shine, Iscariot! You have done well to hold on to it alone for over a year. Now you would do well to make it home alone too!'

He spat at me just before his face vanished, so that I found myself rooted to the ground in disbelief, wondering if I should attempt to scramble back up after them or shout until they had no choice but to return for me. In the end I did neither. The growing realisation that I had got off lightly flooded through me, and I turned to face the gorge which lay ahead of me as an icy gale screamed through the blue stacks.

# LIV

## BANAGH TO CROAGHGORM MOUNTAINS, COUNTRY DONEGAL

*17 – 18 November 1589*

The wind rustled through my hair, and the rain eventually turned into a steady downfall of hail, which peppered my shoulders as my mantle fluttered about my head. I was filled with unease at the sight of the sheer, mountainous surrounds, which rose about me and seemed to hem me in like the walls of a giant, stone prison.

Yet another shriek of the wind was heard, and the reality of my predicament slowly sank in, like a cold, blunt blade through my breast. As I turned away from the harsh bluff, the casket containing the ring bobbed against my thigh, and I was at once reminded of the precious trinket. A deep irritation irked me at the thought of the ring, which had caused my rift with Manglana and his men.

'To think that I don't even have a key to this cursed box,' I whispered to myself, as I slowly lifted it towards my face, then shook it from side to side and heard the ring rattling within.

The sound provided me with relief as well as revulsion, and in a blind rage I fell to my knees and smashed the casket hard upon the ground, desperate to catch a glimpse of the prize I had endured so much to keep hold of, which was denied to me by the corrugated receptacle in which it was held.

'Damn fools,' I growled. 'Damn barefoot, flea-ridden fools to abandon such a priceless trinket so cheaply! And then to wonder why they fail in their struggle!'

The box was smashed again and again upon the cold granite beneath me, until I dropped it, my hands falling helplessly to my sides. With a sigh I stared up at the dark heights that surrounded me, obscured by a flurry of snow which had started to fall.

'They left me here to die,' I whispered in disbelief, 'washed their hands of me like Pilate.'

I had been abandoned without guide or map, left to make my way through an unknown mountain range in the worst of weather. This daunting prospect was only compounded by the chance of crossing paths with hostile kerns or troopers, and it was a scant comfort which was derived from the wintry climate, which would reduce my likelihood of encountering the odd passer-by.

'Curse them,' I rasped as I staggered back onto my feet and slung the strongbox over my shoulder. 'I have endured worse; I will not die.'

My spirits were lifted by the first defiant crunch of the growing snow underfoot as I took a step towards the closest peak. I was resolved to keep to the high places wherever possible, to seek to best avoid hostile eyes and missiles. My sudden resolve was somewhat dampened by the snow, which masked any rocks and hags, and by my tight-fitting brogues, whose soles caused me to stumble with each step and provided no protection from the wet.

It was a terrain to be expected of a mountain region, and the snow covered any tracks which may have existed as I made towards the distant cliff face, which one of the kerns had referred to as Lough Belshade. With each step I fought to banish the farcical hopelessness of my situation from my mind, reminding myself of the harsh weather I had endured on many a Flemish campaign when I had also often gone hungry while on the march.

At the memory of food my stomach groaned slightly, but I ignored the twinge and scaled the uneven upward track. My progress grew swifter as the ground underfoot turned rockier, yet it was still clad with enough heather to cause me the odd tumble, which left me falling onto all fours and doubly frustrated. Amid the clouds of mist caused by my heavy breaths and swearing, the far-off cliff face drew ever closer until I found myself within sight of a cluster of lakelets.

When I reached the edge of the closest one, I briefly paused to refill my skin, ever watchful for any dangers that might be lurking close by. I returned to the uneven path and made towards the larger basin of water which next came into view. I made out the spoor and fur, which filled me with disquiet, since they belonged to wolves which were often made their den alongside bodies of water. The sight brought an added spring to my step, and I swiftly made my way up the rightward rise, which ran along the banks of the lake. I paused at the top to take in the crude diamond outline of the dark blue water below, as well as the cliff faces that guarded its western banks.

I shivered in the freezing bluster that greeted my ascent, then made my way along the edge of a cliff, often slipping upon the hard granite beneath my feet. Upon scaling the precipice, I almost fell over the edge as I stumbled once more, grasping the soaked heather as one of my shoes remained stuck in the thickening snow.

As I reached over to pull out the brogue, the loud howl of a cur was heard from beneath the water below me. The hair rose upon the back of my neck. After the day's journey, a night without slumber seemed almost unimaginable, yet as the wind froze my face, I was uncertain where I would spend the night. Tiered ledges along the cliff face came into view further along from the place where I lay.

'No choice,' I whispered as the howls resumed and the darkness grew.

I ran along the natural buttress, bending low over the ground. My arms wildly flailed against the air as I tried to keep my balance. The peak of the rise slightly dipped as I reached the crags, and I stood above them staring down, trying to pick one which was wide enough for me to shelter in. I chose one and slowly made my way down along the soaked heather upon the ledges which rose out below me, taking care not to slip down the cliff face.

The peril of the errand grew as my hair fluttered about my face, obstructing my vision as my hands clung desperately to the ledges behind me. I made my way down towards the chosen crag, twice hanging just above a ledge which was almost five yards below me before letting go. When at last I could not climb down any further, I hovered silently above the ledge which jutted out a fair few feet below me, and which was fast being darkened by the onset of night.

'No choice,' I repeated to myself.

All hesitation was abandoned as I whipped my mantle off my back and pinned it beneath my knee. My hands gripped the sides of my shirt, which I hauled off as I shivered wildly in the freezing cold. I quickly removed my trousers as my hands started to shake and teeth to chatter as another gust blew over me. I swiftly bound the ends of the garments together, and a hoop was created at the end of the makeshift cord by looping the end of it round and knotting it tightly to the main part of the line.

I placed this newly created hoop about the narrowed edge of the crag which bore me, and I took in a deep breath and then swung about with my eyes closed, praying that my weight would be borne by the knotted garments. For a few moments I swung slowly from side to side against the precipice, naked as a newborn and shivering wildly in the bitter gales. All throughout, I felt like the vile wind was taking bigger bites out of my back and buttocks than the largest, most famished wolf could ever have managed.

My feet slipped clumsily against the icy cliff wall as I slowly released my grip and slid down the cord. My arms and hands screamed with exertion, my gritted teeth feeling like they might shatter. I somehow found it within myself to hold on with the ring's casket, the rifle and the bandolier flapping about my shoulders, and I at last came to the end of the cord made out of garments.

'Holy host of the Madonna,' I cursed beneath my breath, for my feet still dangled helplessly in thin air. For a moment I felt like cursing God for having abandoned me in such a helpless state along the side of a cliff so far from home.

Another wolf howl above me was the only prompt I needed to haul wildly at the makeshift strand of garments which I held, raising myself against it again and again, then letting myself fall with a jolt in the hope of undoing the knot I had tied in the clothing.

When at last the cold was unbearable, I swiftly drew my knife and shoved it between my teeth before climbing up the length of my body and hacking at the line I had devised. The edge of the blade was at least halfway through the mantle's thick cloth when at last the fabric of the loop in the shirt was rent. I tumbled down into the black, releasing a scream of fright before I fell in a heap against the heather underfoot, the wind knocked out of me.

It took me a few moments to regain my senses as I turned over towards the rock wall. I shivered wildly, barely thankful that I had reached the forbidden ledge, which was beyond the reach of any beast known to Ireland. In the dark my trembling fingers reached for the knots binding the clothing and swiftly undid them. I swiftly donned my shirt and trousers before I furled the torn blanket about me and rolled against the cliff edge, still shivering madly and caring not where my rifle and bandolier had landed.

To my great fortune the crag where I lay was shielded by other crags and natural buttresses which lay further ahead. I was thus shielded from the icy blasts, so that it was not long before the harshest edge of the cold was gone and I slowly warmed up again. I breathed as heavily as I could within my mantle, and my hands sprouted from within it long enough for me to warm my ears with their palms.

Meanwhile I viciously rubbed my stockinged feet against one another until it felt as if the flesh beneath them might come away. The resulting burning sensation left me feeling relieved that I had done what I could to ward off the dreaded frostbite which had often claimed the extremities of Dartrymen's limbs. As the howl of the wind and wolves grew across the lake, the snow thickened, and within two hours it had me covered from head to toe. I curled my body into a lifeless ball beneath it and pressed myself tightly against the dank cliff wall.

The glowing cocoon of warmth secured a slumber which freed me from any further angst or preoccupation. My sleep was largely dreamless, though I stirred twice due to the screeching gales. I could also hear the distant howl of wolves in the heights. Each time I passed out once more from sheer exhaustion despite the screech and cacophony of my surrounds.

The next day I awoke with a start, my lips and nostrils raw from the cold and my feet still itchy after a fitful night spent tossing and turning. I found myself short of breath as I beat the snow above me with my fists. As it came away, I shoved my head through it to loud gasps of breath. I found myself still wedged against the cliff face, the snowfall having finally abated. An iron-grey sky was choked with cloud overhead, and it was hard to pick out the sun and tell the time of day.

'A morning reached without much mishap,' I whispered to myself in disbelief.

It was then that I noticed the sharp pain in my side, which had me twisting about in discomfort, suddenly fearful that I had been wounded in my sleep. Yet my fears abated when my right hand pulled the iron casket away from my sore ribs. I grabbed it in both hands and held it above my face, shaking it slowly from side to side and listening to the clatter of the trinket within it.

A scrape and scrabble were next heard behind me, leaving me to swiftly turn around in fright as I clutched the box to my chest. My eyes met the yellowed stare of a wild goat which stood but a few feet away on the ledge closest to me, observing me with a dull stare. I let out a huge sigh of relief. The creature twisted its head to the right but once as I thought to reach for my knife. Then, almost as if reading my thoughts, it set off down the terraces of the cliff side towards the reddish rock below, with a litheness and haste which stirred a deep envy within me.

'Whoreson,' I whispered to myself as I observed its shrinking black-and-white form reaching the banks of the lake below.

The goat paused, then set off towards the hills that lay to the south. It was then that my eyes came to rest upon the tiny form of a man making his way up the same slopes. My stomach twinged at the memory of the riders we had seen the previous day, and the sight of other small figures led me to a grim realisation.

'Holy host of the Madonna,' I whispered to myself as I lay back upon the ground and crept slowly towards the edge of the precipice beside me. 'At least six more of the bastards.'

All thoughts of sorrow and abandonment were banished as I quickly searched for the items I had carried into the mountains. I quickly gathered my knife from against the wall, returned the ill-fitting brogues to my feet and slung the musket, bandolier and my pack back over my shoulders. With a small leap I reached the closest grassy ledge which ran above the crags further on below, resolved to put as much distance between myself and my pursuers.

Almost an hour passed as I avoided the sharp drops along the remainder of the descent. I kept to the gentler slopes with a constant fear that I might come to one sheer cliff face running across the base of the mountain which might bar my descent to the lakeside. I often lost my footing and was left to desperately cling to the heather as I slipped dangerously close towards the edge of a precipice.

It was a great relief when I finally reached the banks of the sky-blue lake, though this relief was replaced by chilling disbelief when the sight of a ladle came into view, lying directly beneath the ledges where I had spent the night. I raced towards it and picked it up, twisting and turning it in my hands. I was shocked to realise that it belonged to me. In an instant I dropped to my knee and removed my other belongings from my back, opening my pack to find out what else had fallen out of it.

I found the balls and match cord within it, as well as the pieces of dried cowflesh which had been stowed away together with the other implements needed to clean the musket. My slight relief at the discovery of these items was replaced by frustration as I sought in vain to find the tinderbox. It soon became apparent that it had fallen out of the bag during my fall from my makeshift rope the previous night.

I made a brief attempt to find it, running back and forth along the edge of the lake, looking all over the sides of the mountain until the inevitable thought struck me that the tinderbox must have ended up in the dark water. With a deep sigh at the thought of its loss, I marched off in the direction of the slopes ahead, resolved to climb away from the lowland where I might be picked out by my trackers.

Eventually the sharp rocks overhead disappeared, replaced by a gentler incline in the shadow of the last high crag which belonged to the sharper slopes. My climb up these slopes soon revealed a gully which led directly to the other heights surrounding the lake. I was grateful for this discovery as I swiftly made my way up it, all the while casting fearful glances to my left for signs of the enemy. This concern was justified when I reached the rocky heights of the next mountaintop, which afforded me a view of the sparkling lake behind me but also of the outline of tents along a southern rise where the enemy had spent the night.

The sight filled me with renewed hope as I was struck by a sudden realisation that I had stirred early enough to steal a march on my pursuers. It was therefore with a degree of optimism that I resumed the difficult trek which lay ahead, offering a short prayer to whatever fates had conspired to deliver me as I crossed a cairn atop a mountainside. I passed huge boulders and rocks with my eyes constantly examining the ground ahead of me, primed to identify a track which would lead to the heights ahead.

The wind produced a strident howl once more, and my clothes flapped about me as I covered the remaining distance towards the next mountaintop. I had to tackle numerous crevices and outcrops as the slope I climbed grew ever steeper, leaving me to clutch at grass to haul myself upwards, often throwing glances over my shoulder to check for signs of the enemy.

When I had finally scaled the fiendish rise, I fell sideways across the ground and caught my breath for a few moments. I turned onto my hands and knees to find myself directly over-looking the gentle slopes of a valley with a lake at its base and a large wood upon its northern bank. The sight of the trees in the middle of the sparse, white valley sparked memories of safer days spent hunting game in Dartry. I bitterly recalled how I had once ridden alongside its deceased queen and her retainers while Muireann led the chase.

'And now you are gone,' I said to myself and then sighed aloud, imagining the ollave seated in front of a great fire in Donegal Castle, her hand rested upon her son's shoulder as Diarmaid's voice carried through the great hall of his lord.

I could also imagine the roseate features of O'Ronayne, standing at her other shoulder, and a slight smile played upon my broken lips when I thought of the great tankard he doubt-less held in one hand. Nial would no doubt be standing but a few feet away from them, with his usual grin noted by all. I felt a twinge of loss as the ivory features of the ollave returned to mind. I hoped that she had traded a swift stare with the bondsman and that she had been at least a bit troubled by my being left to perish in the mountains.

Then the gales about me picked up again, and I banished the thoughts of the Dartrymen to focus instead on the still heights about me and the grey heavens above. Everything seemed as taut as bending glass about to shatter, as deceptively still as the calm before the storm. A slight rattle broke the si-lence as I rose to my feet, and I grabbed the casket despondently in one hand, shaking it from side to side as the ring bounced within it.

'You fool, Santiago,' I whispered with a low snort of disgust. 'They would not spare a thought for you, you profiteering, lying whoreson. They would have bled and died for you, yet you wounded them more deeply than the hardest spear thrust.'

I hurled the casket away from my face so that it dangled helplessly from my shoulder, then restrained a tear as I took a step forward, still berating myself.

'You deserve to die, you blinded ass. And yet now you must seek to finish whatever it was you started.'

A large cloud of mist grew before my face as I released a deep breath, then walked towards the heights which lay ahead. After my efforts to climb the last ascent, it was with great relief that the relatively easy walk towards the next summit was accomplished. As I strode along, I quietly admired the wild, rugged scenery below and the lakes to my left.

At least another mile's distance was covered before the next rise was reached, where I paused to take stock of the great plains and valleys below me. The mountaintops around me appeared as puny hills when compared to the soaring vantage to which I had ascended, leaving me to wonder whether the highest rise of all had been scaled and whether the heights about me stretched far beyond my line of sight like some white ocean spume.

With a sigh I hurled my mantle across my face and continued onwards. Despite the keen winds it was almost mid-morning as I made my way down the sharp descent. I tackled another rise on all fours, due to the steepness of the grassy hill, with more rocks obstructing my path. Together with the scree, it made the lower rise an even greater challenge than the towering mountain from which I had just descended. After regaining my breath I pushed on yet again, moving downhill and then up a gentle rise, which became steadily steeper as I caught sight of small southern lakes below.

These exertions kept my mind from straying into self-pity and fear, and all thoughts of the Dartrymen were banished as my legs burned from the toil of the hard journey. At midday, when I reached the wide summit of the next hill, having traversed its three tops and skirted its small lakes, I sat down along its edge and helped myself to the dried beef within my pack.

As I gnawed at the rock-hard food, the sight of a reddish grouse pecking the grass came into view. I instantly reached for my musket, only to remember that I had no slow match with which to fire a ball. The thought never left me as I hastened down the hillside towards the brown moorland below. I decided that shooting grouse was best avoided, though, since it might alert my pursuers to my whereabouts.

The loss of the tinderbox had me despairing over how to start a fire, but an idea struck me as soon as the foot of the hill was reached. Between me and the next rise were a large number of peat hags. I thought that a secret fire might be chanced among them, and I had scoured the ground for a sizeable rock which could be carried in one hand. After I gathered it, as well as two handfuls of turf and peat, I sought the cover of one of the larger hags.

My kindling and fuel were squashed upon a base of twigs, which protected them from the wet ground. Then a few strips of cloth were cut from the collar of my shirt, which was the only dry material to be had for miles. The pieces of vestment were laid gently over the turf and peat, with some gunpowder sprinkled atop them to aid in the burning. I held the rock just above the cloth, and I struck with my *skene* dagger, producing a sharp scrape against the stone.

After a half-dozen attempts, the first shower of sparks flew onto the kindling; it was another three to four strikes until a low sizzle was heard and a tiny tendril of smoke was emitted. The slightest glow caused me to swoop down and blow lightly upon it until the bluish flicker grew into an orange-yellow flame. As the cloth burned, the heat from the fire overcame the dampness about it so that, before I knew it, a small fire was going which I gently fed with twigs and bits of peat.

I held my palms about it and warmed them for the first time in days. I placed my numb toes against the warmth while my back rested against the damp side of the hag. Something close to a trance overcame me as my feet were freed from cold, leaving me to feel almost completely restored as my shoulders sagged back and my head met the ground amid deep gasps of relief. I must have lain there for close on a half hour until the heat was reduced and I got up to fetch more twigs and branches to put upon it.

As the fire grew, I recalled why I had lit it in the first place, and I quickly snatched up the match cord from the gun to light one end of it. When this was done, I gently blew upon it while loading the musket, then tightly wedged it back into the lock. It was with great reluctance that I proceeded to shove snow upon the fire, since I no longer wished to risk drawing the enemy's attention.

Once the last few tendrils of smoke had petered out, there was nothing left of the flames except a small mound of soggy mud. I returned to my feet and made for the next hill which lay ahead of me. As I walked on I kept low to the ground, ever mindful of the great danger which was presented by the wild and by natives who might be journeying through the hills.

In this way I had covered half the distance towards the next promontory when a muffled voice to my right caused me to throw myself headfirst beneath yet another peat hag, my gun held tightly as I crouched in the mud and held my breath. The voice was soon joined by others as the crunch of heavy boots upon snow alerted me to the presence of more men moving behind me.

'There was smoke, I swear it!' shouted a voice in the Gaelic tongue. 'It came from there!'

Muffled mutterings and grumblings were heard in response to this claim, which belonged to at least a half-dozen men who tramped past me before their leader called a sudden halt.

'Very well then, we must divide ourselves into pairs again and search the vicinity. I will wait here with the boy while you two cover the land between here and the silver hill, and you two until the edge of the lake. Cry out instantly at the first sign of fog or Spaniard.'

As the men trudged off, I cupped my hands about the slow match, hoping to hinder the light tendril of smoke from it long enough that it might not be seen until the searchers had passed. I silently weighed up the advantages and drawbacks of my situation, realising that I had years of skirmishing skills to call upon and that I was caught in a terrain which was wholly unfamiliar to me. The beating of my heart pounded in my ears when one of the troopers spoke up but a few feet away from me, and my arms slightly trembled as the exchange grew louder.

'How precious is this Spanish whoreson that we have to look for him all over these wretched mountains? What with Christmas almost here too! What do we know about this bastard anyway? What does he look like?'

'They say that he is old,' replied the other, 'but also dangerous. A mark of the spider is borne upon his breast; they say the master did it to him.'

I could not stifle a gasp at the man's reference to his master, and the palms of my hands were instantly sweaty as the memory of the Sligo dungeon tore through my head.

*Burke is alive?* I could not help thinking. *How can that be?*

'Is he dangerous?' asked the first trooper.

'I've heard tell that he's a deadly shot.'

'Why, if that is not just splendid tidings,' said the other as he stepped into view half a musket shot away to my left. 'At any time he could blow our heads off while we stand about here like grouse.'

'I doubt he would risk a shot,' replied his portlier companion, casting nervous glances about him, 'and in any event, he is probably already through the mountains and halfway towards Derry.'

I retrained a chuckle at their lofty estimation of the abilities of a lame old Spaniard who was as lost as a pilotless ship without a compass on the high seas.

Indeed, I thought, *I have fainter hopes of survival than a cat hurled into a dogfight.*

'Do we even know whether he was here?' replied the other as they moved on towards the lakeside, having never once noticed my feet's impressions in the mud.

'It is beyond doubt. The agent confirmed it.'

'Ah, him; curse his soul. It'll be a long day then, for he's never wrong.'

As they wandered off, I crept away from the cover of the hag and inched towards another one which lay closer to the next hill. I progressed towards another three hags to get out of the pair's line of sight. I had hardly reached the last hag and slumped across the ground when the exchange of the hapless duo recommenced, and I lay as still as a corpse as they returned to their leader.

'Nowhere to be seen,' grumbled one of them, 'and not even a sign of the fire. Yet you did say that he escaped from Sligo . . .'

'I tell you he is dangerous,' replied another voice, 'not a whoreson to be trifled with. He proved a match for the master if ever anyone did.'

I once more received their reference to Treasach Burke with amazement, thinking of the one-eyed sergeant I thought I had killed in Sligo when I rescued the doomed Riona O'Malley. The thought of how far they had journeyed to avenge him left me feeling somewhat unnerved.

'And we are sure he is the one?' one of them spoke again.

'Yes, he is. The one who sought out the master and left him to burn in the stables. But have no fear, for once the hounds arrive we will pick up his trail again.'

The mention of the dogs further rattled me as the men walked away. As their sound diminished, I dared to slowly raise my head along the top edge of the hag, seeing their shapes drifting off towards the mountain from which I had descended. For a moment I rose to my feet and made to step towards the mountain ahead, but then on a hunch I turned about and closely followed the men.

I kept as low as I could at all times while tracking the troopers. The hapless search performed by the two tosspots had left me hoping that perhaps not all was lost, and that I might yet be able to prevail against the search party. For close to a half hour, I tracked the men's progress at a distance as the pair whose conversation I had overheard fell behind the rest of their party, seemingly ignoring their leader's calls to keep up.

They were almost a musket shot's distance from the rest of their party yet still marching along the edge of the great hills. They were unwittingly paving their way towards the northern heights, which I intended to make for as soon as the Sassanas rounded the next rise. A loud curse was heard ahead of me. One of the two tosspots had stumbled and was holding his ankle as he flopped onto his back.

'What is the matter?' called his companion ahead of him.

'I twisted it,' groaned the portlier one as he rubbed the side of his leg.

I could see fine soldiers' boots of burnished leather on his feet, and I wished that I might exchange them for my own pair of cursed ill-fitting brogues, which had plagued me ever since we had left Rosclogher.

'Do you need help?' called the other soldier as he regarded his companion in annoyance, casting the odd nervous look about him.

'No, do not tarry,' called the other, 'yet you must notify the others.'

'Very well. We'll await you along the lake.'

A nod from the injured soldier was all it took for his annoyed companion to make his way downhill, quickly vanishing from view and leaving the other trooper behind. It was a moment too tempting for me to resist, and I lifted a sizeable stone from the ground while loosening my dagger in its sheath. I slipped the brogues off my bruised feet as I crept over towards the trooper, who was still muttering in annoyance beneath his breath.

'Damned scree.'

When I brought the rock down on his head, there was heard a sound akin to a cracking walnut. He quivered but once until another blow from the stone left him to fall in a heap at my blistered feet. No sooner did he lose consciousness than I set to work hauling the boots off him, followed by his thick socks and heavy jacket. I also removed his gloves and pulled them over my hands, and I plucked a blunted eating knife from his side and wound it through my belt for use as a secret weapon. A flood of relief filled me as I pulled the thick wool over my throbbing feet, followed by the boots, which fitted so snugly that some of the cuts on my feet could no longer be felt.

'Lorcán! Where are you?'

As soon as the cry was heard I was already racing towards the northern heights as fast as my legs would bear me. My new boots allowed me to cover the yards with haste, despite my misgivings at keeping to the low ground where I might encounter hostile tribesmen, or where the enemy might spot me from on high. My path veered east as I ran along the river which rushed ahead of me, and I decided to make my way towards the lake in the valley which I had spotted from the first rise I had climbed.

Upon reaching it I would be able to enter the forest on its northern bank, wherefrom I would be able to reach the next belt of mountains under cover of trees. The cries of rage from my pursuers had long faded away as I kept a steady march in the shadow of the mountains I had previously scaled.

In less than two hours I spotted the edge of the wood. My spirits were lifted and my gun lowered as I hastened towards it. I made sure to keep to the harder ground whenever the dirt underfoot almost reached my ankles. As I reached the first trees, I pushed the boughs aside with a gloved hand and was stepping through them with raised spirits when I heard the sound of a loud bark.

A howl followed thereafter through the trees, far enough ahead to pose no immediate threat, yet far too close for comfort. I exited the wood and made towards the slopes along the eastern bank of the lake, no longer mindful of any bog as I raced towards it. More shouting and barking were soon heard behind me as I reached the edge of the closest mountain, and I was already tearing at the grass with my hands as I hastened to make my way up the steep slope.

In moments I was further up than I had managed in twice the time upon other slopes, my immediate fear acting as the sharpest spur as the sound of my pursuers grew louder behind me. A loud yell was heard to my right, and I cursed, looking over my shoulder to see the party of men I had encountered at the peat hags before turning east. They were already gathered at the base of the mountainside which I was busy climbing, aiming their muskets at me.

'Bastards,' I cursed again. Sparks flew near my face as a ball narrowly missed me.

Other shots struck the grass about me, and in a rage I turned back towards them while blowing upon the cord which was wedged tightly in the jaws of the crude matchlock. I missed the sleek bore of the Marquardt wheellock, which had been destroyed in the horseshoe valley.

The men crouched below me with their hands held before their faces. My finger pulled the serpentine and felled the guide boy who had led them after my tracks, prompting incensed insults to be hurled at me.

'Go hump yourselves!' I shouted back at them, filled both with vindicated anger and dark despair. 'And find another goatherd to bugger!'

I waved two upraised fingers at them, then continued my flight up the hill as more shots and barking rang around the valley. My breathing was ragged as I pushed on past the outcrops and crevices, then half slaughtered myself from exertion over the last steep climb to the top. I used both hands and knees until I collapsed in a winded heap, panting like a stray upon a roadside until I had enough strength to return to my feet.

At the sight of the tiny pursuers behind me I thought to load my rifle and pick them off one by one, but another loud cry behind me made me turn around in bewilderment to face the party of troopers I had seen earlier that morning. They were a dozen strong, small shapes who were approaching me at speed.

'Surrender, Spaniard!' carried a voice over the whistling wind. 'Surrender!'

'Christ wept,' I whispered in despair. 'I cannot keep this up for much longer.'

To my dismay I realised that far from throwing my pursuers off the scent, my gunshot had instead alerted other search parties to my presence. In turn there was little choice left but for me to make towards the next mountaintop to the northwest while trying to think of a way in which I might shake off the three parties which fast closed in on me.

As I raced towards it, the sheer drop of the cliff face where I had spent the previous night returned to view, and I almost despaired at finding myself back where I started. I did my best to keep my balance as I found myself running alongside it once more, sick to my stomach that I had spent the day travelling in a circle and cursing myself for not venturing further west when I had the chance.

I spotted another six troopers upon the other side of the mountaintop; my stomach churned as I realised that I had been caught in a vice from which there could be no escape. I stumbled along the edge of the drop directly above the lake, feeling sickened that my life and the ring would soon be in the hands of my enemy.

The thought of the ring left me with a mad idea, a last desperate hope to which I could cling, if only to prevent the enemy from getting their hands on Hurtado's trinket. With a deep breath I grabbed the edge of the rock upon which I stood, then slowly lowered myself onto a crag below. With a low gasp I slipped down towards another crag, the dark blue lake spread out beneath me as I held the casket out over the water. As I hovered above the lake below, I was overcome by a strange calm despite my great disappointment. I felt almost grateful that the chase was finally ended; my every limb quivered from strain.

'So here it ends for you, Santiago,' I whispered myself, 'in this back of beyond corner of the arse end of the world.'

The drop below me seemed to spin around, so that it took all of my concentration not to topple forward, tempted as I was to end it all rather than return to my foes' power. I grappled both with the effort to keep my balance and with a huge fear of what might befall me, given my vulnerable position and the number of approaching troopers. A scraping sound behind me had me turning around to face a dozen of the sneering enemy, who beheld me with enraged wonder as they raised their crossbows and guns in my direction.

'Don't dare harm me,' I roared at them in my angst, 'or I'll hurl it over!'

At the sight of the raised casket some of the men hesitated, and one of them reached over towards a slow-witted trooper who still took aim at me.

'Stop!' he cried. 'Stop! Do not shoot!'

All weapons were lowered at the soldier's instruction, and he turned back towards me with a cry of fear.

'Stay your hand, Spaniard! And do not leap!'

'And why not, whoreson?' I shouted back. 'So you may further torment me for your own amusement?'

As expected there was no reply, yet the Sassanas did back away until they were out of view. Snatches of agitated conversation could be heard over the crag until a last grudging instruction was called out to me.

'Wait, Spaniard!'

I laughed aloud in a mad despair, as my hand still held the casket over the crag on which I stood precariously. I overheard some deliberation amongst my enemies, and I pondered whether I should not hurl myself over the edge and be done with everything. I told myself that no one would miss my passing and that the Irish allies whose trust I had betrayed would in fact be best served if the ring came to rest with me at the bottom of the lake.

As the midafternoon wore on there was no further sign or sound of the enemy, although the odd head was spotted peering over the top of the cliff whenever I cast a quick look over my shoulder. Then the faces seemed to vanish indefinitely, and I was uncertain how long I stood upon the cliff edge, shivering violently in the cold wind and sleet until I could not even feel my fingers.

The wretched solitude of my situation filled me with dismay, the memories of all the pains I had endured to keep the ring passing through my head. A hot tear of frustration even rolled down the end of my nose. There was still no sign of the enemy behind me, and I wondered what devilry they might be up to as I shivered upon the ledge, suddenly reminded of my sentry duty at Rosclogher when it had been besieged by hundreds of troopers from Dublin.

At least another three hours passed without the sight of a single soul, but then the scrape of boots overhead made me turn about to catch a glimpse of a hooded man leading a horse towards me from the cliffs to my left. I stared back at this traveller who approached from the opposite direction, feeling confused as to whether he was also an enemy or else a traveller who had appeared in the wrong place at the precise wrong time. I stiffened along the edge of the precipice like a cornered cat, ready to leap at the first sign of trouble, when a familiar voice called out to me.

'Hospitalarios! What are you doing there?'

I stared back over my shoulder in disbelief as the man stood directly above me, and when his hood was pulled back I was taken aback by the broad smile of Nial, his full head of golden locks swirling in the wind. Words failed me as I took in the unexpected sight of the bondsman, who proceeded to unfurl a length of gut cord which he flung over the edge towards me.

'Grab a hold, Spaniard,' he called out again, 'and come back up here!'

'What devilry is this?' I asked in bafflement.

"Tis no devilry!' he called back to me. 'Whatever you are fearing is gone!'

'Scores of troopers?' I stammered through chattering teeth. 'Gone?'

'Yes, friend Juan, they are gone.'

'How? Why?'

'I cannot know for certain, although I suspect that the approaching force of O'Donnells would have something to do with it. Great lords do not appreciate the Crown's troopers roaming their own lands without their sanction, and they have a great many spies.'

The tidings were too good to be true, and I pondered over his words a few moments before replying.

'If what you say is true, then why are you here? You abandoned me only yesterday.'

Nial did not stir at my words, instead beholding me with his fists rested upon his hips. He stood as still as a statue, so that it was only the tendrils of mist from his nostrils which betrayed the life that coursed through him.

'I had no choice but to run off with the other kerns and feign obedience to the chieftains' orders,' he said, 'yet I slipped away last night. It had to be the right place and the right moment, for you yourself know how hard it is to lose the kerns in the wild. For all I know, they might already be on my trail.'

'Why did you return to me?' I snapped.

'I am returned to tell you that I fully understand your design,' he replied in a lowered voice, 'that I know why you could not conceive of a future in Dartry. I, too, share your belief that the time of the chieftains is at an end.'

'At an end?' I replied, taken aback. 'But how can you think this?'

Nial was silent for a few moments.

'I do not think this, Spaniard; I know this. So I would also leave this constant warfare behind, to journey with you to the Indies.'

I stared back at him in wordless bafflement as he continued.

'You said that you were to board a ship for the Indies before you were forced to join the Armada. A better opportunity to secure freedom and fortune will not soon befall me, if indeed it ever does.'

Despite all the surprises I had encountered throughout the last year, this declaration was the one that left me the most dumbfounded. Nial's expression did not change as he witnessed the shock on my face, yet he instantly sought to allay any concerns I might have.

'If you would have me join you, I could be of great service. We would reach Derry tomorrow, before the day is out, and then find a boat to Scotland. I can disguise us so that no one could tell our origins, and you know that you will not get far alone. Now seize the rope and let us refrain from talk, for we must find a safe place to spend the night.'

'How can I trust you?' I called back, still fearful of treachery.

'What choice do you have?' he called back in annoyance, though he proceeded to drop all of his weapons to the ground.

He next hitched the end of the cow gut about his horse's belly before stepping away from it and standing along the leftward side of the precipice so that I had full view of him.

'Take up the cord and keep this at the ready,' he said, flinging me his flintlock pistol, 'and at the first sight of an enemy you may discharge it upon me.'

I met his stare for a few moments, then leant the casket along the edge of the crag and loaded his pistol. When this was done I returned the casket over my shoulder, then hesitantly stood up and walked over towards the cord, which dangled off the cliff face, seizing it in one hand. As the bondsman goaded the horse, I was soon lifted off the ground, pushing at the rock wall with my feet while aiming the gun at the bondsman. Nial never once stirred as I kept him in my sights, both of us knowing full well that I could swiftly blow his head off with ease from the distance at which he stood.

I was slowly hauled back up towards the top of the cliff, ready to release my hold of the cord and fling the casket towards the lake at the first sound of trouble. Yet as my head was raised over the cliff edge, I could see that the bondsman spoke truth and that there were no troopers anywhere. The great fear which held me in its grip seemed to dissipate in the relentless wind that howled through the hillsides about us. I released a huge sigh of relief, and for the first time in days a half smile grew on my face.

'If you speak truth,' I said, 'then perhaps my fortune is finally turning.'

A crunch was heard from Nial's boots as he walked up to me and rested his gauntleted hand upon my shoulder.

'I have watched you suffer much in past weeks, Spaniard, but I know you are no fool. I also know that your intentions are no different from those of any other man – to seek out a better life, one free of gore and desolation.'

His words struck a chord, for after long months of sacrifice I felt vindication, as well as relief that I could finally share my woes with another. I realised that I was not mad to have kept the ring hidden for as long as I did, that perhaps my interminable sacrifice had been one that was worthy. Nial stared directly into my face, seemingly reading all that passed through my head as I seized his arm in a firm grip and addressed him once more.

'Well met, *dhá chlaíomh*. We had best continue our journey.'

# LV

## CROAGHGORM MOUNTAINS TO DERRY SURROUNDS

*18 – 19 November 1589*

Nial handed me a blanket as the night set in, which I gratefully wrapped about me as he readied to take the first watch.

'How are you feeling?' he asked with concern in his voice as my head collapsed back upon the grass.

'Sore and weary,' was my reply. 'Although I could be worse . . . even dead.'

The bondsman gave a grunt of agreement as we lay low in the frosted rushes alongside the rumbling river, blowing up small puffs of mist as our faces shone in the glow of the small fire upon the snow. The warmth from the flames had left me feeling restored, with new life returning to my limbs and feet.

'How is the leg?' I asked.

'Getting worse,' he scowled as he grabbed his ankle and rubbed it hard as if in afterthought.

The unfortunate incident had occurred not an hour after we had descended from the heights that shielded Lough Belshade, then forded the river in the valley below to journey on through the cover of forest. We were not halfway through the wood when the deserting bondsman got his foot stuck in brambles hidden beneath the snow. Nial wrenched his foot free but twisted his ankle badly, then lay upon the ground in a heap until he somehow returned to his feet and marched on with his usual stoic resolve.

Yet after a time a hideous grimace had marked his usually jovial face for so long that I insisted on surrendering the horse to him, so that he might rest as we pressed on through the wood. To our left we stole glimpses of the two rises he called An Gáigin and Sliabh Mullach as the wolves howled in the distance. The sound urged me to press on and jerk the horse until it proceeded at a canter with me jogging alongside it.

'Save your vigour,' Nial whispered to me, 'for we have a long journey ahead of us yet.'

'We must retire to safety for the night,' I replied, yet he said nothing.

The heights behind us soon dwindled, and we broke into a country which was less rocky and which would have been greener had the heavy snowfall not resumed. The bondsman and I drew our hoods on tightly about our heads, moving along the banks of the river until it joined with another, then made towards another, wider confluence. Nial stared back at me blankly when I looked at him askance, then groaned aloud as I stepped towards the water.

'No choice but to ford it,' I grumbled, then felt my teeth about to splinter against one another as my shoes sank into the dark water ahead of me.

It was so icy that my feet could not be felt below the knee until the opposite bank was reached. Upon climbing back onto the snow, I used the hard marching to restore some feeling back into my legs and feet. As a cold, northern wind sliced through us, my step only faltered at last Nial called out to me and returned to his feet despite my protestations.

'Let us retire here,' he insisted, 'for there is less than an hour left until nightfall.'

He reached for the horse's back and pulled a pack off; it contained a tent of hide which we set about pitching along the gushing water. When this was done the horse's reins were hitched to another stave driven into the ground. We set about retrieving twigs and wood which we piled together just outside the tent, setting it aflame with the use of the bondsman's tinder-box and some of his powder. Amid the welcome crackling of flames, I removed my boots and socks, then placed them within the cover of the tent, yet as close to the flames as was possible.

'Cursed mountains,' I muttered, shaking my fist at the distant heights of Croaghgorm, which rose behind us and which I was so glad to have abandoned.

Nial sighed wearily as he took two handfuls of fresh meat from out of his pack.

'Trapped a hare before I found you,' he said with a grin, then skewered the flesh with the ends of his *skene* dagger and held it over the flames, turning it from side to side until it was sufficiently cooked.

He passed me the braised meat, and my heart quickened as my teeth sank into it and I bit off a large mouthful. In instants my share of supper was gone. Nial finished his not long afterwards, as the howl of wolves echoed about us.

'Will we be safe here?' I asked hesitantly.

'Who can say for certain?' he replied, then finished off his last strip of rabbit and reached for his waterskin. 'I doubt there is much human threat, what with the cold and the O'Donnell force making for the mountains. As for the wolves, well, we shall just have to keep watch.'

The flames were fed with enough sticks to keep a low fire going, without allowing it to grow into a raging blaze which might be seen beyond the high grass in which we had set up camp. I was overcome by weariness as a last exchange was traded with the bondsman, who lay alongside me with his returned pistol held before him and his drawn swords placed to his right.

'Where are we headed?' I asked.

'Derry,' he replied, 'to seek out the bishop.'

'Reimundo Termi?'

'Yes, him,' said Nial, 'the same O'Gallagher who helped other Spaniards reach Scotland.'

The full realisation slowly dawned upon me that the end of my days in Ireland was close at hand. Memories of Spain returned to me as we sat in the darkness, and I felt an inevitable stirring inside me at the prospect of my return. The thought of it took the edge off the pain I still felt at having been abandoned by the Dartrymen. It seemed to me that every sacrifice made to retain the ring in the face of so much adversity suddenly all seemed worthwhile.

In the middle of the night I was shoved awake, met by the gaunt face of Nial, who immediately collapsed to gain his own repose. I rubbed my eyes hard between furious blinks as I sought to keep awake, for I was still weary from the previous day's exertions. I snatched my musket and placed twigs and stalks upon the dying fire until the first light of dawn, when the howls of wolves had subsided after a few uneventful hours. Nial still slumbered as I shoved snow onto the sizzling brands, and after I had put on my boots again, I stamped out the last living embers.

I turned towards the bondsman, wondering whether or not to stir him while I recalled the fortunate escape I had had in the mountains, as well as his fortuitous midafternoon appearance. It was then that my eyes fell upon the pistol which lay at his side, and I marvelled at its fine workmanship in the early morning light, since I had been too agitated in the mountains to study it when he had handed it over to me. Despite my best efforts it was difficult to resist inspecting its design more closely, so I leant stealthily over the bondsman and picked it off the edge of his blanket.

I quietly examined the bore and the lock as I ignored Nial's low snores. Its craftsmanship left me to wonder what had become of my pistol, which had been lost during the battle of the horseshoe valley, and it suddenly struck me that the gun in my hand was the very same type of weapon. I staggered backwards in disbelief, staring at the pistol in astonishment and wondering whether it was mine or Ramos', when a loud grunt from Nial gave me such a fright that the pistol fell from my hands.

As the bondsman smacked his lips and rolled over, I fell to my knees, filled with dismay when I saw that the gun had landed deep in the snow outside the tent. A sudden fear filled me as Nial stirred, but before his eyes opened I had snatched up the gun and wiped it hard with my shirt, then placed it back alongside him. With a sigh of relief I returned to my seat before the tent, even as the bondsman blinked in the wan sunlight and slowly lifted his head.

'Any curs?' he asked, and I shook my head by way of reply.

Nial seemed to stare into space for a few moments as he always did, then slowly raised himself onto his feet and winced as I stared up at him.

'Does it still hurt?'

'Yes,' he groaned. 'Yes, it does.'

So saying, he limped off towards the river, where he washed his face and hair in the ice-cold water, then returned to find me striking the tent.

'Will you not also wash your face?' he asked.

'No, it can wait,' I replied, for even the very thought of the icy water made me tremble.

After the tent had been folded and slung over the horse's back, I helped Nial climbed back onto the saddle.

'Where to now?' I asked as he stared over the snow-covered grassland which lay ahead of us, covered with many clumps of trees.

'I believe we should keep to the Finn for at least another ten miles,' said Nial, 'yet travelling along the river for too long is perilous, and I shall seek to hire a guide at the first opportunity.'

'Would that not also be perilous?'

'Peril lurks in every shadow of this land,' he replied, 'and we have no choice.'

We set out east once more, with the heights of Croagh-gorm behind us shrinking with each mile we covered. My dry feet and good boots made the going easier, as well as the food I had eaten the previous night. After an hour a sizeable cluster of huts were sighted ahead of us, and the bondsman told me to refrain from marching.

'Lie behind those bushes,' he said, 'and do not stir until my return. Should there be no sign of me after an hour, you should venture on as best you can, always using the river as your guide. If you reach Derry, you should ask for Bishop O'Gallagher. Tell him that you were sent by the Jesuit O'Ronayne.'

I trembled with anger at the mention of the Jesuit, who had accompanied me on the journey north, knowing that I would be abandoned to my death in the mountains. Yet I still heeded Nial's instructions, falling fell onto my knees and lying low in the grass, my rifle primed and my hand upon the casket at my side. A deep anxiety seized me as the bondsman kicked his horse on towards the settlement, his cloak and fair hair billowing in the freezing westerly.

No sooner had he vanished from view than I berated myself for not having told him about his wet pistol. The realisation only made the waiting worse, and I made a quick sign of the cross while whispering a prayer to the Virgin that he would come to no harm. In the event my prayers were answered, for the distant figure of a horseman could be seen once again heading at a canter in my direction, along with a slight figure on foot. As they drew nearer Nial called out to me, and I rose to my feet to find a young, barefoot boy wrapped in a blanket standing alongside him, his face as keen and as flushed as it was grubby.

'This is Matthew,' said the bondsman, 'a local goatherd. His mother has lent him to us for the day, to guide us along lesser-known passes.'

I nodded to the boy, who stared at me in wonder, though he nodded back at me with a ready smile.

'And what was the asking price?' I replied.

'The last of our conies,' replied the bondsman drily.

I grimaced in annoyance as the whiskerless stripling waved for us to follow him. He brought us to the bank of the river and proceeded to wade through the water.

'Not again,' I sighed, while behind me Nial made to dismount.

'No, do not leave the horse,' I snapped, turning around and keeping him from dismounting.

I took three steps forward and closed my eyes as my foot sank into the water, instantly numbed by its ice-cold current. A kingfisher and a woodcock were disturbed as we forded the Finn, after which we struck out along a north-easterly path. The wind behind us only grew in cold and strength, and our hair was buffeted about our heads.

'It's a Protestant wind that blows no one any good,' I muttered. Behind me the bondsman said nothing as we skirted a lake and tramped on through the largely white and brown grassland, with gentle rises to our left.

Young Matthew proved a hard walker who knew the country well, often seeking the cover of trees as he never once tarried from the path. Whenever we entered the forests, we paused to collect faggots of firewood, which were tied with twine and placed upon the hobby's back. This was accomplished in relative safety, for not a soul could be seen for miles during our march, which was of great comfort to me as our journey brought us within sight of a hill to our left, with another spotted to our right not long after.

'Cruachán?' called Nial to the boy, pointing to the rise to our right.

Matthew turned on his heel and nodded, a hesitant smile spreading beneath his brown fringe.

'Yes, sire. We stand close to Magh Ithe. That is the hill where the great warlord of yore was laid to rest, after the battle fought in the famous plain by the Milesians.'

Nial flashed him a kindly smile and gestured to him with a gauntleted hand.

'You may head back home now, boy. Yet take this reward before you make off, for you have earned it well.'

All shyness was gone as the young goatherd smiled openly at us.

'Not yet, sire,' he replied. 'I shall lead you but a while longer, for treacherous bog lies ahead of us, and I must first guide you through it.'

The bondsman appeared taken aback by the boy's selflessness, and I served the lad with a nod of appreciation. Thereafter Matthew proved as good as his word, nimbly leading us over the softer ground which lay ahead, keeping us clear of the dangerous mire while we often found ourselves up to our ankles in mud. When the last marshy stretch had been covered, we found ourselves less than a mile distant from the hill which they had referred to earlier, and with the sun being at about noontime height, I smugly surmised that good progress had been made.

'Yonder lies An Cruachán,' said the boy as he stopped in front of us and gestured towards the hill. 'Beyond it are Leifear and then Derry. You could reach them both before the day is out.'

'You are a good lad,' said Nial with a terseness in his voice. 'Take these sweetmeats and be off with you, and bear our thanks to your mother.'

Matthew smiled broadly as he took the treats from the bondsman's hand, then bowed deeply to us with a final salutation as he made back the way we had come.

'Godspeed to you both, kind sirs.'

When he walked off the first snowflakes started to whiten our heads and shoulders again, and Nial jerked his head towards the rise before us.

'We can rest there for the night, then resume our journey in the morning.'

'Need we tarry for that long?' I replied.

'We shall not soon encounter a safer spot, and from that vantage we can observe any movements for miles about us.'

With a nod I turned to resume our progress, holding the horse by the reins as we proceeded to scale An Cruachán. When compared to the heights of Croaghgorm, the steep hill felt like a gentle rise, and it was less than an hour before we had passed a cairn and then struggled through the gorse to reach the heather-clad top of the summit. After the steed was hitched, I helped Nial to dismount. I handed him the bundles of sticks and twigs to start another fire against the jagged remains of an ancient wall, and I set about pitching the tent in front of an ancient Celtic stone cross which stood atop the hill.

'Well, here we are, Spaniard,' said the bondsman when the tent was pitched and the first crackle of twigs could be heard, 'lodging alongside the bones of our common ancestor.'

'Where is Ithe's tomb?' I asked, staring about me.

Ne Dourough tapped the grass beneath us with his knuckles. 'Right there. At least that is what the bards say.'

"'Tis a good spot,' I replied as I stared about us, taking in the sight of the plains and distant hills, together with the small town which stood to the east. 'You can see everything for miles about.'

'A good spot for a marksman.' Nial smiled, then raised his head and closed his eyes as he sniffed the buffeting wind that rustled my hair and the grass at our feet. 'Can you smell that tang in the air, my friend?'

'Yes,' I lied, for in truth I had a slight cold and could not smell much at all. 'It is almost brackish.'

'The sea.' He slowly rose to his feet and hobbled towards the tent. 'Soon we shall see it again.'

Nial told me that we were safe in the ruins of an old hill fort, which was not used by the local tribes. No sooner had he given me this assurance than I lay down and slumbered for a few hours at his urging, for I had marched for most of the day.

'Have a good rest, Spaniard,' he whispered, 'for it may be the last one you might have for a while.'

When I stirred once more, the glow of the sun could be seen despite the thick cover of clouds, being well past midafternoon height. Low snoring was heard at my back, and I turned to find that Nial was fast asleep upon his left side. I fed the fire and relit the slow match upon my musket with the end of a burning stalk, then placed my hand upon the casket which hung from my side.

My fears for my own safety had dispelled any thoughts of the ring ever since we had left the Croaghgorm range behind, yet I felt frustrated as I raised the iron box, an emotion which only grew as the object it contained rattled from side to side once again. With a great annoyance I seized the padlock and twisted it hard, but it held firm as I jerked it up and down and tugged it repeatedly. In another attempt to wrench it open, I took up the wooden ramrod, shoving its end through the lock and pulling repeatedly until I feared that the end of the stick might crack.

'Holy host of the Madonna,' I cursed as I stared at the remains of the ancient rubble wall ahead of us, seeking a rock which might break open the steel box.

'Fiendish devil, isn't it?' came a voice from behind me, and I turned in surprise to find the bondsman grinning at me.

'And what of it?' I asked, feeling displeased that he had watched me wresting the lock.

'Pass it to me,' he demanded suddenly with an outstretched palm, his *skene* dagger drawn from his side.

I stared at his open hand and then the blade on his lap, wondering whether he was attempting to take the ring from me by force.

'Do you not even trust me now?' Nial asked in an exasperated voice.

For a moment I hesitated, then handed him the box with a nervous chuckle, feeling flushed with embarrassment at my initial reluctance and worried that I had irked him.

'Here it is,' I said with a low chuckle. 'You just baffled me when you drew the knife is all.'

Nial silently took the box and lifted the padlock up towards him, eyeing it carefully before placing the point of the knife through the keyhole. With a few twists of his wrist, he prodded the inside of the lock, then closed his eyes as he quickly jerked his hand sideways, which produced a click as the lock came undone.

'You did it!' I exclaimed as he drew the bolt out through the grooves on the top of the strongbox and flung the sprung lock aside.

'Hold your hands out.' He smiled as I cupped my palms together and held them out before him.

He raised the box over them and then turned it upside down. The smile on my face grew and then instantly vanished as a blackened acorn fell against my fingers and rolled into the middle of one palm. For a few moments we sat in dumbfounded shock as we beheld the object which I picked out of my palm, then held up between us. We gaped at it in stricken silence, as if it were the most horrid aberration that we had ever seen.

'What . . . what is this?' I finally managed as I let the shrivelled nut fall onto the ground. I seized the opened box and shoved my face against it, desperately seeking out any other contents within it.

The bondsman sighed aloud. 'It is in vain, Spaniard. They have outfoxed us.'

'But I saw them,' I snapped. 'I saw them put it inside it.'

Nial sighed again. 'Well, it is evidently no longer in there.'

'Then where is it?' I growled, feeling both stupid and increasingly enraged at the duplicity of the chieftains. 'What do you know that you have not yet told me?'

The bondsman grabbed his weapons and slowly heaved himself to his feet, then hobbled over to the stone wall behind us and stared out across the plain.

'All I know is that you were meant to be left in the mountains. O'Rourke said that it was too perilous to keep hold of the ring or to even seek to pawn it. He said that we should feign to help you to reach Derry, then abandon you at the first opportunity in Lough Belshade. We were also to ensure that the enemy discovered our plans. That is all that I was told.'

I flung the iron casket upon the ground as I angrily rose to my feet, kicking up the grass and cursing aloud again.

'Christ's blood! All very well then, if that is what you were told! Yet did you not suspect or overhear anything which betrayed their duplicity?'

At my outrage, Nial whirled upon me with a startled look which seemed to stare into the very depths of my soul. As his stare turned into a glare I stepped away from him warily, for I had never seen him display such a fearsome expression.

'I said I knew nothing further,' he whispered, 'although it is jaw-dropping to listen to you accusing the chieftains of duplicity – you who hid the ring from them for so long, who caused all manner of grief to them and their peoples.'

His accusation stung me since it also rang true.

'My suspicion,' he said as I turned away from him and wandered along the hilltop, 'is that you were used as some sort of distraction, to turn the pursuing troopers away from whoever bears the ring now. My suspicion is that Muireann now bears it.'

'Are you certain?' I blurted as I turned towards him again, feeling further betrayed by the minute and barely able to speak from the pain of my disappointment.

'Who else can it be?' he replied. 'She is MacGlannagh's most trusted relative.'

'But why would he have given it to her?'

'Who knows?' said Nial. 'Maybe he sought to purchase mercenaries from Ulster or to forge an alliance with the O'Donnells.'

'So much for it being too dangerous to hold,' I spat, then fell to my knees and held my face in my hands. I fell over to my side and lay there like a kicked hound for what seemed like ages.

'They are here,' said the bondsman at last.

I raised my head at his words, curious as to their meaning. I saw him turning away from the Gaelic cross on the other side of the hilltop and walking over towards me without the slightest limp. I beheld his steps in my direction in utter astonishment, which left me wondering whether I was trapped in the middle of some terrible nightmare. My astonishment grew further when he raised the flintlock pistol before my face.

'Stand up,' he growled, his stare hardening further as I struggled to get back to my feet.

'You made me walk all that distance for nothing,' I whispered as I looked at the pistol bore.

'I am sorry, Santiago,' he said in a mocking tone which I had not previously heard from him, 'although I daresay you deserved worse than a hard march.'

'The Binghams?' I said at last.

'No.'

'Viceroy FitzWilliam?'

'Walsingham.' His curt reply left me entirely stunned. 'He wants it too. It shall fetch the treasury a great ransom. And yet I must feign alliance with the Binghams' agents until I can send word to London. They owe him their hides after he protected them from the viceroy; they shall not deny him anything.'

The ease of his duplicity left me speechless, as with each passing moment he seemed to increasingly turn into a stranger before my own eyes.

'And what of the MacGlannaghs?'

'They shall not see out the year.' He shrugged. 'They are surrounded by too many of the enemy's eyes and ears. The times have changed too quickly for them and the O'Rourkes.'

The bondsman shot a glance over his shoulder, then gestured at me with the pistol to follow him.

'Now let us be off, for Burke wants you alive.'

I was so shocked by his words that the ground seemed to rise and dip around me, leaving me to snatch ragged breaths.

'Abel de Santiago,' chuckled Nial as I walked alongside him. 'Who could have known? Alba's very own angel of death!'

For a moment I thought of begging him to set me free or asking whether we could feign some sort of escape. I could not fathom being returned to the power of the demented renegade sergeant, whom I thought I had left behind in a wrecked and burning barn in Sligo Town. As we approached the edge of the hill I could hear the distant rumble of mounted troopers; their swords pricked the air and clouds of mist flared from their mounts' nostrils as they crested a gentle slope and then hurtled on towards us.

Less than a musket shot's distance ahead of them I could make out the small figures of travellers who were seeking in vain to elude the riders. My heart quailed when I recognised the faces of Lochlain and Muireann in the company of the Jesuit, who hurried in vain across the open country with a half-dozen kerns watching their backs.

'Burke is here early.'

Nial's callous, indifferent tone left me cold as the chargers drew nearer to our fleeing former comrades, and my arms trembled at the sight of the leading trooper, entirely clad in black. Despite the distance, I could already somehow tell that it was Treasach Burke.

'So he is indeed alive,' I said as we commenced our descent down the slope.

'Who? Burke?' answered Nial. 'Yes, 'tis a miracle that none could have foreseen. They say the very thought of you returned him from the brink of death.'

I nodded once when he said this, and my fear slowly turned into anger.

'So the path through the bog, the poisoning, Dervila's ambush. All of it was you?'

'Yes, for the most part. Except for the queen's ambush. Cathal turned late on in the story.'

My teeth were bared in rage, and as I stopped, he winded me with a blow to the stomach, shoving me to my knees, then jamming the pistol's nozzle against my forehead. Around us the wind sounded like the whispered lament of a long-dead warrior, who told of his defeat whilst urging me not to readily accept mine.

'Get back on your feet,' growled Nial, 'and no more sudden moves.'

In that instant I realised the ironic sight of a fencing master bearing a gun, and I stared up at the ivory sky, praying for at least a drop of rain which might serve to disable the flintlock. Then I remembered dropping the pistol into the snow that morning, and for an instant I wondered whether my captor had since dried it out.

'I said get up,' he hissed once more. 'Don't make me tell you again.'

I hurled myself at him with the speed of a wildcat, his finger squeezing the serpentine as my arms were wrapped tightly about his. No shot followed the lock's dull scrape as we rolled downhill, our foreheads smashed into each other's faces until I released him. The full force of his fist missed my head by a whisker, yet his knuckles grazed my crown. As he reached for his blades I shoved an elbow into his chin with a fury that sent him flying back onto the ground.

He was dazed for but an instant, long enough for me to snatch up one of his swords while he shot back to his feet and drew his second. I deflected his fierce attack long enough to stagger downhill but on the back foot. A seething hiss left his lips as he came at me again and again, his thrusts inching ever nearer to my shoulders and face until he nicked one of my cheeks.

I knew he would attempt another downward thrust, yet it still sent me falling backwards as I jumped away from it. The vigour of his swing left him stumbling forwards, so I kicked out a foot and sent him stumbling into a heap alongside me. As I hurled myself onto him, the full force of his forehead crashed into the side of my cheek, and a howl left my throat. As I collapsed sideways, he reached over and pinned me onto the ground, all the while reaching for his sword.

'Surrender, Spaniard!' he gasped as a trickle of blood rolled down his chin. A pinch at my navel reminded me of the eating knife I had taken from the trooper I had attacked in the mountains.

As Nial raised his sword, I whipped out the small blade and plunged its point through his cheek. His eyes almost tripled in size, then grew further as I smashed my knee into his groin, sending him flying over me and rolling on furiously downhill.

His roar of agony rose above the howling wind, and I coughed heavily amid ragged breaths. My mouth was full of the taste of my own blood as I spat out a tooth. For a while I lay in a winded heap, then returned to my feet and staggered uphill towards the Gaelic cross. A glimpse over my shoulder revealed the lifeless body of the bondsman almost at the foot of the hill. The cries from the plain left me in no doubt as to the danger of my situation, and I resolved to reach the hobby as quickly as I could, though my ears still rang from the blows I had received.

When at last I reached the top of An Cruachán, I hurried over to the horse and unhitched its reins, then quickly picked up the empty casket and slammed it shut. As I climbed atop Nial's mount, the distant shouts and cries reached my ears from below. In a daze, I stared behind me, beyond the heights to my left, where there stretched the great woods of birch that surrounded the town of Derry. My knuckles whitened around the reins when two loud bugle blasts were heard, followed by the strident scream of a woman.

'Help! Heeeeeeeeelp!'

It was the first time that I had ever heard Muireann calling for aid, and I shook my head in disbelief as I spat blood onto the grass and grumbled to myself.

'You would call for help now, damned Mac an Bhaird.'

Billows of wind swept through my dishevelled hair as the hobby set off downhill at a canter. I slammed its flanks with my ankles, also lashing it with its reins, so that my steed made good haste towards the enemy. I had almost crossed half the distance between us when I saw two troopers and all the wood kerns lying wounded upon the grass. The surviving riders had made quick work of the Irish guards, having already dismounted to kill those who writhed on the ground. As I drew nearer, I made out the blood-streaked face of Fergus, who served me with a stare of disbelief as his throat was slashed open.

Muireann's face was the picture of fury, though her arms were pinned behind her by two of the enemy while a third tore open her cloak. The rest of her company were hardly faring any better. The Jesuit lay trembling on the ground with the foot of a trooper rested upon his cheek while Lochlain struggled in the grip of a burly Sassenach. Sheets of vellum fluttered in the air as a grinning Sassenach snatched them out of the Jesuit's pack, even as O'Ronayne issued loud protests from the ground.

'Stay your hand! Those are the annals of Dartry!'

The prelate's protest was stifled when he was booted across the face, just as my horse drew closer to the enemy. I seized the MacGlannagh's strongbox, which bounced upon my back.

*'MacGlannagh Abù!'* I screeched as defiantly as I could manage, holding up the casket for all to see.

The half score or so troopers instantly turned towards me, flinging their captives to the ground like straw dolls as they vaulted onto their mounts without a second thought. My hobby made off at a gallop across the snow, my heels plunged in its sides countless times while Burke's men commenced their chase. I cursed the absence of a goading stick, abandoning the forlorn hope that we might outpace the heavy chargers at our backs.

A thud of hooves seemed to drum against the back of my bruised head while I rode into the darkening moors which lay further inland. The weather had also turned, the sun having long been eclipsed by cloud. Flecks of earth flew as my mount veered to the right, while Burke's charges whinnied and wheeled onwards.

The scattered trees ahead had almost thinned out altogether when a hail of shot and bolts struck the ground about me. As my charger collapsed beneath me, I was flung across the mud where I lay for a few instants, suddenly noticing a corpse which lay a few feet away from me. It was then that I recognised Matthew's white and stricken features; bile still gathered at the boy's lips, though his widened eyes were glazed over and his limbs contorted. His fingers were still sticky from the poisoned sweetmeats which the bondsman had given him.

'Motherless, sodomised whoreson,' I spat beneath my breath, furious at Nial for having slain one so young and innocent.

Blood spurted from my mount's haunches as it screeched and thrashed upon the ground behind me. With a sigh I heaved myself back on my feet. I tore through the high grass as my pursuers closed in, sure of their kill. I ran past a lonely ash and then made an abrupt sprint towards a beech. I had just passed its crooked branches when a sword thrust sliced the air overhead, leaving me to crouch in low bushes. I had just thanked all the saints above for having spared me when a bolt skewered me above the knee, dropping me to all fours like a beast.

My throat still ached from my yell, and I all but gagged in pain, clawing at the muck with mud-spattered hands. I decided to make for where the bare stalks of the cotton grass sprouted.

Amid grunts of pain I could shift myself forward no further, finding myself up to the shins in the filth. There followed a great cry as the riders thundered towards me, leaving me to despair that I was not close enough to the plants. With fists balled and eyes shut, I cringed before the inevitable pain that would ensue. Just then, a whinny was heard from the forerunner as the enemy's horses buckled and squirmed. The mounts ignored all jerks of their reins, for the mud was already up to their knees, and their riders were hurled about into the mire that trapped me.

The troopers sank into the stinking sludge, dragged down by their heavy armour, issuing cries and wails of dismay. I suddenly recognised Treasach Burke alongside me, his pink, blotched skull specked with clumps of hair. His one eye boiled with rage as he strained against the mud towards me, a shard of metal still wedged hard in his forehead; the flesh around it resembled charred vellum. One of his arms had been rendered a stump, yet the revenant sergeant drew his sword as I tried to kick away from him with my good leg, my arms flapping around wildly to keep me afloat.

Burke was but a yard away as he sank into the black swill which claimed us, the bodies of chargers straining about in the bog. The shriek of the mounts was horrific as they desperately twisted and turned, up to their chests, their struggle making the stench thicker. My feet felt like they rested on the bladders of a hundred stray sheep. All my senses recoiled at the stinking bog, my body left rigid with cold and fear as the sergeant throbbed with rage and lunged at me madly.

His sword whipped the thin air before my head and splashed dirt into my face, while behind him the arm of a trooper reached out from beneath the muck, then quivered a last time and dropped. I cursed aloud as the sludge reached up to my chin. I sought in vain to swim against the thick mud, yet I lacked a leg with which to rise above it sufficiently.

Burke's mouth fell open and mud slid into it, and his burning eye soon vanished as bubbles rose to the surface and burst. The swamp froze my limbs and my legs into blocks of ice, sucking me in deeper whenever I squirmed so that my nostrils were somehow strained above it. My eyes shot from left to right, my strength having long abandoned me, and in fear of death I relieved myself. The scream of sinking troopers and horses still rose from the deadly bog, and my heart sank each time one slipped away from view.

A noose of sheep gut cord fell before me, and I somehow slipped my hand through it as my head sank beneath the mire. My nostrils were filled with mud and my sight was blurred as the cord tightened about my wrist, and my hand turned bloodless when a great tug was felt upon it.

Just when it seemed like my hand might be torn off, I gasped shock and relief and clean air again, though I was unable to see anything. My hand turned completely numb as the cord bit harder into my wrist, but my feet came unstuck as my whole body was somehow dislodged from the bog.

'Holy host of the Madonna!'

I screeched the cry of blasphemy as my skewered leg left the bubbling filth, the cord feeling like it had cut down to the very bone of my wrist. Blood gushed from beneath my palm as I was dragged over the mud past the kicking hooves of a horse, where I also heard the odd moan of a wailing trooper.

My hand was a whitened claw devoid of feeling by the time I saw a Sassenach the size of a wardrobe grimacing over me. I tried in vain to free my arm as I was hoisted upon a firm peat hag. The remaining trooper disabled me with an almighty punch to the stomach, then rested the edge of his dagger against my throat. His foul breath stank of rancid barley, and he all but suffocated me when he rasped into my face, 'Give it up or I'll skin you.'

'Give up what?'

I groaned when the point of his blade drew blood, though the force of his thrust eased when he looked up and stared ahead in amazement. Although it was veiled by mist, I made out a shadow slowly skipping from tussock to tussock, seeming to rise out of the silhouette of a small horse behind it. My captor gasped at the sight.

'Kelpies?'

He lifted my wildly shivering form back towards him and cursed.

'Give me that cursed stone or I'll slit your throat!'

I could barely even talk when the twang of an arrow was heard. The bolt struck the ground alongside the Sassana's foot, so that his grip was instantly released as he fled with a curse. My breathing quickened at the approach of the female form, a prayer forming in my throat as I readied to be claimed by the dreaded spirit said to haunt the Irish countryside.

As she stepped in front of me, the ollave regarded my helpless form caked in blood and dirt. The strands of her dishevelled hair fell about the torn cloak, which rippled about her. The bow fell from her hands as she hobbled over towards me, then knelt down and raised me against a solitary stump.

Muireann touched the bolt through my knee; then, noticing my violent shivering, she snatched a blanket from the back of the flown trooper's horse and flung it upon me. My eyes tarried but a moment upon her torn bodice. Fear of further agony made my leg quiver before she snapped off the end of the bolt, which she cast away before we beheld each other in awe and gasped for breath.

A purple welt rose on her cheek alongside her bloodied nose, and her lips were bloodied. Her eyes fell upon the ground as I tried to raise my arm, yet it fell away, sapped of strength. With a tremendous effort I lifted my muddied hand onto my lap and managed a whisper.

'You took it.'

Her eyes studied me, and she still appeared unable to speak for the horror she had somehow survived. She finally reached for her quiver and drew out the ring, holding it out before my face between thumb and forefinger and twirling it from side to side as a teasing smile grew on her lips.

'I accept your gift, Spaniard.'

Amid ragged breaths I noted her mocking tone with a raised eyebrow.

'Even one coming from a landless alien?'

There was heard the slightest hint of a simper above her smudged chin.

She finally managed a whisper. 'Better a loyal alien than a disloyal freeman.'

She trussed the trinket back into her ruptured girdle, and I stared at it until it was hidden from view, then wrenched my eyes away to return her stare. We were silent as dusk descended about us, until I found the strength to speak again.

'Have a care for the bauble, my lady, for I owe it my life.'

The ollave's eyes gleamed as she leant forward and gently wiped the mud off my forehead. Her breath was warm on my lips when she whispered a reply.

'Forsooth, soldier. Then that is the reason why I owe it mine.'

# RECOMMENDED READING

If you got this far, I'm guessing you found the sixteenth century setting interesting. If you'd like to read more on the period, I can recommend the following works, which are the main sources I read when creating the pentalogy:

## Non-Fiction

*Ireland: Graveyard of the Spanish Armada,* T. P. Kilfeather (Saint Paul, Minn.: Irish Books & Media, 1967).

*The Defeat of the Spanish Armada,* Garrett Mattingly (New York, NY: Houghton Mifflin Harcourt, 1984).

*England, Spain and the Gran Armada, 1585-1604: Essays from the Anglo-Spanish Conferences, London and Madrid,* eds. M. J. Rodriguez-Salgado, Simon Adams, John Donald (Ann Arbor, Mich.: University of Michigan Press, 1991).

*Languages and Communities in Early Modern Europe,* Peter Burke (Cambridge, England: Cambridge University Press, 2004).

*Medicine and Society in Early Modern Europe,* Mary Lindemann (Cambridge, England: Cambridge University Press, 2010).

*Captain Cuellar's Adventures in Connacht & Ulster, AD 1588,* Francisco de Cuellar, Hugh Allingham, Robert Crawford (Creative Media Partners LLC, 2018).

*The Road to Rocroi: Class, Culture and Command in the Spanish Army of Flanders, 1567-1659*, Fernando González de León. (Boston, MA: BRILL, 2009).

Comentario del coronel Francisco Verdugo: de la guerra de Frisia, en xiv anos que fue gobernador y capitan general de aquel estado y ejercito, Vol. 2, M. Rivadeneyra (Netherlands, 1872).

*Aristocrats and Traders: Sevillian Society in the Sixteenth Century*, Ruth Pike (Ithaca, NY: Cornell University Press, 1972).

*Armed Forces and Society in Spain, Past And Present*, eds. Rafael Bañón Martínez & Thomas M. Barker (Boulder, CO: Social Science Monographs, 1988).

*Crime and Society in Early Modern Seville*, Mary Elizabeth Perry (Lebanon, NH: University Press of New England, 1980).

*The Army of Flanders and the Spanish Road, 1567-1659: The Logistics of Spanish Victory and Defeat in the Low Countries' Wars,* Geoffrey Parker (Cambridge, England: Cambridge University Press, 2004).

*The Dances of the Processions of Seville in Spain's Golden Age*, Matluk Brooks (Kassel, Germany: Edition Reichenberger, 1988).

*The Duke of Alba*, Henry Kamen (New Haven, CT: Yale University Press, 2004).

*William the Silent*, Frederic Harrison (New York, NY: Macmillan and Co., Ltd., 1897).

*Jewels in Spain, 1500-1800,* Priscilla E. Muller (New York, NY: Hispanic Society of America, 1972).

*Distinguished Irishmen Of The Sixteenth Century*, Frank J. Sullivan,

*The Adventures of Captain Alonso de Contreras: A 17ᵗʰ Century Journey*, Alonso de Contreras. (Saint Paul, Minn.: Paragon House, 1989).

*Renaissance Essays*, Hugh Trevor-Roper (Chicago: University of Chicago Press, 1989).

*A New History Of Ireland,* Moody, Martin, Byrne

*Anglo-Irish Trade in the Sixteenth Century,* Ada Kathleen Longfield (London: G. Routledge, 1929).

*Catholic Priests Of Elizabethan Ireland - James Archer, Nicholas Sanders, Diarmaid O Hurthuile, Richard Creagh* (Books Group).

*Cattle Lords and Clansmen: The Social Structure of Early Ireland*, Nerys Patterson (South Bend, IN: University of Notre Dame Press, 1994).

*Connaught*, Stephen Lucius Gwynn (London: Blackie and Son, Ltd., 1912).

*Early Irish and Welsh Kinship*, Charles Edwards (Oxford, England: Clarendon Press, 1993).

Elizabethan Ireland, Grenfell Morton (London: Longman, 1971).

*Elizabethan Ireland: Native and English*, G. B. O'Connor (Dublin: Sealy, Bryers and Walker, 1899).

*Elizabeth's Irish Wars*, Cyril Falls (Syracuse, NY: Syracuse University Press, 1997).

*From Kings to Warlords: The Changing Political Structure of Gaelic Ireland in the Later Middle Ages*, Katharine Simms (Suffolk, England: Boydell and Brewer, Ltd., 2000).

*From Rosclogher To Rooskey – The Leitrim Story*, Lorcan O Runai

*Gaelic Ireland*, Duffy, Edwards, Fitzpatrick

*History of Sligo, County and Town: From the Accession of James I to the Revolution of 1688*, WG Wood-Martin (Dublin: Hodges, Figgis & Co., 1889).

*Ireland in the Age of the Tudors, 1447-1603: English Expansion and the End of Gaelic Rule*, Steven G. Ellis (London: Routledge, 2016).

*Bardic Poetry*, Osborn Bergin (American Committee for Irish Studies, 1969).

*The Bog of Stars: And Other Stories and Sketches of Elizabethan Ireland*, Standish O'Grady (Norderstedt, Germany: Hansebooks, 2017).

*The Brehon Laws: A Legal Handbook*, Laurence Ginnel (London: T. F. Unwin, 1894).

*The Course of Irish History*, T. W. Moody, F. X. Martin, and Dermot Keogh (New York: Roberts Rinehart Publishers, 2012).

*The Elizabethan Conquest of Ireland: The 1590s Crisis*, John McGurk (Manchester, UK: Manchester University Press, 1997).

*The Great O'Neill: A Biography of Hugh O'Neill, Earl of Tyrone, 1550-1616*, Seán O'Faoláin (Cork, Ireland: Mercier, 1986).

*The Irish Wars, 1485-1603*, Ian Heath (New York: Bloomsbury, 1993).

*The Making of Ireland and Its Undoing, 1200-1600*, Alice Stopford Green (London: Macmillan, 1908).

*The Year In Ireland: Irish Calendar Customs*, Kevin Danaher (Cork, Ireland: Mercier, 1972).

*Antique Firearms*, Frederick Wilkinson (Novato, Calif.: Presidio Press, 1977).

*Antique Guns in Colour to 1865*, Robert Wilkinson-Latham (London: Blandford Press, 1977).

*The Age of Chivalry*, Vol. 3, Liliane Funcken and Fred Funcken (Hoboken, NJ: Prentice-Hall, 1983).

*Sixteenth-Century Irish Swords in the National Museum of Ireland*, G. A. Hayes-McCoy (Dublin: National Museum of Ireland, 1977).

*Sniper: A History of the US Marksman*, Martin Pegler (New York: Bloomsbury, 2007).

*The Collector's Illustrated Guide to Firearms*, Martin Miller (London: Barrie & Jenkins, 1978).

*The History of Sniping and Sharpshooting*, Major John L. Plaster (Boulder, CO: Paladin Press, 2008).

*A History of Spanish Firearms*, James D. Lavin (London: H. Jenkins, 1965).

*The Warhorse, 1250-1600*, Ann Hyland (Gloucestershire, England: Sutton, 1998).

*The World of the Galloglass: Kings, Warlords and Warriors in Ireland and Scotland, 1200-1600*, Seán Duffy (Dublin: Four Courts Press, 2007).

*Tools of War*, Jeremy Black (London: Quercus, 2007).

*War and Society in Renaissance Europe, 1450-1620,* J. R. Hale (Baltimore: Johns Hopkins University Press, 1986).

*Warfare in Early Modern Europe 1450-1660*, ed. Paul E. J. Hammer (London: Routledge, 2017).

*Weapons and Warfare in Renaissance Europe: Gunpowder, Technology and Tactics*, Bert S. Hall (Baltimore: Johns Hopkins University Press, 2002).

*Granuaile: The Life & Times of Grace O'Malley, c. 1530-1603*, Anne Chambers (Dublin: Wolfhound Press, 1998).

*Love Songs of Connacht,* Douglas Hyde (London: T. F. Unwin, 1905).

*Mary Queen of Scots and Her Hopeless Husbands*, Margaret Simpson (New York: Scholastic, 2010).

*Women in Early Modern Ireland*, Margaret MacCurtain and Mary O'Dowd (Edinburgh: Edinburgh University Press, 1991).

*Women in Renaissance and Early Modern Europe*, Christine Meek (Dublin: Four Courts Press, 2000).

*Women, Armies and Warfare in Early Modern Europe*, John A. Lynn II (Cambridge, England: Cambridge University Press, 2008).

*The Time Traveller's Guide to Elizabethan England*, Ian Mortimer (Washington, DC; National Geographic Books, 2013).

## Scholarly Articles

*Some Survivors of the Armada in Ireland*, Martin A. S. Hume (London: Royal Historical Society, 1897).

*Sir Richard Bingham and the Mapping of Western Ireland*, J. H. Andrews, *Proceedings of the Royal Irish Academy: Archaeology, Culture, History, Literature*, Vol. 103C, No. 3 (2003), 61-95.

*Taking up Office in Elizabethan Connacht: The Case of Sir Richard Bingham,* Rory Rapple, *The English Historical Review*, Vol. 123, No. 521 (Apr. 2008), 277–99.

*Remarks on Certain Passages in Capt. Cuellar's Narrative of His Adventures in Ireland after the Wreck of the Spanish Armada in 1588-89, Followed by a Literal Translation of That Narrative,*

J. P. O'Reilly and Francisco de Cuellar, *Proceedings of the Royal Irish Academy (1889-1901)*, Vol. 3 (1893-1896), 175-217.

*The Spoken Languages of Medieval Ireland*, Edmund Curtis, Studies: *An Irish Quarterly Review*, Vol. 8, No. 30 (June 1919), 234–54.

*"Doctors of the Military Discipline': Technical Expertise and the Paradigm of the Spanish Soldier in the Early Modern Period,"* Fernando Gonzalez de Leon, *The Sixteenth Century Journal*, Vol. 27, No. 1 (Spring 1996), 61-85.

*Gaelic Domestics,* Hamilton Manuscripts, *Ulster Journal of Archaeology*, First Series, Vol. 3 (1855), 117–26.

*The Wild Irish: A Study of Some English Satires against the Irish, Scots, and Welsh*, Edward D. Snyder, Modern Philology, Vol. 17, No. 12 (April 1920), 687-725.

*Derry in 1590: A Catholic Demonstration*, F. X. Martin, *Clogher Record*, Vol. 6, No. 3 (1968), 597-605.

*The Collapse of the Gaelic World,* 1450-1650, Steven G. Ellis, *Irish Historical Studies*, Vol. 31, No. 124 (Nov. 1999), 449–69.

*The Poetic Brehon Lawyers of Early Sixteenth-Century Ireland*, Katharine Simms, *Ériu*, Vol. 57 (2007), 121–32.

*The Exploitation of the Mines of Ireland in the Sixteenth Century*, M. D. O'Sullivan, *Studies: An Irish Quarterly Review*, Vol. 24, No. 95 (Sep. 1935), 442–52.

*The Composition of Connacht in the Lordships of Clanricard and Thomond, 1577-1641*, Bernadette Cunningham, *Irish Historical Studies*, Vol. 24, No. 93 (May 1984), 1-14.

*An Introduction to the Study of Political Ideas in Early Modern Ireland,* Hiram Morgan, keynote address, *Ireland 1598:*

*Contexts, Representations and Revolts*, University College Cork, May 1998.

Special thanks to Dr Anton Caruana Galizia, Lecturer in History at Newcastle University, for sending me many of the above articles.

## Podcasts

Tudor & Stuart Ireland Conferences.

# About the Author

James Vella-Bardon was born and raised in Malta, an island nation influenced by thousands of years of imperial history - from the Romans to the British - where his passion for exciting and dramatic historical events was formed. After reading law and history at the Universities of both Malta and Sydney, James qualified as a lawyer and completed a doctoral thesis on the rights and freedoms of peoples at international law.

He emigrated to Sydney in 2007 and turned his hand to novel writing. His debut novel *The Sheriff's Catch* (2018), which recounts the adventures of a Spanish Armada castaway in Tudor Ireland, won the 'best novel' and 'best historical fiction' categories at the international Royal Dragonfly Book Awards and was also named an 'Outstanding Historical' by the Independent Author Network Book Awards in 2019.

James was heralded as 'the new king of historical fiction' by British newspaper *The Scotsman,* in their review of his novella *Mad King Robin*, about Robert the Bruce.

*www.jamesvellabardon.com*

Also by James Vella-Bardon

**The Bruce Books**
*The Cream Of Chivalry*
*Mad King Robin*

**The Sassana Stone Pentalogy**
*The Sheriff's Catch*
*A Rebel North*
*Hero Of Rosclogher*
*Trials In Tumult*